WHITE TREES
CRIMSON SNOW

THE EIGHTH BOOK IN
THE MARY CROW ADVENTURES

by

SALLIE BISSELL

LOCUSTHURST
PUBLISHING
ASHEVILE, NC

WHITE TREES
CRIMSON SNOW

Other titles in the Mary Crow series:

For Cynthia Perkins

I'd like to thank Margaret Steiner for casting a talented and dedicated eye on this manuscript.

CHAPTER 1

Friday, January 15
Murphy, North Carolina

Her breasts, she wasn't sure about. Her face looked okay—her skin was clear, her teeth straight, and she'd managed to trim her hair to just below her jawline. But her breasts seemed way too small to attract much notice. She'd struck a pose she'd seen in an ancient issue of *Playboy*, pinching her nipples erect as she lifted one arm above her head. But even that didn't make her breasts look as big as Alenna Prosper's, her Micmac friend in Maine. "More than a mouthful is too much," Alenna had told her with authority, cupping her own bosoms in both hands. "Good thing my Noel has a big mouth, eh?"

She pulled up the picture Bryan had sent her for Christmas. God, he was hot. Sun-bleached hair, amazing abs, jeans pulled down just to where things got really interesting. *I put on some muscle last summer when I worked on a farm*, he'd written. *My hair's not that light anymore. Merry Christmas, anyway.*

She gazed at the image. She'd written him off at first, heeding the Warden's warnings about the internet, figuring he was some fat, forty-year old pervert trolling for young girls. But Bryan had kept texting, never sounding like anything but a teenager, never suggesting anything more concrete than meeting "someday." He'd also sent lots of pictures—of himself, with his friends, in his green football jersey with the number 35 on the front. As the weeks passed, she slowly decided that he was for real. The fact that in three days they would meet was unbelievable.He had Monday off from school, for Martin Luther King Day, and his Uncle Jake had promised to drive him all the way from Kentucky to North Carolina. She'd sent him directions to a nothing little place in the mountains called Unaka.

Enlarging the picture, she focused on his face. His mouth looked plenty big—he wouldn't have any trouble fitting it over one of her breasts. The thought of it sent a delicious shiver through her insides.

She looked up from her phone, alert for the Warden. Walmart was having an after Christmas sale. People were waddling across the parking lot bundled up like wrapped packages, laden with half-price tree lights and decorations they could use next year. She wondered if the Warden would ever think of making such a far-sighted purchase, then decided not. They lived like gypsies—tending a camp in Maine last summer, wintering at another one here in Carolina. Next year they'd probably be somewhere even duller than here. *I hear Alaska's really cool*, the Warden had said last week, that stupid dreamy look on his face. *The Aurora's amazing up there.* Alaska is fifty times colder than Maine, she wanted to tell him. Full of crazy trappers and starving polar bears. We are Eastern Cherokees. We have no business in Alaska. But she knew better than to express her opinion to the Warden. He did what he wanted, always. Right now he was probably standing in line, irritated at the shoppers ahead of him, who were foolishly stocking up on tinsel and wrapping paper instead of serious essentials like lamp oil and duck tape.

A truck pulled up beside theirs, jarring her back to present. She clutched her topless selfie to her chest as the driver climbed out. A boy her age, skinny, cheeks pink-chapped from the cold. He wore a bright gold Murphy Bulldogs cap. "Hi," he said, grinning. "Happy New Year, a little late."

Before she could answer, he looked up as someone yelled across the parking lot. Lily turned to see two girls wearing gold Murphy hoodies, waving for him to join them.

"Gotta go," he said. "See ya."

He ran to catch up with the girls. After they all hugged, he scooped one of them up into his arms and kissed her. Then they all loped into Walmart together, their laughter ringing bright on the cold air.

She watched them until they disappeared inside the door, wondering what it would be like to have that many friends. What would it feel like if Bryan swirled her around and kissed her before he took her to Kentucky? Every night she prayed to her dead mother Ruth *please let this happen; please let this work out.* But even if Bryan didn't work out, at least she would not be trapped there. She could leave Kentucky and go anywhere she pleased. All she knew was that she was done with the Warden. She couldn't stand another year of being ogled by lecherous old fishermen who shook her father's hand but winked at her when his back was turned.

She looked at her phone again, studying her own image. Compared to those girls in the parking lot, her breasts seemed ridiculously small. "Bryan might not even like the way I look," she whispered. What if he got the picture and backed out of coming? Wrote that he got sick or his Uncle

Jake's van had broken down? Or worst of all, what if she never heard from him again? What would she do then?

Her fingers trembling, she looked up. Another shopper caught her attention. A tall man in a camo jacket, walked towards the truck carrying a big brown sack and a length of cotton rope. Her heart sank. The Warden had finished his shopping.

"Shit." If she was going to send the selfie, she needed to do it now. They wouldn't be back in town for another week, and she'd never be able to upload it from the ridge. Taking a deep breath, she logged on to her secret Kimmeegirl account.

This is me, she wrote, her thumbs flying over the phone. *See you in three days!* She offered another quick prayer for luck and pressed *send*.

She looked up, checking for the Warden as her selfie uploaded. Some woman in a pink ski jacket had stopped him halfway to the truck, holding a map in front of him. The Warden was pointing across the parking lot, giving her directions somewhere.

"Come on, come on," she whispered, returning to her phone. Why did these pictures take so long to send? She checked to see what the Warden was doing. He'd finished talking to the woman and was hurrying towards the truck. A few more seconds and he would be here.

She watched the *send* icon spinning; just as the Warden unlocked the driver's door, a ding from her phone went off. Her selfie had launched. Bryan Thompson of Henryville, Kentucky, would soon be getting a real close look at Lily Walkingstick.

CHAPTER 2

———

Mary Crow stood at the side entrance of the Tsalagi County courtroom and buttoned the jacket of Deathwrap, her trademark suit. It had been years since she'd worn it and it felt a little tight in the waist. Better cut down on the apple strudels at home, she told herself. Or you won't be able to button it at all.

She'd convicted nine killers in this outfit, earning her nickname Killer Crow. Cal Whitman, Maxine Lukes, seven beyond those. She could see each of them, smirking and cocky, until their verdicts were read. Suddenly their arrogance vanished, and they left the courtroom sad-faced and shackled, their justice delivered by her, a half-Cherokee woman in a black silk suit.

"Hope I can do it again," she whispered, brushing a speck of lint from her sleeve. "Lots riding on this one."

She waited until the last case cleared out; then she squared her shoulders and strode into the courtroom. Tsalagi Countians filled every seat, knowing that the docket of DUI's and the B&E's had been just warm-ups for the main event. Her case was what they hungered to hear—the State of North Carolina v. Teofilo Owle, a twenty-year career drug trafficker who'd not only managed to avoid conviction on a number of felonies, but who'd also never spent more than an hour behind bars. The DA's office regarded Teo as "the curse", and the prosecutor who could put Teo in jail for even one night would be regarded as a hero in this small, westernmost county of North Carolina.

Mary walked to her table, relaxing her poker face long enough to smile at her friend Ginger Cochran, who was covering the trial as a stringer for the *Charlotte Observer*. The story had garnered a lot of ink. The Attorney General in Raleigh had asked Mary to take over a drug trafficking case that stalled out in mid-discovery when Tsalagi County DA Drusilla Smith was found floating face-down in Hiawassee Lake. The SBI had worked double-time trying to link Teo to her death, but when they couldn't come up with anything more actionable than a suspicious drowning, Mary decided to continue with Drusilla's original drug case. Even so, she knew putting Teo behinds bars would be a long shot. The next attorney scheduled to take over this case had jumped ship and taken a private job in Charlotte. The single remaining ADA with any knowledge of the case was undergoing treatment for breast cancer. In desperation, the state AG had called Mary. A continuance would likely mean they'd never see Teo in Tsalagi County again.

As Mary put her papers on the table, a loud murmur went through the crowd. She looked up to see two men take seats at the table opposite from hers. One was tall, elegant William Bradford Breedlove, a pricey defense attorney from Raleigh. The other was Teo himself, the short, dark Mexican/Cherokee eluder of justice. Mug shots of Teo usually showed him glowering with a red bandana around his neck, a razor-thin scar going from the right corner of his mouth to his right ear. Today Breedlove had spruced him up in a suit and tie. Mary exchanged a collegial nod with

Breedlove before she glanced at Teo. She was expecting the usual frown, or a surreptitious middle finger salute. But Teo did neither. He appraised Mary as if she were naked, then, with his lips making a sucking motion, gave her a lurid wink. The instant he did that, she felt her old hatred flare. It had ignited the day her mother was killed; she guessed it would simmer inside her until she drew her last breath. Murder and murderers were personal for Mary Crow.

She returned Teo's wink with an icy stare that telegraphed its own message. *I am the last person you want to mess with, you worthless turd. I will hurt you more than you can imagine.*

The bailiff conferred with Judge Hamilton Morton, a tall, barrel-chested man who wore rimless glasses, and announced the case. "Continuance of Case 00-612, the State of North Carolina versus Teophilo Owle."

Mary stepped up to the microphone. In her crisp, courtroom voice, she read Drusilla's old indictment, which claimed that Teo conspired to transport and vend various illegal substances in and through the state of North Carolina. Mary knew from Drusilla's notes that she also had evidence against Teo for robbery, arson, and murder, but had opted to go to trial with the drug charge. Mary figured Drusilla had planned an Al Capone prosecution, where you put a killer away on a more easily proven indictment.

Bradford Breedlove stood up. "Your Honor, as I said when the late Ms. Smith brought these charges, the state has no evidence linking my client to these crimes. Since almost seven months have passed in the continuance of this case, we move to dismiss."

Mary shot back. "Your Honor, the State will show that before her untimely death, District Attorney Smith had built a strong case that irrefutably substantiates the charges against Mr. Owle." Though Mary tried to sound confident, she knew this was iffy. Drusilla had collected good enough drug evidence, but she'd pieced it together like somebody who'd dipped into the evidence locker. Mary was still finding little bits of police reports stuck in books, possible witness lists crumpled in the drawers of Drusilla's desk.

Bradford Breedlove started to protest again, but Judge Morton cut him off. "We did much of this last summer, Mr. Breedlove, so let's get going. Has Mr. Owle changed his plea?"

"No," Teofilo said, cutting hard black eyes at Mary. "I'm not guilty. This woman don't know what she's talking about."

Mary held up her casebook. "This is the evidence file, your Honor. It grows thicker by the day."

Judge Morton looked at Mary over his glasses. "I suppose you want him remanded?"

Mary frowned. Here was Teo's evil genius—when someone filed an indictment against him, strange things started to happen to people connected with the case. Witnesses' barns caught fire, a cop's favorite hunting dog was poisoned, and Drusilla, who'd once swum backstroke for Duke, wound up drowned in four feet of water. Nobody was immune to these curious runs of bad luck.

She said, "Given the seriousness of this indictment, I think all of Tsalagi County would rest easier with Mr. Owle in jail."

Breedlove protested. "Judge Morton, you granted bail to Mr. Owle seven months ago. He has lived within its parameters, and has incurred no further charges. I see no reason to incarcerate him now."

Mary stopped Breedlove from going further. "Your Honor, I'd like to remind the court that Mr. Owle has a well-known history of witness intimidation, obstruction of justice and interfering with police investigations." She held up a long sheet of paper. "Since this case was initiated, sixteen complaints have been filed by witnesses connected with this case."

Breedlove laughed. "Then why haven't you charged him with anything else?"

Mary addressed the judge. "Witnesses are afraid to come forward, your Honor. But there is a clear pattern here. I can show it and we can all follow it."

"Unless he's been charged, it's inadmissible, Ms. Crow," said Morton. "You know that."

Mary went on, playing the one trump card she'd managed to come up with. "Then let me remind the court that Mr. Owle is part Cherokee and lives in an extremely remote area of the Unicoi Mountains. This location affords him easy access to the old Cherokee trails that still honeycomb the area. Mr. Owle could easily escape trial by following these trails."

"I don't know anything about no trails," squawked Teo. "I got bone spurs in both feet, anyway."

Ignoring him, Mary asked the judge, "May I approach, your Honor?"

Morton nodded. Mary stepped forward, carrying a map on a large piece of foam core. She turned it so that both the judge and rest of the courtroom could see.

"Your Honor, this is a map of the eastern United States. As you can see, the old Warrior Path leads from North Carolina up to Canada, and south to the Gulf of Mexico," she explained, pointing to the routes she'd marked in red. "Mr. Owle has relatives and business connections in both the Nuevo Leon and Jalisco regions of Mexico. All he needs to do is follow this trail down to lower Alabama, get on a boat, and he's home free."

A murmur of surprise went through the courtroom. Apparently no one had ever considered old Indian Trails and Teofilo Owle's family connections.

Leaving her map in full view of the courtroom, Mary returned to her table. She knew that if Judge Morton let Teo loose, he might get voted off the bench come the next election. But if he put Teo behind bars, he might wind up floating in the Hiawassee like poor Drusilla. Mary did not envy him his decision.

After what seemed like eons, Morton ruled. "Ms. Crow, you've certainly done your homework, and your theory has merit. But Mr. Owle has obeyed the strictures set by his bail. He could easily have used those trails to avoid the little get-together we're having right now. I find that without additional cause, there's no reason to remand now."

The courtroom spectators gave a soft groan. Disappointed, Mary Crow looked down at her papers. She had hoped to serve notice to Tsalagi Countians that Killer Crow had come to town. Instead, she'd just become another prosecutor who'd struck out.

Judge Morton continued, squinting at his computer screen. "I'm going to re-set this trial for Monday, March 4, 10 a.m." He looked at Mary and Breedlove. "Let's be ready to go then, counselors. This has lingered too long." With a theatrical rap with his gavel, he said, "Court adjourned."

Everyone stood as Morton returned to his chambers. Breedlove and Teo waited a moment, then turned to leave out the side door. As they did, Teo leaned toward Mary, pointing his finger like a gun.

"Hanuwa, jigili!" he whispered in Cherokee.

She gave him another cold smile; the courtroom came to life–people talking, shuffling to the exit. As she packed up her briefcase, she heard a familiar voice behind her.

"Any comments, Ms. Crow?"

She turned. Her friend Ginger stood there hugely pregnant, balancing a reporter's notebook on top of her expanded belly.

Mary knew she had to be diplomatic here. After struggling for a comment that did not convey her disappointment in Morton's ruling, she finally said, "I'm glad we got an early trial date, and I'm eager to present the State's case in court."

"That's it?" Ginger frowned. "Seriously?"

Mary nodded.

"Okay," said Ginger. "I've got to go file this now. But let's talk later."

"Okay."

Ginger hurried to the door. As she did, a tall man sauntered up from the other side of the courtroom. Victor Galloway, now stood dressed in a jacket and tie, SBI badge around his neck. When Mary left him in bed this morning, he'd had nothing on but a pair of green plaid boxer shorts.

"So what did you think?" she asked, her tone subdued with disappointment. She'd hoped to dazzle Victor with her courtroom prowess.

"Formidable," he said. "I've never seen you as Killer Crow before."

Mary grabbed her map. "I didn't break the curse."

"You were going up against an expert at the weave and dodge."

She smiled at him, knowing how hard he'd worked to link Teo to Drusilla's death. Though the coroner confirmed that Drusilla had drowned with a blood alcohol level of .16, everyone in law enforcement was certain Teo had something to do with it.

"What did Owle say to you when he left?" asked Victor.

"*Watch out, bitch.* In Cherokee, no less."

He scowled. "Are you kidding me?"

"Victor, I've heard far worse in Atlanta. So have you. Comes with our jobs."

"Except most threats come from jail," he said. "This asshole's running loose."

"And I'm living with an SBI agent who has a mighty big gun." She smiled. "I think I'll be okay."

"I suppose." Still frowning, he jingled the keys in his pocket. "Hey–want to go out tonight? There's something I'd like to talk about."

His words caught her by surprise. In her experience, a man wanting to schedule a talk seldom meant good news. "Like what?"

"Just stuff," he replied, lowering his gaze to the bar that separated them.

She knew he was dodging the question, but she couldn't go into it now, in the middle of the courtroom. "Okay. I should be back in Hartsville around six."

"Great. I'll pick you up at your office." He looked as if he wanted to say something else, but instead he turned and headed for the front door. As she packed Drusilla's evidence file alongside her map, a thought occurred to her. This truly had been the first time Victor had seen her in Death Wrap, as Killer Crow. Could he be feeling queasy about that aspect of her? Her old love Jonathan Walkingstick sure had. *I love you*, he'd always said. *But you just go too flipping crazy when murder's involved.*

No, she told herself as she gathered up her coat. Victor would stand up and cheer if I put this bastard behind bars.

CHAPTER 3

Two states away, in Henryville, Kentucky, Leroy Summers sat in his bedroom, staring at his laptop. The email he'd been waiting for had arrived at work, but he'd managed to resist the temptation to open it. Personal emails were forbidden at the call center, but more important was that he didn't want any of his brain-dead colleagues leaning into his cubicle, gawking at his screen. Everybody at work thought he was just a dateless geek, in his Spiderman tee shirt and polyester pants. They had no idea what he was in reality.

"Okay, Kimmeegirl," he whispered, a frisson of anticipation tightening his balls. "I'm finally gonna see what you look like."

He'd learned early on that most of the cuties sent fake selfies—the girls who bit on his bait were too fat, too pimply-faced or just too butt ugly to risk revealing their real faces. But Kimmeegirl had seemed different from the start. She didn't write in the usual adolescent slang and she never complained about stupid crap like geometry homework or what the mean girls had done to her in gym class. At first he'd worried that she'd been FBI or a rogue cop who'd gone vigilante. But as the months passed, he realized that as polished as Kimmeegirl's writing was, it still betrayed the dreams of a teenager. Like all the others, she sought friends, yearned to break free of parental tyranny, and desperately wanted someone to love.

So he wrote to her as one of his old stand-bys, Bryan Thompson, who was everything he himself had not been in high school—athletic, zit-free, and popular. He'd gone with his usual Bryan bio—a lonely orphaned boy who lived with his bachelor uncles. At fifteen Bryan was a sophomore at Henry High, where he played JV football and enjoyed English class. In reality Leroy was 42, a paunchy telemarketer who lived with his brother Chet on a seventy-acre farm, most of which was leased out to an agribusiness concern. Five days a week he successfully hawked everything from time-shares to automobile maintenance plans. But nights and weekends, from a mean little house that squatted on the edge of a soybean field, he sold love to homely teenaged girls who panted to meet boyfriends who didn't exist.

Despite his gifts of persuasion, it had taken him months to crack Kimmeegirl. She was wary as a fawn, and only after he'd sent her hundreds of fake pictures and told her that he'd flunked algebra (true), smoked weed when he could get it (sometimes true) and had never had sex with a girl (false, though none of his conquests had survived the experience) did she reveal that she was home schooled, that she lived in a log cabin and referred to her father as the Warden. Sensing his opening, he'd pounced. *Is he that bad?*

Yes, she'd replied. *He's awful. He'd chain me up if he could.*

He had Bryan respond sympathetically, hoping she'd reveal her location. *That must suk. Where do you live?*

In the middle of nowhere, she'd replied, cleverly avoiding his trap.

From then on, Kimmeegirl became a challenge. He'd pursued her relentlessly, sending her pictures of Bryan (really a photo of Troy, the

WHITE TREES CRIMSON SNOW

muscle-bound kid he paid to mow his front yard), texting her funny little love notes with emojis. Finally, it had worked. She'd revealed that her name was Lily Walkingstick and she lived with her father at Paint Creek camp, near Murphy, North Carolina. Today the photo she'd long promised him had arrived. If she wasn't too much of a dog, he might make good on his promise to meet her.

"Okay, Lily Walkingstick," he whispered, cracking his knuckles for luck. "Let's see what you got."

He opened her email with half-closed eyes, preparing himself for the inevitable disappointment. But when he got a good look at the picture, he gasped. If this girl was for real, he'd hit the jackpot. Dark hair, caramel skin, deep dimples in both cheeks. Her face was beautiful, but beyond that, she'd lifted one arm over her head, allowing plump, young breasts to peek from a white blouse. Immediately, his penis stiffened, hot and hard, demanding his attention. He unzipped his pants, covered his lap with the dishtowel he kept by his computer. Moments later his bottle rocket fired with a gush that left him weak.

He sat in the chair, drained, feeling as if heart had just exploded. He stayed that way for a while, opening his eyes only when he heard the low rumble of a motor approaching the house. He turned, watching out the window as a monstrous truck cab came growling up the rutted driveway, yellow lights glowing in the early evening darkness.

"Chet," he whispered as the cab rolled to the rear of their property. Back from taking some load of something to God knew where. If Chet was feeling familial, he would come in the house, nuke a burrito and drink beer until he passed out on the living room sofa. If he was still pissed about little Spitfire, he would hole up in his rig, smoking weed and feasting on fried pork rinds. By morning, the smell would be unimaginable.

Leroy waited, wondering if Chet would emerge from the cab. When he didn't, he grabbed his laptop and zipped up his jacket. Pissed or not, Chet needed to see this new cutie. She was something special.

Turning his collar up against a blustery wind, he walked towards the truck. Yards away, he could hear *Poor Twisted Me* blasting from inside the cab. That meant that Chet must have driven north, to Indianapolis or even Chicago. Red Bull and heavy metal music were what got him through the dull, ruler-straight roads of Indiana and Illinois. Taking a deep breath, Leroy walked up and banged on the door of the cab.

"Hey, Chet," he yelled above the din inside. "It's Leroy."

The music blared on. He knocked again. "Chet, open up!"

Metallica continued to yowl. Growing angry at having to trudge through the cold to talk to his little brother, Leroy picked up a rock from the driveway and heaved it at the side of the cab. It made a terrible thud. Abruptly, the music stopped, leaving his ears ringing in the sudden silence.

The door burst open, revealing a six-foot, blue eyed, near-clone of himself. Only hair and body fat differentiated them—Chet kept his head shaved, his muscles toned while Leroy had fuzzy brown hair and a gut that already hung over his belt.

"What the fuck do you want?" Chet shrieked, his eyes looking like two fried eggs. He was wired on something way beyond Metallica.

"You want some supper? I made a meat loaf," Leroy lied. His notion of a home-cooked meal meant shoving a TV dinner in the microwave.

"I already ate."

"You want to come to the house and watch TV? Indiana's playing Kentucky."

"No."

Leroy realized his friendly overtures were falling flat, so he cut to the chase. "You up for the cutie run of your life?"

"And get killed for real this time? No thanks."

"That wasn't my fault, Chet." Their most recent cutie run had nearly ended in disaster when they'd been surprised by deer hunters. They'd managed to escape capture despite the screaming, kicking girl, but just barely.

"But you told me it was okay. You told me you'd checked it out." Chet wore only jeans and a wife-beater tee shirt, but he seemed to radiate heat like nuclear waste.

"I did check it out. Those fuckers were poachers."

"Yeah. Poachers who could have called the law on us. I'm still scared to drive through Pennsyl-fucking-vania."

Leroy clutched the laptop and spoke softly. "I've told you before, Chet. Anybody poaching game isn't going to call the cops over anything. Get over it."

"Screw you, Leroy," Chet muttered, turning to climb back inside the cab.

"You really need to see this one, Chet. She's *special*."

"So's fresh air and freedom, Leroy. And not spending twenty years getting cornholed in prison. That's pretty damn special, too."

"She looks a little like Darlene."

Leroy watched as Chet stopped halfway up the ladder. Darlene was Chet's ex-wife. Black-haired and black-hearted, the thought of her still stopped him cold. Leroy never could tell if it was from hatred or desire. Chet paused a moment, then turned and said, "Let me have a look."

Leroy gave a small, secret smile as he followed Chet into the cab. The trick to anything was figuring out which button worked on which people. Once you pushed it, you could get them to do anything you wanted.

Inside, the cab both looked and smelled like a garbage dump. Fast food detritus—McDonald's bags, Hunt Brothers Pizza boxes littered the floor, while Chet's ashtray sprouted a forest of stubbed-out Marlboro butts. Chet scooted over to the driver's seat, still eying Leroy with suspicion.

"Okay. Let's see this magnificent piece of poontang."

Though Leroy hated to cede his nice laptop to his ham-fisted brother, he handed it over. As soon as Chet opened it, the picture of Kimmeegirl filled the screen.

Chet stared at the image, clicking the top of his favorite Zippo lighter as he gazed at the girl. Finally, he admitted Leroy was right. "Damn–she does look a little like Darlene. Same dimples. Darlene's tits were bigger, though."

"Ever see a cutie that juicy?" asked Leroy.

Nervous, Chet clicked the lighter open and shut. "Makes me wonder if it's too good."

"A trap?"

"Yeah. People are still looking for Spitfire. We might be on the cops' radar now."

"Not possible," said Leroy. "I had the camper painted, got a new Ducks Unlimited license plate. Besides, I've talked to this girl for months. She's for real."

"Where is she?"

"North Carolina. I'm going there tomorrow."

"You?" Chet laughed. "By yourself?"

"I've got plenty of rope, dope and ammo. She's expecting me Monday."

Chet looked at him as if he'd lost his mind. "Who's she expecting? Leroy the love-salesman?"

"Bryan. He works well with this type. I'll play good old Uncle Jake."

Chet glanced at Kimmeegirl once again, and handed the laptop back to Leroy. "Good luck, man. I hope it works out for you."

"You seriously don't want in on this?" asked Leroy.

He used the lighter on a cigarette, blew out a long stream of smoke. "Ain't worth it. I'm not playing this game anymore."

"Well, Mom always said you were the timid one." Leroy sighed as he climbed out of the passenger seat. "I guess that was one thing she got right." He put the laptop under his jacket as he stepped away from the cab. "See you."

Lifting a hand in farewell, he started walking back to the duplex. If he knew his brother, the word *timid* would stick in his throat like a chicken bone. He would fret all night about it, and unless Metallica had caused Chet to grow a set of balls big enough to stand up to him, by morning he would be banging on his backdoor, begging to come along.

CHAPTER 4

All the way home, Lily felt as if someone had lit a slow-burning fuse inside her. Even after they finished the rest of their errands and the Warden took her to Marco's for a large pepperoni pizza, she remained jittery. All she could think about was the selfie she'd sent. Had Bryan gotten it yet? Did he like it? Or was he laughing at her, showing her nakedness to all his friends?

They pulled up to the camp just after dark. Lily unlocked the gate and opened it wide enough to allow the truck to pass through. Then she re-locked it and rode standing up in the back of the truck as they jounced along the rutted, mile-long road to the cabin. Spreading her arms wide, she pretended she was in Hawaii, surfing.

After the Warden parked, she helped carry their supplies into the kitchen. Canned tomatoes, orange juice, two more boxes of tampons. She almost laughed—the Warden's notion of a menstrual period was something akin to a leg amputation. Already she had enough pads and tampons to last her into her twenties. Thank God Alenna's mom had showed her how to use them. She cringed at the thought of a female anatomy chat with the Warden.

"You okay?" He broke the silence that had stretched between them since they left Murphy.

"Fine."

"Want to play a game of Scrabble?"

"No." With a heavy sigh, she went to her room and closed the door behind her. Jesus–how many games of Scrabble had she played in the past five years? She had no idea—just that they'd worn out two dictionaries and she had a ready arsenal of words like quidnunc and zooty. Once she got away from the Warden, she would never play the stupid game again.

She flopped down on her bed and checked her phone, hoping some miracle had occurred and she had enough bars to reach cyberspace. But the thing was useless as ever, the eighty million trees that surrounded them smothering the signal. She would have to wait until tomorrow, when she could scurry up the ridge behind the cabin. Sometimes, if the internet gods smiled, she could get a signal there.

She turned on her light, grabbed a book from the pile by her bed. *Between Shades of Gray.* She started reading. It was unlike *Fifty Shades of Grey*, which she and Alenna had read by flashlight at a sleepover. This story was about a Lithuanian girl, shipped to a Gulag by the Russians. She turned the pages quickly, caught up in the story, thinking how like this girl she was. They'd both been taken from their homes, forced to live lives they didn't want. But the girl in the book loved her mother and wanted desperately to reconnect with her father. Her own mother Ruth was dead, killed by the bitch Mary Crow. Though the Warden had told her a bullshit story about her mother having some kind of breakdown and pulling a gun on Mary, her Grandpa Moon had told her what really happened—that Mary Crow had grabbed that gun and shot her mother, just so she could get her father back. Once she heard that, her love for Mary had soured into hate. Nothing had changed her opinion since.

A noise outside caught her attention. She looked out the window to see two raccoons picking at the lock on the smokehouse door. She banged on the window. They turned and scurried away, hunchbacked and galloping.

The spell of the book was broken then, and her thoughts flew back to Bryan. Again she checked her phone; again she got nothing. Sighing, she looked at the picture he'd sent. He was standing beside a lawn mower, his blonde hair long, his grin slightly crooked. He looked confident, assured. A boy who could handle anything, from catching a pass to mowing forty acres.

She expanded the picture and traced his arms, wondering how tightly those muscles would hold her, how his lips would feel on her skin. *Eating at the Y*, Alenna had told her, was when boys kissed you *there*, between your legs. "It's awesome," Alenna reported with great authority.

"Has Noel done that to you?" asked Lily.

"Three times," Alenna said proudly. "In the parking lot behind the skating rink. I nearly died it felt so good."

She touched herself, wondering how different a tongue might feel than a finger. Softer, certainly. Warmer, too. Quickly, she pulled her finger away and rose from the bed. What a freak she was! Fifteen and kissed only once, by Marc Freneau, who stuck his thick, slimy tongue halfway down her throat, just before the Warden caught them and scared Marc so bad he ran all the way home. All her friends in Maine had been kissed many times, now. And by many different boyfriends. They were in love, having sex, probably planning weddings. All she'd done was traipse after the Warden like a pet on a leash.

Angry tears came to her eyes—she felt as if her life was some bright stream that was flowing past her, sweeping Alenna and Bryan and everything she loved away. She went to her dresser and pulled a red wool sweater from a drawer. Maybe she would walk to the lake. Or hike to the ridge, on the outside chance she could link to the internet there. All she knew was that if she stayed in this cabin a minute longer she would scream.

She laced up her boots and put her phone in the back pocket of her jeans. When she emerged from her room, she found the Warden in the kitchen, washing sweet potatoes for supper.

"I need to go out," she announced flatly.

"Now?" He looked up from the sink, warming up his parental NO.

She played the trump card that worked every time. "I've got cramps. I sat in the truck most of the day. I need to get some exercise."

"Oh." He dried off the potatoes, his resistance evaporating. She knew he regarded menstruation as a mysterious land of hidden dangers; never did he cross the border or question the guards.

"I'm just going to the top of the ridge. I'll be back in time for supper."

He glanced at his watch, then handed her his knife. "Take Ribtickler. I saw coyotes up there last week."

They both knew most coyotes would slink away from humans, but she took the knife just the same. If it shut him up, who cared?

His "be careful" followed her as she slammed the front door behind her and stepped into the January night. She hurried around the cabin, sliding on a frozen puddle. Up into the woods she went, the slush from old snow crunchy beneath her feet. She came up here a lot, storming out of the cabin whenever the Warden pissed her off. The trail was steep but apparently smelled of humans. She'd never seen anything bigger than a possum up here.

With Ribtickler digging into the small of her back, she ran. Once something scuttled away from her in the brushes, but beyond that, only the woods stretched, stark and silent, into the night. And miles away, west of the Appalachians, was a boy in Kentucky who maybe by now had seen her mostly topless.

"Wonder if he's already written me," she said, starting to hurry. "Wonder if I've got a message waiting, right now."

Twenty minutes later, sweating and breathless, she reached the top of the ridge. Fifty feet from the trail was a broad stump of an oak tree felled by lightning. She hurried to stand in the middle of the stump and looked up. The moon had risen, a white orb over the distant mountains, surrounded by a halo of ice crystals.

"Ring around the moon, snow coming soon," she whispered, repeating one of the Warden's dopey weather maxims. God, what would she do if Bryan couldn't get up here? What would she do if stupid snow ruined her plans?

"Just see if he's even sent you a text," she told herself. "He may not think you're worth coming to see."

She pulled her phone from her back pocket and stared at the screen. She was almost too scared to check her messages. What if he gave her some lame excuse? Said his uncle bailed on the trip, or he'd gotten back together with an old girlfriend? Or worse, said nothing at all?

"Come on," she whispered. "Don't be such a chicken."

She turned on the phone. With another silent prayer to her dead mother, she closed her eyes and lifted the phone to the sky. For an agonizing minute she heard nothing, then amazingly, she heard the *DING* of a message alert. For once, the internet was working up here! With trembling hands, she lowered the phone and looked at the screen. She had one message, from *tracksterBryan*.

Her heart beating wildly, she clicked on the message. She saw first a line of heart emojis, then the text–U R BEAUTIFUL. ILY. CU in 2 Days.

A wave of utter joy engulfed her. Embracing the phone, she gazed up at the ring-girded moon. For the first time, on this night, at this moment, a boy had wanted her. Whatever else might happen to her, she would remember this moment forever.

CHAPTER 5

Mary Crow drove home to Hartsville in a mood as gray as the weather. She'd blown her triumphant return as a prosecutor, and now Victor wanted to talk. She couldn't imagine what might be troubling him, unless he'd argued with Alton Spencer, his spit-polished, anal boss who regarded Agent Victor Galloway as a dangerously loose cannon. "Some days just dawn crappy and never improve," she whispered as sleety rain began to pepper her windshield.

She found a parking space a block away from her office and lugged her briefcase up the street. Her secretary Annette had already gone, but had left a page of notes–mostly about JimAnn Ponder, a fifty-something mountain woman whose husband of thirty years had taken her out to a fancy dinner and told her he wanted a divorce. JimAnn bent Mary's ear regularly about that humiliation, and now she'd apparently begun to hector poor Annette, who'd noted that Mrs. Ponder had referred to her soon to be ex as a "pissant ridge runner" and that she was "mean mad enough to wring his chicken neck."

Imagining their conversation, Mary had to laugh. Annette sounded like an announcer for the BBC while JimAnn Ponder could win the local hollerin' contest. Annette probably wished for a translator every time JimAnn called.

"Good grief," whispered Mary as she reluctantly made a note to call JimAnn in the morning. "I'd rather do one good murder than a hundred divorces."

A knock on the door startled her. She opened it to find Victor, still dressed in the coat and tie he'd worn to court. Though it was freezing outside, his face was flushed and a sheen of sweat glistened on his forehead.

"Hi," he said. "What are you working on now?"

"Helping a mountain gal who's madder'n a wet hen," Mary imitated JimAnn as she put a hand on Victor's forehead. "She's nigh fit to bustin' over her rotten mister. Do you have a fever?"

"No, I'm fine. So are you going to take her rotten mister to the cleaners?"

"After she's washed his socks and run his flea market for thirty years, I'm not letting him leave her with nothing," said Mary.

"You go for it, counselor." He turned toward the door, frowning. "Are you ready to eat?"

"I am. I haven't had anything since breakfast."

"Then let's go. I've got reservations at Lulu's."

As Mary turned off her lights, her heart gave a sour little beat. Lulu's had been the site of JimAnn Ponder's dump-off dinner. Victor was acting so subdued, she wondered if he had a similar plan for her, tonight. Don't be silly, she told herself. Victor's no Cletus Ponder.

The restaurant was only two blocks away, so they walked, arm-in-arm, along sidewalks wet with an icy rain. Hartsville seemed in drab hibernation—all the bright Christmas decorations had vanished, but the stores had been slow to replace them with Valentine hearts. Hurrying through the depressing gloom, they jaywalked across Main Street, dodging a red pickup truck. Mary looked back at the driver just before they ducked into the warm redolence of Lulu's. As they followed the hostess to a small booth in a corner nook, Mary realized that this was the perfect break-up table. Softly lit, but secluded, so that angry tears and strident voices would not disturb the other diners. But it was also a romantic nook, perfect for hand-holding over a bottle of wine. Mary didn't know what to think.

The waitress came to the table. Victor ordered the IPA on tap. After the long, frustrating day, Mary decided to self-medicate, fast. "A double martini. Sapphire Gin, Noilly Prat. With a twist."

As the waitress left, Victor gave her an odd look. "You're usually a Malbec girl. When did you switch to double Martinis?"

"When I blow a case in court. Killer Crow got her wings clipped today."

"Are you kidding? You looked like the right hand of God up there. That stuff about the Indian trails was terrific."

"Yeah, well, that bastard Teo's still a free man."

"I feel like that's my fault," said Victor. "I followed every lead I could find, and still came up with nothing. Spencer pulling me off on those other cases didn't help, either."

"You did a great job, Victor. Drusilla's secretary warned me that catching Teo was like trying to bottle smoke."

Victor's frown did not lift. "I still should have done better."

"We've got almost four more months to work on it," said Mary. "Surely we can come up with something."

The waitress brought their drinks. Mary clicked her martini against

Victor's beer and drained half of it. As the gin began to warm her insides, she looked at Victor and mustered her courage.

"So what did you want to talk about?"

He loosened his tie. "Don't you want to eat first?"

"No. I'd rather have our talk." If Victor was going to dump her, she did not intend to react like JimAnn, and start bawling over a plate of pork chops.

"Oh. Well. Okay." He ran a hand through his dark hair. For a moment he stared at the dark green candle that glowed between them, and cleared his throat.

"Mary, by my last count, I've asked you to marry me six times. You've turned me down six times. Tonight," he paused for a deep breath, "things have got to change."

"Okay." This is it, she decided, taking another slug of her Martini. Here it comes.

He took another swallow of beer. "The Richmond, Virginia, police department has made me an offer— they'll put me on salary as detective and pay for the rest of my training as a profiler. I will no longer be at the end of Spencer's short leash."

"That's great!" She tried to sound happy but her heart clenched. Victor was moving to Virginia.

"That's the good news," he said.

"Okay. What's the bad news?"

"I have to let them know by next Friday."

"Oh." Mary blinked. "Why is that bad? I know how much you hate Spencer."

"Before I go, I need to do this." He reached in the pocket of his jacket and pulled out a small, black velvet box. He opened it to reveal a ring; a single diamond surrounded by small rubies. It reminded Mary of glittering pieces of ice and fire, all mixed together.

"Te adoro, Maria Cuervo," he whispered, leaning across the table. "For the last and final time, would you do me the honor of becoming my wife?"

She stared at the ring, stunned, unable to form words.

"If you don't love me, just say so." Again, he swallowed hard. "I'd rather end everything tonight."

She felt like an idiot. She'd tossed back most of a double martini to soften the blow of a kiss-off. Now he was proposing.

Her cheeks on fire, she struggled to come up with the right words. "Victor, I love you more than anything. But..."

"It's Walkingstick, isn't it?"

"Walkingstick?"

"You still look at red pickup trucks. You looked at that one on the way over here."

"It almost ran over us."

Victor went on. "Every time you see a red pickup, you look. I used to think maybe you just had a thing for trucks, but Cochran told me that Walkingstick drove one."

"Victor—"

"Look, I know Walkingstick played a big part in your life. I know how much you loved him."

He rattled on, expanding on a theory about how some deep hurts can emotionally lame people for the rest of their lives. Finally, he gave up the psycho-babble and grabbed her hand. "Look—forget Walkingstick. I don't know that much about him and I don't care. What I do know is that you are kind and funny and smart and beautiful and even our worst moments have been the best moments of my life." He slipped the ring on her finger. "Marry me," he whispered. "I will never, ever love anyone the way I love you."

She stared at the ring— it perfectly reflected everything she felt for him. Love and passion, need and desire. Her head clearing a bit, she pressed his hand against her cheek. "Victor, I love you but I don't know if I can marry anybody."

"Why not?" he asked. "I'll never ask you to quit being Killer Crow."

"Victor, it has nothing to do with my job." She looked into his eyes—the candlelight made them dark and fierce, but also kind. "I'm just scared."

"Of what?"

"Of it not working out. Of having something wonderful turn to dust." Losing Jonathan Walkingstick had felt like someone dissecting her own beating heart, inches at a time. After that she'd sworn that she would never again love anyone that deeply.

Gently, he covered her hand in such way that she could not remove the ring. "Then let's do this. Wear this for a while. Think hard about everything I've said. Tomorrow I go to Raleigh for that SBI seminar. When I get back, we'll talk again. If you say yes, I'll forget Richmond and happily stay here kissing Spencer's ass until we toddle off to the nursing home together. If your answer's no, I'll move on."

She kissed his hand—how she loved him! What would her life be without him? She couldn't stand the thought of losing him, but neither could she stand the thought of the two of them someday turning into another JimAnn and Cletus Ponder.

"Let's go home, Victor," she finally whispered. "Let's forget about dinner and go home. Then we can pretend I've just said yes."

CHAPTER 6

Saturday

The next morning a pale, anemic sun rose on Leroy Summers, who was speeding south on I-75, heading from Kentucky into Tennessee. He was driving their old camper, now sporting new decals (NRA, USA) that would identify them as sportsmen and patriots. Inside, it displayed a different array of decals—flags from each state where they'd grabbed a cutie, had fun with them in their upper berth and finally dumped their bodies miles away from where they'd grabbed them. For the past ten years, their system had worked perfectly. A dozen different states. Leroy had lost track of the cutie count.

"So tell me about Little Miss Poontang," said Chet, lighting another cigarette. Just as Leroy had figured, the word *timid* had gotten inside Chet's head, and at dawn he'd shown up at the camper, guns and gear in hand.

Leroy pulled a battered black album from under the driver's seat. Usually, he kept it shoved beneath his mattress at home. It held all their mem-

_es of their cuties—little hair ribbons and woven bracelets
_y kept as trophies. In the wrong hands it would send them both to
death row; never did he leave town without it.

"Her info's in the back. She lives in southwest North Carolina, on
the lam with her father. Claims he's dragged her up and down the
Appalachian Mountains for years. She's sick of it."

"A child custody thing?"

"She's never said," replied Leroy. "She's not chatty like most of 'em."

Chet peered at the pages devoted to Kimmeegirl. "Never given you any
bullshit about all her cute boyfriends, or rich parents, or being a cheer-
leader?"

"Nope. She claims she sits home every night playing Scrabble with her
old man."

"That's pretty weird. You sure she's not scamming you?"

"What makes you say that?"

Chet studied her picture. "She's way too pretty to be sitting home playing board games. She's probably some cop, setting you up. Maybe even
the FBI."

For a moment, Leroy had a pang of doubt. Had Kimmeegirl scammed
him, the ultimate scammer? He considered it for a moment, finally deciding no. He'd texted her for months. He knew real when he heard it. He
could sniff out deception like a bad fart.

They rolled on, Chet flipping through the album, chuckling over a few
of his favorite pictures. Suddenly he started squirming in the seat, finally
pulling a white plastic hair barrette from under his butt.

"Look what you forgot, Mr. I Got Rid Off All The Evidence." He held
the barrette up. Two long reddish hairs still clung to it.

"That was Spitfire's," Leroy said softly.

Chet flicked at a tiny brown spot with his fingernail. "There's sti. some blood on it."

Leroy flashed back to Spitfire. Fierce as a little wildcat, she'd fought them from the get-go, all teeth and claws. When those deer hunters wandered up and banged on the camper door, she'd screamed like a banshee, quieting only after Chet took a hammer to the back of her skull. They'd dumped her body in some park in Pennsylvania and beat it back home, practically shitting their pants every time they saw a cop.

"We'd better get rid of this," Chet told him."Cops ever find this, we're cooked. They have stuff that lights up bloodstains like a laser. And they're still looking for that girl."

"Toss it," said Leroy. "Spitfire sure doesn't need it anymore."

Chet rolled down the window and heaved the barrette out, along with his cigarette. Leroy watched as the last remnant of Spitfire bounced into the early morning darkness, just another piece of junk on the highway.

The sleet that had greeted them at the Tennessee state line now began to cover I-75 in a fine, icy snow. The pavement grew white as they passed Knoxville, with mean little flakes slickening the road and making the camper's rear end swing wide on the curves. Chet curled up in the back bedroom while Leroy drove on, dreaming about Kimmeegirl. What a treat to have all that young flesh, completely under his control. He was thinking of all the things he would do when the gas light on his dashboard came on. He pulled off at a truck stop, and after he filled the tank and emptied his bladder, he texted Kimmeegirl. *On my way. CU soon!* When he got back in the camper, he found Chet sitting in the driver's seat.

"Show me where we're supposed to go," he said. "And you can sleep while I drive."

Leroy pointed at a miniscule spot on his map. "There. Unaka."

"Unaka? As in *you naked?*"

"Yeah," said Leroy, remembering when he'd asked Kimmeegirl the same question. "Kind of."

Chet gave a bray of a laugh. "All right! I'm down with gettin' this girl naked!"

They went on, Chet driving as Leroy curled up on the bed, trying to sleep through a ride that grew more and more like the Tilt-A-Whirl on a midway. After almost getting tossed to the floor twice, he gave up on sleep and made his way back up to the passenger seat.

"Where the hell are we?" he asked, watching huge flakes of dizzying snow hit the windshield.

"Highway 64. Following the Ocoee River."

"We've left the interstate?"

"Miles ago," said Chet. "You put the snow tires on this crate?"

"Last month," said Leroy. "But we've only got the donut for a spare."

"Terrific," Chet said with a grunt.

Leroy buckled himself in the passenger seat. As they crossed into North Carolina, the bad twisting road turned into a worse one, dipping into low spots where standing water had frozen to ice.

"Shit," said Chet as he downshifted, teasing the camper up a mountain. For hours they crept along, when finally, at a wide curve in the road, their headlights flashed across a bank of trash dumpsters.

"Hold on," said Leroy. "This might be it. Let's see if we can find a sign or something."

Chet stopped to let Leroy climb out of the camper. Immediately his feet flew out from under him, and he hit the ground hard, flat on his ass. Chet leaned on the horn, doubled over in laughter.

"Fuck you," yelled Leroy, his tailbone burning. He got to his feet and limped over to the dumpsters. When he stooped down and wiped the snow from the biggest one, it revealed the stenciled letters UNAKA RECYCLING. He smiled, gratified. Kimmeegirl had told him the truth, just like every other stupid girl in love. Carefully, he picked his way back to the camper and hopped in the warm cab.

"This is it. We meet her here at noon tomorrow."

Chet looked at him, incredulous. "At a bunch of trash dumpsters?"

"That's what she said."

Chet stubbed out his cigarette. "Leroy, unless that girl is an Eskimo, there's no way she's meeting us here tomorrow."

"She knows snow, Chet. She's lived in Maine. Canada, even."

"I don't care if she's lived with penguins at the South Pole. This is a goddamned blizzard. If we stay up here overnight, we'll get snowed in big time."

Leroy frowned. Chet was usually an intrepid driver, rarely spooked by bad weather. "So what are you saying?"

"I'm saying I think we should let this chick go and get the hell back home," said Chet. "These snow tires drive like they're bald and according to you, we've only got a damn donut for a spare."

Leroy sank back in the seat. He wanted Kimmeegirl badly—she was so special, so different from the pudgy, pimply-faced others.

Chet pressed his case. "Leroy, there's a ton of cuties out there. Don't you have three or four others on the line right now?"

"None this pretty." He tweaked his brother with a sly glance. "None that come close to Darlene."

"Pretty isn't worth taking a header into one of these ravines. Not even Darlene's worth that."

Chet started to make a careful, snow-crunching U-turn in front of the garbage bins when Leroy put a hand on his arm.

"Wait," he said. "I Googled this girl's camp—I think I know where it is. How about we just go get her?" He grabbed the album, turned to a page with a map. "It's not that far. We go in, grab her, and beat it before the weather gets worse."

His brother gazed at him as if he'd lost his mind. "What about her old man?"

"I don't know. Tie him up. Pop him if we have to." Again Leroy pointed at the map. "We're so close. We can go in there and be out of this mess in time for dinner."

"This one's really gotten in your head, hasn't she?"

Leroy shrugged, suddenly embarrassed."Yeah. I guess she has."

Chet leaned over the steering wheel, gazing up through the windshield. The sky looked as if it was shaking thick pieces of itself to earth. After a long moment, he said, "How far is it exactly?"

"According to her, an hour's walk," Leroy replied. "An hour's walk in good weather is what–probably an hour's drive in the snow?"

"Are you sure you know where it is?"

"Totally," Leroy lied. Screw the snow. He wanted this girl, bad.

Chet let a breath out through his teeth that sounded like the hiss of a snake. "I'll give it a go," he finally said. "On one condition."

"What?"

He flicked his Zippo and grinned. "I get her first."

Leroy didn't like those terms, but the important thing now was just to get there, any way they could. He could think of how to outwit Chet later.

"Okay," Leroy conceded. "This one's all yours, right off the bat."

CHAPTER 7

For the first time in months, Lily woke up smiling. Jonathan didn't know if her cramps had abated (she seemed to have cramps a lot, but what did he know about it?) or if their weekly trip into town had lightened her mood. Whatever it was, she rolled out of bed around noon, singing as she headed to the bathroom. He was astonished—she hadn't said three words yesterday and had spent most of last night outside, on a solo hike up to their ridge. He wondered–had the sweet little girl who'd vanished at age twelve returned? Did he dare hope?

He waited until she'd returned to her bedroom, and tapped on her door. "It's almost lunchtime," he said softly, afraid of breaking the spell. "You want something to eat?"

She opened the door in sweatpants, smelling of soap and tooth-paste."Sure, as long as it's nothing gross."

"How about pancakes and bacon?"

She smiled, dimples crinkling both cheeks. "Sounds good."

He hurried to the kitchen and lit the stove. Maybe if he was careful and did nothing to upset her, this new old Lily would stay. He'd always refused to give in to her stormy rages and petulant silences, but he never knew if that was the right approach. Teenaged boys were simple math—muscular young bucks fueled by sex and competition. Teenaged girls, or at least Lily, were more like calculus—complicated equations, seemingly veering into quantum physics. Though the books he'd read chalked it up to hormones, he knew Lily was a special case—a headstrong young girl tethered to a stern and watchful father, fleeing the law along the Appalachian Mountains.

"It's still better than Oklahoma," he told himself, trying to assuage a sudden pang of his recurring guilt. In Oklahoma she would be thirty pounds heavier, meeting boys at the mall, smoking weed and drinking beer. That would have been her life if he'd given her to Fred Moon.

He fmixed up the pancake batter he'd learned from his grandmother. The pancakes were small and crispy with the tang of bacon grease. The first batch was warming in the oven when Lily came into the kitchen, dressed in jeans and the blue wool sweater Krisjean Prosper had knitted her in Maine. Jonathan missed Krisjean. She was the only person who understood the hard choices he'd had to make.

Aware that the wrong word could sour Lily's mood like vinegar in milk, he asked, "How many pancakes can you eat?"

"Six. Ten. I don't know," she replied, unwilling to commit. "What are you going to do today?"

"Closing up the shutters of the boathouse," he said neutrally, then decided to risk an invitation. "Why don't you get your skis and come with me? The snow's already getting deep."

"The snow?" She bolted up from the table and ran to look out the kitchen door. "Oh, shit." She turned to him, panicked. "When did it start snowing?"

"Before dawn."

"Is it going to snow all day?"

He shrugged. "The moon had a big halo last night." He almost added that he'd felt the wind shift to the northwest, and had seen squirrels digging up acorns yesterday, but she hated it when he "went all Cherokee."

"What's the big deal?" he asked. "You love snow."

"Not today I don't," she cried, tears suddenly rimming her eyes. "I hate snow! I hate pancakes. I hate this stupid life!"

She ran back to her room and slammed her door so hard the windows rattled. Then, not two minutes later, she ran out the front door and headed back up to the ridge she loved so well. He stood there watching her go, still holding her plate of pancakes. Then he went over and peered out the window, wondering what could have upset her about this particular snow. It looked like regular old *gutiha*—big white flakes quickly carpeting the ground beneath the trees. Yet Lily had reacted as if it had spoiled a pool party on the fourth of July.

Sighing, he turned off the stove and took the sad little plate of pancakes to the table. There was no point in cooking more. He would eat what he'd made and go work on the boathouse. Maybe later Lily would get her skis and join him. Or maybe she would come back from the ridge and hole up in her room for the rest of the day. With Lily, he never knew.

"Krisjean would say not to worry," he told himself as he poured maple syrup over the pancakes. He thought of last winter in Maine, when the two of them had watched their daughters skate on a frozen pond. Lily and Alenna had raced across the ice, the blades of their skates scraping like razors against a leather strop. Lily had reminded him of a bright, graceful bird, consigned to fly in too small a cage. It would be over soon, though. In three years she would be eighteen and could go where she pleased. Somedays he doubted he would ever see her again.

"But it's still better than Oklahoma," he muttered again, swirling a bite of pancake in the syrup, wondering if Lily would ever understand.

As Lily Walkingstick trudged up to her beloved ridge, Mary Crow woke from a deep sleep. Eyes still closed, she rolled over in bed, extending an arm to wake Victor. But instead of finding a warm sleeping man to nestle against, she found only cool sheets and a note taped to his pillow. She sat up, read it. *Leaving early to get my snow tires on. Consider yourself engaged and kissed,* he'd scrawled, drawing hearts around the sentence. *I'll call you from Raleigh.*

She looked over at the empty sheets beside her. This is what it would be like if he took that job, she realized. No love, no laughter, no silly sparring over wet towels on the bathroom floor. She would reach for him but he would be gone—far away in Virginia, learning to parse the inner demons of criminals.

She sighed. This morning she'd hoped to recapture a bit of the amazing magic from the night before, but now she was glad he'd left early. Raleigh was six hours away and mountain roads were always treacherous in snow.

After staring at Victor's pillow for another moment, she got up and looked out the window. Half a foot of snow capped the railing of the balcony and the stuff was still coming down, hard and fast.

"Unaji," she whispered. "Or is it gutiha?" She couldn't remember—her Cherokee had grown rusty since she and Jonathan had split up. She was amazed she'd understood Teo Owle yesterday in court, but maybe the hateful words stayed with you longer than the sweet ones. She'd learned *bitch* early on, from some of the girls at Cherokee High.

She watched the snow until she realized there was no point in staying here and missing Victor. She could walk to her office and get some work done on the Owle case. It would be fun to walk in the snow and on Saturday her office would be free of distractions.

She showered quickly, pulled on jeans and boots and headed downtown, her engagement ring nestled inside a blue wool mitten. Hartsville was in a full-blown Southern panic, with people lined up to get ice melt at the hardware store, bread and milk from the grocery. Mic and Mac's were already busy–apparently some people were planning to drink out the storm. After buying coffee and a strudel at Sweet Monkey's bakery, Mary hurried upstairs to her office.

Inside, everything was cast in a cool, colorless snow-light. No messages blinked from Annette's phone and Drusilla's old evidence files remained where Mary had dropped them last night.

"The only thing different is now I'm engaged," she said, pulling off her mittens. "At least for the next three days."

She crossed the reception room and went into her office. Nibbling the strudel, she flipped through the files from yesterday, newly aware of the ring on her finger. One minute it felt heavy and cumbersome; the next minute she didn't feel it at all. She tried to read Drusilla's notes, but her thoughts kept bouncing between the ring, Victor, then to the possible absence of both the ring and Victor.

Finally, she gave up on Drusilla's hen scratchings and drank her coffee. As she did, she gazed at the tapestry that had graced every office she'd ever had. Her mother had woven it years ago, a mélange of shades of green and blue with flashes of silver. She was in high school when her mother started it, and she remembered watching her weave the colors together.

"The blue is for the mountains, because the *dodaluh* are as old as the sky. The green is for the trees," Martha Crow told her. "The silver thread is you."

"What do you mean it's me?"

Her mother gave her a curious look. "It's your path. Who knows where it will go?"

Mary stared at the tapestry. Back then she'd been certain her path would include Jonathan. A year ago she'd thought it would lead to the DA's office. Neither of those things had worked out. Jonathan had long ago skipped out on her in Oklahoma, and the incumbent DA had won re-election by a mere 52 votes. She looked at the ring sparkling on her finger. Was the silver thread now leading to a wedding? Was that her new path? She couldn't say, she didn't know. She couldn't remember a lot of what Victor had said last night.

"This is what happens when you knock back a double Martini on an empty stomach." She sat there, trying to remember exactly what had transpired between her and Victor when the phone shattered the silence of her office.

She grabbed the thing before it could ring twice. "Mary Crow," she answered, hoping it was Victor.

A scratchy croak of a female voice came over the line. "Mary? This is JimAnn. You got a minute to talk?"

Mary sank back in her chair. Without Annette screening her calls, she was stuck with JimAnn. The woman would spoil the comfortable solitude of Mary's office, relating every detail of the last skirmish in the war between her and Cletus Ponder. Half-listening, Mary put JimAnn on speaker-phone and leaned back to listen. Look on the bright side, she told herself as she lifted her left hand to gaze at the ring that glittered from her finger. At least you're not comparing notes on how you got dumped at Lulu's.

CHAPTER 8

Leroy's optimistic hour-long jaunt through the forest turned out to be a slow crawl, with the camper getting stuck twice in snow so thick that they finally just began to guess their way. Three times they had to stop and use bolt cutters to slice the chains that closed off Forest Service roads for the winter. Leroy was about to concede that maybe they should have turned around at Unaka when, just after dark, their headlights flashed across an aluminum gate that spanned two tall pine trees. From the top rung of the gate hung a small, birdshot sign that read "Paint Creek Camp—Private."

"Stop!" cried Leroy, re-checking his Kimmeegirl notes. "On November third she wrote *Paint Creek is a real dump.* This is it!"

"It fucking well better be," growled Chet. He nursed the skidding camper past the gate and pulled off at a wide spot in the road, some twenty yards away. He cut the engine and leaned back in the driver's seat, rubbing the back of his neck.

"I've driven through rotten weather in every state east of the Mississippi, but this beats 'em all."

"Have a smoke," suggested Leroy. "Relax a few minutes."

"Are you kidding? I want to get this over with." Chet stood up and dug a small bottle of white capsules from the pocket of his jeans. He swallowed two, washing them down with a slug of Red Bull.

"What are you taking?" asked Leroy.

"Shit that keeps me going but doesn't show up in my piss." He offered Leroy the bottle of pills. "Want one?"

Leroy shook his head. Substance-wise, he was the virgin to Chet's slut. Where his brother would drink, smoke or shoot up most anything, Leroy had seen their old man crazy drunk too many times. Ever since his father dangled him head first over an old well, he took only aspirin and seldom even drank beer.

While Chet waited for his pills to kick in, Leroy rolled down the window, listening for the sounds of any nearby humanity. But the woods stood silent and the only sound he heard was the low moan of the wind as it swirled the snow into little eddies of fluff. A moment of sudden doubt gripped him—what if Kimmeegirl had lied about living here? What if she'd faked him off and really lived somewhere else? If they had come up here for nothing, Chet would beat him senseless.

"I'm good to go," said Chet, interrupting Leroy's nightmare. "You pack the pigeon shit suits?"

Leroy nodded. "Under the bed."

"Okay."

They pulled on the gray and white winter camo suits that Chet said looked like they'd been splattered with pigeon crap. Then they laced up boots, broke out their weapons and two small bottles of chloroform. When they finished they looked like two beefy, broad-shouldered snowmen armed with dark purpose.

"How are we going to do this?" asked Leroy. Ordnance decision he

ceded to Chet, who'd spent six years in the National Guard. He was better at strategy—more of a big picture guy.

"You take the pistol and the zip-ties." Chet gave his brother the Ruger
that had belonged to their father. "I'll take my new bullpup."

"What the hell's that?" asked Leroy as Chet pulled a short-barreled
automatic rifle from under the bed.

"It's like an AK-47, only lighter. They're standard issue for a lot of
armies in Europe." Chet shouldered the weapon. "I'll cover you with the
bullpup while you cuff the girl. If the dad gives you any grief, I'll take him
out."

"Shouldn't one of us go reconnoiter first?" asked Leroy. See if this
camp really exists, he thought.

"It's too cold, Leroy. We need to move fast. We fart around scouting
and the snow will just get deeper."

"Okay," Leroy said, praying that there actually was a camp at the end of
the road.

"Once we grab the girl we'll hustle back here and get out of these
mountains."

Leroy smirked at his brother. "Not taking your first turn with her
immediately?"

"No way," said Chet. "My first turn starts when we're on dry pavement
or flat land."

They pulled white ski masks over their heads, strapped on night vision
goggles, and went out into the snowy night. As the pristine white world
turned a sick greenish-yellow, they ducked under the gate between the
two trees. On the other side, Chet said, "You take the left side of the road,
I'll take the right. Stay hidden, just in case somebody's crazy enough to be
outside."

After a fist bump, they started off, crunching through foot deep snow. They slipped and slid through trees and coiling rhododendrons. Again, Leroy's stomach clenched at the real possibility that Kimmeegirl had tricked them; that they were going nowhere, except down a mountain path in the middle of a blizzard. His goggles began to fog up; he'd just pulled them off when he saw Chet motioning him to the center of the road. Clutching the pistol, he hurried forward.

"You smell anything?" Chet asked in a whisper.

Leroy lifted his ski mask to take a deep sniff of air. The faint aroma of wood smoke reached his nostrils. "A fire?" he asked, hopeful that the camp actually existed.

Chet nodded. "We must be getting close to their cabin. Let's stay on one side of the road. I'll go first, just like we did in Missouri."

Though Miss Missouri had been five summers ago, Leroy remembered it well. Heat, sweat. Crawling through midges and mosquitoes for a chubby teenager who had some kind of leprous skin disease. He gave an inward shudder. Of all their cuties, that one had been the worst.

Crossing over to Chet's side of the road, Leroy gave him a ten-step lead and began to follow him, two shadows moving through a field of white. After a couple of twisty turns, the road widened into a small parking area. Thirty yards past that stood a cabin where soft yellow light spilled from the windows, casting pale blue shadows on the snow. Leroy felt a flood of relief. The cabin was real; so far Kimmeegirl had told the truth.

Chet dropped to his knees, Leroy flopped down after him. Sleet pinged on Leroy's jacket as Chet turned towards him.

"I'll go see what we're up against," whispered Chet. "Stay hidden, but watch me. If anything goes down, use that pistol."

Leroy nodded as Chet slipped into the trees. He took the safety off the Ruger and watched from behind a tree. Chet ran towards the cabin, stopping behind a woodpile in the side yard. After a few moments, he burst forward again, this time diving into the shadows at the side of the cabin. As Leroy watched, his breath again started fogging his goggles. He took them off in time to see Chet slowly creeping up on the porch and sidling up to one window. Keeping his back to the exterior wall, he risked a cautious peek through the glass. After a moment, he turned and vanished around the corner of the cabin.

Leroy remained at his post, watching and waiting. He wondered what Kimmeegirl was doing. If she'd gotten his last text, she was probably packing her bags and thinking about Bryan. If she hadn't received it, then she was probably brokenhearted that her boyfriend had dumped her. He didn't care. It didn't matter. Kimmeegirl would be meeting Bryan and Uncle Jake far quicker than she'd ever dreamed.

Suddenly, a figure emerged from the other side of the cabin. He tightened his grip on the pistol until he realized it was Chet. He watched as his brother glanced in another set of windows and disappeared into the woods. A few moments later he made his way back to the tree, slipping in the snow, gasping for breath.

"What did you see?" Leroy whispered.

Chet lifted his ski mask to gulp more air. "A girl and a man, playing a board game in front of the fire. She looks thin, average height. He's big, watchful. I think he might have heard me when I was on the east end of the house."

"Does she look anything like her picture?" asked Leroy.

Chet gave a sly, lupine grin. "You were right about this one, bro. She is special."

Leroy smiled. "Any weapons?"

"I only saw a bow and arrow." Chet giggled. "Can you believe it? One old-fashioned bow and a damn quiver of arrows."

Leroy frowned, unbelieving, until he remembered Kimmeegirl said she was Cherokee. Apparently, every word the girl had written was true.

"How about other people?"

"The two bedrooms are empty," said Chet. "Everybody in that house is sitting right by the fire."

"Fish in a barrel."

Chet leaned close. "Okay, let's do this. We'll sneak down there, then on my mark, we'll come through the front door, guns drawn. That way we'll cut 'em off from their big bad bow and arrows. You got the chloroform?"

Leroy patted his left breast pocket. "Right here."

"Good," said Chet. "You take the girl while I wrangle the dad. Any problem, I'll take care of it."

"Just be careful and don't shoot her," said Leroy.

Chet held out his fist for another bump. They touched their gloved knuckles together with a whispered *argonish*, the battle cry of their childhood and started toward the cabin. Leroy wished, for a moment, that he could peek in the window and see Kimmeegirl as she was right then. For a few more moments she would have the beautiful look of wide-eyed innocence. That would change pretty fast, though. And once he and Chet came through the door, that look would be gone forever.

CHAPTER 9

———

"Want to play again?" Lily asked as Jonathan totaled up their Scrabble scores.

"I don't know." He squinted at the score sheet. "You won by a hundred points when we played in Tsalagi. Two hundred when we played in French. You're making me feel pretty stupid."

She put their dessert, a plate of chocolate chip cookies, on the table between them. The snowstorm had made the day so dark that they'd turned their cabin lights on early and had eaten their supper in the late afternoon. "Then let's play with no borders."

"No borders?"

"We can make words in French, English or Tsalagi."

"Why not Mic Mac and Russian, too?"

"Ha, ha." She gave an exasperated sigh at his small Dad joke.

Jonathan leaned back in his chair and regarded his daughter. After the morning's pancake debacle, he figured she'd spend the day in a pout, on her beloved ridge. Instead, when he got back from the boathouse, he'd found her baking cookies and making a pot of chili big enough to last several days.

"You want to play for some stakes?" he asked, chalking her sudden good humor up to hormones and chocolate chips.

"Nah." She looked at him with an oddly wistful smile. "Let's just play like we used to. When I was a kid."

That would have been when we lived with Mary, he thought as he started flipping over the tiles. They had been happy with her; Lily had been a sweet child with a good life. But then her grandfather Fred Moon sued him for custody of Lily and it all went to shit. Did he dare tell her that he wished she would be like that kid again? Back before bras and cramps and Tik Tok? No, a stern inner voice warned him. Say that and this new, happy Lily will vanish like smoke.

He turned his attention to the snowy world beyond the walls of the cabin. In the middle of their French game, as Lily was sinking his ship with the word *quinze*, he'd heard a noise. A soft, brief creak on the porch. After he'd come back with *voila*, he'd gotten up to look out the front window. Snow was pummeling down like a ripped pillow, obscuring any chance of seeing tracks. Finally he decided it was probably just Opie, their resident opossum, trying to get warm under the porch. Still, he'd slipped his knife Ribtickler in the back of his belt. No point in being careless, even in a snowstorm.

"Game on," Lily announced, turning over the last tile. "Any language you want. Losers go first."

He chose a tile, flipped up an E. She turned over an M.

"Ha!" she cried. "My streak goes on." She spelled out a-m-i-e. "French for friend."

He reverted to English, spelling d-a-n-c-e on her a. Back and forth they went, his words prosaic and practical, hers frilly and romantic, all having to do with love or friendship. *Amour, baiser, desir.* When she spelled the word *beau*, he could keep silent no longer.

"You trying to tell me something here?"

"What do you mean?"

"All your words are mushy French stuff."

A rare blush crossed her cheeks. "I called Alenna when we were in town yesterday. She has a new boyfriend."

"I didn't know she had an old boyfriend." Jonathan tried to picture Krisjean Prosper's reaction. She had vain hopes of her smart, but hot-to-trot daughter going to college.

"She's got three old boyfriends." Lily gave a big sigh. "Now she's got a new one."

"And you're feeling left out?" He tried to pose the question as neutrally as possible. Beyond that scumbag Marc Freneau in Maine, boys had been a distant threat to Lily, like the coyotes that remained invisible during the day, but howled wildly at night.

For a long moment she stared at the tiles on the board, as if they might conjure her answer. "No," she finally said. "But I do miss my friends."

He'd realized that might become an issue as soon as they moved here. In Maine she had friends. Here the only kids she saw were ones they passed by in town. He felt another hard knot of guilt in his throat, as if he were keeping an animal in a cage, just to prove some stupid point. "Would you like to go back to Maine? I could probably find another job up there this summer."

This time she hesitated so long he feared she might suggest going home to Hartsville, or worse, back to the Moons in Oklahoma.

"Maine is okay." She looked at him pleadingly. "But couldn't we go someplace not in the mountains?"

52

He stifled a groan, figuring the next word she said really would be Oklahoma. "Like where?"

"I don't know." She shrugged. "Kentucky, maybe. I hear it's pretty there."

"Kentucky?" He sat back, surprised. It seemed as if she'd chosen Kentucky as randomly as she might pick up a tile in this game. "Kentucky's pretty enough. But so's Utah, or Wyoming."

"It's just a suggestion," she said, a tinge of acid returning to her voice. "We'll go where you want to go, anyway. We always do."

"We go where I can get work, Lily," he said, trying to keep her good mood from curdling. "When you're eighteen, you can go anywhere you please. I'll buy you a plane ticket and help you pack your bags."

"But that's three years from now!" she cried. "Alenna will probably be married and I won't have even had a date!"

She folded her arms, in a huff. As she did, Jonathan heard a sudden thump on the porch. He looked up just as the front door exploded in a deafening roar, pieces of the lock and door knob flying across the room. In a blast of snow and frigid air, two men wearing winter camouflage stormed in. They looked like monstrous, hooded snow men. One aimed a handgun while the other pointed a weapon the size of a small assault rifle.

"Atli!" Jonathan yelled the code word he'd drilled into Lily's head from day one. "Atli now!"

He leapt to his feet, kicking over the table, the Scrabble tiles scattering like broken teeth.

Lily jumped up and ran towards the kitchen. As the man with the handgun started after her, Jonathan drew his knife and heaved it at his gut. With a thrussshhhh like scissors cutting cloth, it sheared through the man's jacket and into right side of his abdomen. Blood spurting, he fell screaming to the floor.

"Atli! Atli!" Jonathan kept yelling. He lunged toward the gunman, trying to pull Ribtickler from the man's side and plunge it into his heart. His fingers had just grasped the handle of the knife, when another thunderous blast made his ears ring. A fiery pain sizzled through his right shoulder as he flew over the wounded man and landed on the floor beside him. As blood and bits of his own flesh spewed into his face, the rifleman ran over and pointed his weapon at Jonathan's heart.

"Get the girl back here or you're a dead man."

His lips looked clownish–a fleshy red circle moving behind a ski mask of mottled white. Jonathan tried to speak, tried to tell them that the girl would not be coming back here ever, but the fire in his shoulder made his tongue useless, the words float in his brain. His one sentence came out garbled, as if he were drunk.

Rifleman turned to his partner, who lay writhing on the floor. "How bad are you?"

"I don't know." Handgun gasped, his voice high and breathy. "This hurts like shit."

"Give me your zip ties," said Rifleman. "I'll take care of him and go after the girl." He grabbed Jonathan's right arms. The right arm felt normal, but the left flopped like a disjointed chicken wing. Jonathan heard bones crunch and felt another hot spurt of blood on his face as the man fastened his wrists together,in front of him. *I am going to bleed out*, he thought airily. *Right here in the living room. Where did Lily go?*

He watched, bleary-eyed, as Rifleman slipped through the blood on the floor and headed toward the kitchen, in Lily's direction.

"You goddamn bastard," Handgun cursed beside him as the coppery smell of blood enveloped them like a cloud. "You're gonna pay for this."

Jonathan lay there, his shoulder on fire, the room swirling around him. *Atli, atli, atli the word echoed in his brain. Cherokee for go. Had Lily remembered that?*

His head cleared for a moment, and he wondered if he dared make another grab for his knife, but he heard more footsteps, coming from the kitchen.

"She ran away,"announced Rifleman.

Jonathan breathed deep, grateful. *Lily had remembered atli. She knew what to do.*

"Where the fuck did she go?" Handgun's voice cracked."There's a foot of snow out there."

"Her tracks lead into the woods," said Rifleman. "We should have covered both doors."

Rifleman knelt down beside his partner, wrapping a kitchen towel around the man's wound as they conferred in whispers. Jonathan caught the words *cutie* and *freezing.* Handgun mumbled something he couldn't understand, but Rifleman said, "I'm going after her. She can't have gone far."

Yes, she can, Jonathan thought as he felt himself start to float somewhere near the ceiling. *Lily had remembered atli. She can go as far as she needs to. She'll take off for Maine, or maybe even Kentucky. She's heard it's pretty there.*

CHAPTER 10

———

Lily fled, in her deerskin house shoes and U of Maine hoodie, her ears still ringing from the blast of the gun. What had happened? Edoda had been yakking about where to go next when the cabin exploded. For the first time in her life he'd yelled the code word he'd imprinted in her brain for years. *Atli! Go! Run and don't look back!*

She rushed out the back door, racing for the trees behind the cabin. She was halfway there when she heard the back door slam. She glanced behind her—the man with the rifle was coming after her! Lowering her chin, she altered her course toward the woodshed, hoping she might grab the axe that hung on the wall. But the Rifleman was too fast; already she could hear the raspy wheeze of his breath, the snow crunching beneath his feet. With her lungs on fire she again changed direction, now heading down the narrow gap between the woodshed and the smokehouse, praying that such a large man might find it too narrow. But he came right after her, not slowing down but running faster. She was about to reach the trees beyond the small out-buildings when she felt his fingers clamp around her right ankle. Squeezing tightly, he twisted her leg as he jerked her backwards. Pain shot up to her hip and she hit the ground hard, face down in the snow.

Instantly, he was on top of her, heavy and stinking of sweat. "Calm down, cutie," he growled. "You're only about to get what you've been asking for."

Thrashing like a squirrel caught in a trap, she kicked hard with her left foot. She connected with something soft—a butt or a stomach or maybe even his nuts. He gave a loud grunt, and for a second, she felt his weight lift. She wiggled away from him, her right ankle throbbing. As frigid air seared her throat, she scrambled to her feet and hobbled toward the dark trees, her father's words echoing in her head. *Atli, Lily. Run smart like jula, the fox.*

She zigzagged through the pines, wincing with every step, desperate to lengthen the distance between her and the Rifleman. If she could just get far enough ahead of him, she could wade through the little stream that emptied into lake. The water would be like ice, but it would hide her trail. In this snow, her tracks were so deep and clear that a blind man could follow them.

As pine branches slapped against her face, she risked another glance over her shoulder, hoping the man had given up. The trees had slowed him down a little, but he was still coming after her, running in his camouflage and goggles like some monster from the movies.

Ignoring the pain in her ankle, she limped on, her left foot just brushing the top of the snow. When she reached a small embankment that edged the creek she jumped, thinking that might confuse him. As she plunged into the creek, the frigid water came up to her knees, first turning her legs numb, then strangely hot. She didn't care–people left no tracks in water; this creek could well save her life.

She hurried, but carefully, knowing that a fall in this water would mean hypothermia for sure. Behind her, she heard the sound of limbs breaking. Incredibly, the man was still coming after her!

She went on. When the creek made a slight bend to the left, she saw what she was looking for. A rotting log that protruded over the water. She found it last fall, a hidey-hole away from the Warden, where she could write in her journal. If she could squeeze inside that log now, she might be able to hide from him.

She reached the protruding end of the log, ducked under it and threw herself belly-down on the creek bank. If she left no footprints, a simple break in the snowfall might not catch the man's attention.

With her jeans filling with snow, she crawled up the bank. The huge old log was hollow with a long, low crack running the length of it. She rolled closer to it, wrangling her shoulders inside first, then pulling in her frozen legs. Though she was completely hidden, she could barely move and had no way to look out and see if he was coming. All she could do now was wait and listen.

"And pray," she whispered, her teeth clacking like castanets. She hugged herself for warmth, her ears keen for the sound of someone approaching. For what seemed like hours she heard nothing but the frantic drubbing of her own heart. The numbness in her feet left, replaced by a hot, painful tingling. *He's given up*, she finally decided. *He must have stopped at the creek and gone back to the cabin.*

Thinking she was safe, she started to wiggle her legs out of the log when she heard it. A faint splash, followed by another, then a third, each one a little louder than the one before. The Rifleman. It had taken him some time, but he'd figured it out. Once again, he was coming after her.

She pulled her legs back inside the log and held her breath. His footsteps squeaked in the snow; his camouflaged pants legs rustled with every stride. No deer hunter here, she decided. But he was still dressed for a winter kill.

She lay still, listening, freezing, her ankle aching. The footsteps grew louder, then stopped.

Suddenly, a shadow fell across the slit of snow light that seeped into the log. The man had stopped right beside her! She waited for him to order her to come out, to threaten death if she didn't, but all she heard was the thundering of her own heart.

Could he not know I'm here? she wondered. She listened, every muscle tensed as she readied herself to bite, kick, to do whatever she had to. But as the minutes crept by, nothing happened. The shadow remained outside the log, patient as a hound waiting for a fox to leave its burrow.

Go away, you bastard, she silently willed. *Go away and leave me alone*. Just when she thought she could stand it no longer, the shadow receded. Once more she heard the squeak of footsteps, now growing fainter as he moved away.

She started to crawl out of the old log, but something stopped her. What if the man hadn't gone but a few feet away? What if he was out there, now playing a game of cat and mouse?

So she waited, shivering, straining to hear any kind of noise a person might make, but the only sound she heard was the eerie squeak of tree branches, rubbing together in the wind.

Ten minutes later, her shivering stopped and she wanted nothing more than to go to sleep. Her eyelids grew heavy and strangely warm, desperately wanting to close when she jerked awake, realizing that if she didn't get moving soon hypothermia would kill her as surely as if the man had put a bullet in her head.

She struggled out of the log as quickly as she could and headed for her cache. With one ear listening for footsteps behind her, she limped through the trees, hurrying to the massive old oak where the Warden had built the deer blind he called Atli central. When she neared the tree she turned and searched the darkness once more, looking for any flicker of movement that might indicate the Rifleman. But the woods remained still, silently enduring the cold caress of snow. Relieved, she hobbled to the tree and started to climb the wooden slats nailed into the trunk. As she scaled the makeshift ladder the irony of all this struck her. Just last week she and the Warden had conducted their monthly check of this blind; the whole time she'd been impatient, bored with the stupid ritual, wanting to scream at his fanatical attention to detail. Now, every step up the ladder made her more grateful for his concern.

She reached the blind and unlatched the trap door that kept out coons and foraging bears. Once inside, she re-locked the door and collapsed on the floor, the tears that she'd held back beginning to flow. When she was nine Atli drills had seemed incredibly exciting–heroic adventures aided by protective spirit animals in the woods. Now, when she was doing Atli for real, she was so scared she wanted to vomit. What did these men want? Why had they broken into the cabin with guns? And what should she do now?

"First get warm," she told herself sternly, wiping away her tears. "Then see how badly he fucked up your ankle."

Pulling off her wet hoodie and jeans, she crawled over and opened the footlocker that held her provisions. Inside lay all the winter supplies she'd acquired in Maine——snowshoes Kitchee Boudreaux had made her, a Canadian Army coat, rabbit skin mittens they'd bought from a trapper named Gold Rush LaForge. Last month the Warden had wanted to add his old .22 rifle to the equipment, but she had sneered at the suggestion. *I'm not running around with a gun*, she'd told him, disgusted. *I'm not in some stupid white militia group.*

She dried off with the heavy coat, quickly donning the new set of wicking long johns she'd gotten for Christmas. Over those she layered wool pants and a couple of sweaters. When she stopped shivering, she examined her ankle. It was swollen, a purple bruise already darkening the outside of her foot, but she didn't think it was broken. But what to do now? Tape it up and go through the woods sock-footed? Or shove it in a boot that might cut off the circulation? She didn't know, she couldn't think. A part of her brain kept expecting to wake up, to sit up in bed gasping for breath, relieved that this had been just a nightmare.

But she did not wake up. Finally, she decided to treat the sprain as best she could. She wrapped her ankle in a bandage, covered it with two wool socks and slowly pulled on one of her mid-calf boots. If she laced the boot loosely, she had some flexibility in her leg and the ankle didn't throb quite so fiercely. After that, she checked her other supplies. She had a well-loaded backpack, a sleeping bag, an extra bow with a quiver of a dozen arrows. She pulled one out. It was not the old-fashioned kind her father made out of cedar and turkey feathers, but a dark, carbon shaft with a broadhead point, sharp as a razor.

These are man killers, she remembered her father saying. *Not for targets or game. Use them only to save your life.*

She ran a finger along the lethal edge of one point. Though she could hit most any target, she'd only ever killed a rabbit, and had cried copious tears after she'd done that. Could she now shoot one of these through the Rifleman's heart?

"No problem," she whispered, remembering his stink and the sneer in his voice.

She put the arrow back in her quiver and gathered the rest of her supplies. If she carried out Atli as her father had trained her, she should run southeast, to the little town of Murphy. But this morning, she'd gotten

Bryan's text. He was supposed to be meeting her at the Unaka recycling bins—he might even be waiting for her now. If she met up with him there, he and his uncle could drive her to Murphy and get help. But what about the Rifleman? Had he gone back to the cabin? Or was he still out there, hunting her? It didn't matter; it would serve neither her nor her father to wait until first light. She needed to go now.

She checked her supplies one final time, snugging a small hatchet on to her pack frame. Traveling through blowing snow was always dangerous; she could use the thing to blaze a trail, or if she had to, bury it between the Rifleman's eyes.

Finally, she donned the Canadian army coat. It hung on her, big as a bearskin, but it would keep her warm and dry. She checked the inside pocket and found the five hundred-dollar bills and cell phone that the Warden kept zipped inside. She turned the phone on, just as she had last week. It was charged and ready, programmed with the one number she hoped she would never have to call.

"Okay," she whispered, taking a deep breath. "Atli."

With a prayer to the great warrior Tsali, she opened the trap door and descended into the darkness below. If the Rifleman didn't get her first, she would soon be meeting the boy she loved. Together, they would get help for her father. Her Edoda.

CHAPTER 11

————————

"Are you wearing your ring?" Victor's voice sounded tinny and distant.

Mary sat back at her desk, admiring the diamond on her left hand. "I am. It's even more gorgeous today than it was last night."

"Have you told anyone we're engaged?" Victor asked hopefully, as if sharing the news might make her more inclined to say yes.

"I haven't seen anyone today," she replied. "Everybody's out buying milk and snow shovels."

"How bad is it?"

She walked over to the window that overlooked Main Street. Hartsville had quietly removed Johnny Reb, the Confederate statue that had guarded the courthouse for over a century. Now the base of his statue, soon to be replaced with a more politically palatable doughboy, was just a mound of white snow. "We've got almost a foot," she told Victor. "But it keeps on coming down."

"Hadn't you better get home?"

"I want to get a little more done on the Teo case. Then I'll pack it in. What's on your schedule?"

"Dinner and a lecture. Sociopathy and Fetal Alcohol Syndrome."

"That sounds zippy," said Mary.

"Yeah, well, I'm supposed to go out with some guys from Richmond afterwards. How about I call you in the morning?"

"Wonderful." She smiled. "Have fun and be safe, sweetheart. Watch out for the alcoholic sociopaths."

"Why don't you stay at my place? You can keep a better eye out for Teo."

"Will do. Talk to you tomorrow."

She clicked off the cell and sat back down at her desk, her gaze again going from the ring on her finger to the tapestry that hung on the wall. All day she'd tried hard to concentrate on Teo, but her thoughts swung between the distant past and the near future. The ring glittered, beckoning her to a life she hadn't planned on. The tapestry felt like an accounting of her life—success mixed with failure, bright joy coupled with dark anguish. She had not thought of either Jonathan or Lily Walkingstick in months, but they had flashed through her head all day, much like that silver thread that twisted through her mother's work.

What did it all mean? Years ago she had loved Jonathan; in some weird way she guessed she loved him still. But she loved Victor, too. And Victor was here, and Victor wanted her. Why couldn't she call him back and tell him yes? Book a church and line up a preacher?

"Because you are one screwed-up chick," she said aloud. "Who can't quit looking at stupid red trucks."

Suddenly, someone laughed outside her door. For a moment, Mary panicked, afraid that JimAnn Ponder had come up here in person, for the latest update on Ponder v. Ponder. But then the door swung open to reveal Ginger Cochran, bundled up in a coat that strained to cover her baby bump and an orange scarf that almost matched her hair.

"God, I just love it when Annette's gone." Ginger laughed, throwing back her hood. "I can tiptoe up here and hear exactly what's going on inside your head. Do you realize how much you talk to yourself?"

"No," said Mary, her cheeks warming with embarrassment.

"You're as bad as an old woman with a houseful of cats. The last time I did this you were lying on your couch, musing about Nick Stratton having sex with the wrong person. Now you're talking about red trucks. I should come up here every day. You're better than Netflix!"

"You'd better be careful. You might hear something you won't want to know," said Mary.

"I'm a reporter. Something I don't want to know hasn't been invented yet." Ginger stepped inside the office. "But I really didn't come up here to eavesdrop. I was on my way home and saw your light on."

Mary eyed her protruding stomach. "Should you and Jerry Junior be out in weather like this?"

"Jerry Junior loves it. He's kicked all day." Ginger patted her belly. "But no kidding, why are you up here in the middle of a snowstorm? Yesterday your case got booted to March."

"No rest for the wicked. Or those trying to put the wicked away."

"But what does Teo have to do with stupid red trucks?"

Mary sighed, giving up all evasions, knowing Ginger was relentless. "Nothing. I'm trying to make a big decision."

Ginger brightened. "Oooo-did they offer you a permanent position in Tsalagi County?"

Mary took a deep breath and held out her left hand. "Victor offered me a permanent position of a different nature."

Ginger's eyes grew wide. "He proposed?"

Mary nodded, sheepish. "Last night."

"Oh, Mary!" Ginger rushed over to hug her. "I can't believe this! He's perfect for you. Totally perfect. Smart, handsome, funny. Plus he loves to nail criminals almost as much as you do."

Mary laughed. "A match made in heaven."

Teo Owle forgotten, Ginger immediately morphed from crime reporter to wedding planner. "When are you going to get married? I've got to tell Jerry. I've got to buy a dress. Heck, you've got to buy a dress. Let's go have a drink and talk."

"Don't you need to get home?" said Mary. "To Jerry and Chloe?"

"Jerry's working the blizzard and his mom has Chloe. Come on—this is important!"

Mary knew it was pointless to continue with Teo Owle. After she saved her files and shut down her computer, Ginger steered her towards Robard's, a quiet little restaurant that happened to be conveniently located next door to Tarcila's Dress Shoppe.

"Look!" Ginger cried as they neared the store. "Tarcila's putting out her spring stuff right now."

They stopped, watching as Tarcila, a small, pretty woman with a wide smile, grappled with the mannequins in her front window. Gone were the velvet and brocade gowns of Christmas parties and winter weddings. Tarcila was anticipating spring with vibrant, silky frocks in sheer fabrics. She'd just finished zipping up a pale peach gown when she noticed Ginger and Mary outside, gawking at the display.

"Want to come in and look at something?" she asked, her voice coming softly through the window. "It's awfully cold out there."

Ginger poked Mary with her elbow. "How about it, Bridey?"

Blushing, Mary shook her head. "No, thanks," she called. "We'll come back later. Your window looks lovely, though. Just like spring."

Tarcila gave a thumbs-up and went back to her mannequins. Mary grabbed Ginger's elbow and pulled her into Robard's.

"What's the matter?" Ginger laughed as they strode over to the best table in the nearly deserted restaurant. "You don't want to look at wedding dresses in the middle of blizzard?"

"Not today," Mary said.

They sat down. Ginger ordered hot tea and a slice of carrot cake; Mary did the same.

"Hot tea?" Ginger cocked her head. "No wine? No martini? Good Lord, are you pregnant?"

Mary shook her head. "I over celebrated last night."

When the waitress brought their tea, Ginger pulled her chair close. "I know when you order hot tea things are serious. So why do you not want to look at wedding dresses? Surely you're not going to get married in that black Killer Crow suit."

Mary sighed. "I'm not sure I'm getting married at all. Twenty-four hours ago I was totally focused on being the interim prosecutor of Tsalagi County. Then Victor pulls out this ring and gives me an ultimatum."

"What kind of ultimatum?"

Mary explained about Victor's new career move now in the offing. "Richmond needs an answer from him by Friday. He needs an answer from me before then."

"Richmond's not that far away," said Ginger. "Couldn't you do a long distance thing until you see how the Tsalagi County job works out?"

"This isn't the first time he's proposed," Mary admitted. "But he told me it would be the last. For him, I guess it's fish or cut bait."

"What have you told him before?"

"That I wasn't ready," said Mary. "Which was true."

Ginger took a bite of cake. "At the risk of getting personal, let me ask the most important question of all."

"What?"

"Do you love him?"

Mary looked at the little candle that flickered between them."Yes," she answered firmly. "Very much."

"Well, it's not like he's some ninety-day fiancé. You've known him for a couple of years."

"True."

"So what's stopping you?"

Mary sighed. What was stopping her? Errant red trucks? She'd thought about that all day. Finally, she looked at Ginger and said, "Honestly, I think I'm scared."

"Of?"

"Of change. Of it not working out. Of us winding up like JimAnn Ponder and her rotten husband."

Ginger frowned. "Nothing comes guaranteed, Mary. You just pay your money and take your chances, as they say."

"They also say if it's not broke, don't fix it. Victor and I are happy now, just the way we are."

"But he wants more, Mary. He wants a commitment."

Mary frowned, remembering her crushing sadness when Jonathan left, taking Lily with him. She waited days, months, for some word, some communication. Nothing ever came.

"It took me a long time to get over Walkingstick," she whispered, her emotions bubbling close to the surface. "And when I finally did, I swore I would never let myself be that vulnerable again."

Ginger reached to squeeze her arm."So maybe you're not totally over Walkingstick?"

"Oh, I'm over him," Mary replied. "I'm just not over all that pain. It depresses me to even think about it."

They sat in silence for a moment, then Ginger said, "What do you think your mother would say about your marrying Victor?"

Mary took a sip of tea. What would her mother say? First she'd probably cry, happy that she'd found a good man to love. Later she would spout some blessing in Cherokee and reserve the chapel at the Methodist Church. Her grandmother would be pleased with Victor's Atlanta roots. Irene Hannah, her old mentor, would wink, and say I always told you the right one would come along. She could almost picture all of them at the table, beaming. "Everybody I love, past and present, would approve."

Ginger lifted her hands, palms up. "Then you've just got to jump and trust that you'll land okay. You can't litigate your life like a case in court. In matters of the heart, the law does not apply."

"Are you saying I micro-manage things?"

"No. I'm saying that you've been horribly hurt, and you're don't want to get hurt again. You look under every rock, which is why you do so well in court."

"And that's a bad thing?"

"It is when you miss some glorious sunrise because you're busy looking under a dumb rock."

Mary laughed. "You sound like a greeting card."

"Pregnancy sets my inner poet free." Ginger drained her teacup, and spoke seriously. "Look, honey, I can't advise you. Nobody can. But Jerry and I both love Victor and would be thrilled to welcome you two into the ranks of the happily married."

Mary finished her cake and squeezed Ginger's hand. "Thanks for listening. You're a pal."

"We're both going to be frozen pals if we don't get home. Come on, I'll give you a lift. Where are you tonight?"

"I promised Victor I would stay at his place," Mary replied. "He thinks

I'll be safer from Teo Owle there. Tomorrow I'm going to lock myself in my office and try to send Teo up the river for good."

Ginger waved for their check. "I'm telling you, girlfriend, Victor is a plum. You don't marry him, some Richmond honey will."

CHAPTER 12

As badly as his knife wound hurt, it was the ski mask that was driving Leroy crazy. It was scratchy and tight in the warm cabin, and he wanted nothing more than to pull it off, claw at what felt like a thousand flea bites, and dunk his face in cold water. He would have done exactly that, except he was afraid to leave the Indian alone. As soon as Chet took off after Kimmeegirl, the guy had started yammering about the girl never coming back so they'd better just take him and claim the money. "Moon will never find her," he kept repeating. Figuring the bullet that shredded his shoulder must have knocked a few of his marbles loose, Leroy had tied him to the sofa and taped his mouth shut. Now all he did was sit there, glaring at him with hard, angry eyes.

Leroy turned away from the Indian as a new trickle of sweat stung his right eye. The mask had to go, right now. He couldn't stand another minute of it. He checked the rope that secured the Indian and headed for the kitchen. There, he pulled off his mask, filled the sink with icy water and plunged his head in. Though the sudden cold made him gasp, it felt wonderful to be free of the hot, itchy wool. His face dripping, he lifted his head and gazed out the window, wondering where Chet was. Had he found the girl and decided to take first dibs, right out there in the snow? Or maybe he'd grabbed her and taken her back to the camper. Maybe right now he was laughing at him while he enjoyed Kimmee-girl. His cutie! The one he'd groomed for months!

"If he's doing that, I will kill him," Leroy soberly promised his reflection in the window. "Brother or not, he's a dead man."

As the wind gusted more snow against the window, he dried his face and rolled his ski mask into a watch cap. Suddenly his belly wound heated up and began throbbing again, pulsing to the tempo of his heart. He lifted his jacket and examined it—a raw, angry looking slit that was still oozing blood.

"Damn it," he whispered. "Why did he have to tag me?"

He went into the bathroom and opened the medicine cabinet. The cabinet looked like the feminine hygiene aisle of a drugstore, overflowing with pads and tampons and two bottles of something called Midol. He unwrapped one of the thicker pads that boasted *no leaking–even on your heaviest days*. It smelled like baby powder—clean and unstained. Virginal. Just like Kimmeegirl, he thought.

He rubbed the pad against his cheek, enjoying its softness against the stubble of his beard, then he lifted his shirt and attached it to his wound with a line of Band-Aids.

"Don't know how heavy this day is gonna be," he muttered as he shook out two Midol tablets and washed them down with water from the sink. "But at least I'm not gonna leak."

Weary of guarding the Indian, Leroy pulled the cap low on his forehead and decided to explore the rest of the cabin. You could learn a lot about people, just from looking at their stuff. The room next to the bathroom belonged to the girl. She'd taped pictures to the walls, along with some yellow crepe paper flowers. An old-fashioned quilt covered the bed, and a pile of books was stacked on a desk. In the closet a bright red Maine hoodie dangled from a hanger, while a bulging green backpack leaned against the back wall. He pulled it out, unzipped it. On top of a pile of clothes was a computer printed picture of Bryan and a note, addressed in purple ink to someone named Edoda. He opened it.

By the time you find this I will be gone. I have met someone and am going to be with him. I love you, but I cannot live this life any longer. Please don't look for me. Just go back to Maine and be happy. I can take care of myself.

Lily.

"Ha!" he whispered, triumphant. "I knew she was coming to meet Bryan."

Chuckling, he tucked the picture and the note in his pocket and crossed the hall to the other bedroom. Here jeans and a brown flannel shirt lay draped over a chair, just above a pair of leather work boots. More books lay piled beside the bed, and on the night table was a photograph of Kimmeegirl with a pretty Indian woman.

"Must be the mommy," said Leroy, peering at the photo.

Wondering if the Indian kept a weapon beside his bed, he pulled open a drawer of a small table. Inside, he found cough drops, a crossword puzzle book, and a yellowed newspaper clipping. Curious, he reached for the article, and started to read.

It was an old story from an Oklahoma paper concerning a custody dust-up over one Lily Walkingstick. Someone named Fred Moon was offering a ten thousand dollar reward for her abductor, Jonathan Walkingstick.

"So that's what the bastard keeps talking about!" Leroy cried, stunned at the lightning strike of good luck. "Moon's not *the* moon. Moon's the grandfather. The Indian thinks we're bounty hunters!"

SALLIE BISSELL

Kimmeegirl had said they were on the lam, but she had never said why. Leroy read the article twice and folded it up with the girl's farewell note. Even if Chet fucks up Kimmeegirl, we've still got the father. Ten grand for hauling his ass to Oklahoma! Warming up his telemarketer voice, he hurried back to the living room and tore the duck tape from the Indian's mouth.

"You got a nice little hideout here, buddy. Real cozy for you two."

The Indian did not reply.

"You know, Moon thought you'd gone to Mexico, but I said no.These days nobody heads to Mexico. Everybody down there's in a gang, just hunting for Americans to kidnap."

Again, the Indian remained silent.

"You know, I get why you didn't want to leave your kid with that old man." Leroy remembered the news clipping. "And this long on the lam is damn good. You gave us a run for our money."

The Indian made no comment.

"I'm sorry your girl freaked out so," he said sympathetically. "We didn't mean to scare her."

"She'll be fine." The Indian broke his silence, his voice gruff.

"I sure hope so." Leroy tried to plant a seed of doubt. "It's cold as shit out there. And the snow isn't slowing down at all."

The Indian gave him a curious look. "We saw worse in Maine."

"Oh?" Leroy said quickly, searching his mental files for every fact he knew about the state of Maine. "My partner figured you were on the coast. Portsmouth or Portland. One of those P towns.."

The Indian gave a sneering laugh. "Some trackers you are."

"Yeah, well you're the one tied up," Leroy reminded him."With your kid running around in a blizzard."

74

"My kid will be okay," said the Indian. "Your partner is the one in deep shit."

After that, all expression left the Indian's face. He closed his eyes and bowed his head, as if in prayer. Leroy doubted he was telling his troubles to God, though. More likely he was plotting some way to kill them both and get his daughter back.

Soon the Indian's automaton pose grew even more unnerving than his dark, hateful glare, so Leroy returned to the kitchen. He switched on the back porch light, hoping to see Chet lumbering up with Kimmee-girl. But outside he saw only white—snow had already covered the tracks they'd made earlier in their mad dash out the door. It occurred to him that the Indian might have a point— Chet could be more in danger than the girl. Though Chet fancied himself a survivalist and had all the high-tech equipment, he was still a flatland trucker, unfamiliar with these mountains and the dark woods that covered them. What would he do if Chet never showed back up? If he was stuck here with the Indian, all by himself? That Midol shit hadn't touched the throbbing in his belly—what if he got really sick?

"Oh, come on," Leroy whispered, fighting down a moment of panic. "Chet's probably back at the camper, taking Kimmeegirl on her maiden voyage."

As much as he hated the thought of Chet's hands on all that young flesh, he hoped it was true. He would be bitterly disappointed not to get her first, but at least his brother would not be lost in the snow. He would need Chet to get them out of here, alive.

A mile to the west, Lily Walkingstick was snowshoeing along the Salt Lick trail. At first she'd been tempted to hurry to the park access road and follow it to Unaka, but that would take longer and she figured such an easy, clear path would only make it easier for the Rifleman to track her. She'd seen no trace of him, but a creeping edginess kept her looking over her shoulder. At least, she told herself, she wasn't leaving boot tracks in the snow. The snowshoe grids were harder to see and her ankle felt steadier on the little woven platform.

The snow fell as hard as ever. It did not drift here, under the trees, but instead bent the gorse and prickly vines low to the ground. Briars and brambles clutched at her coat as she fought her way forward.

And the trail, which three days ago had been an ambling, winter-drab path of gray and brown, was now an icy maze of white. With no moon or stars, she used a small flashlight to get her bearings as she hacked out blazes on the trees every twenty yards or so. Even the sounds of the woods had gone—no owls hooted, nor did she hear the scampering of any animal fleeing from her approach. Everything stood cold and silent, as if she were the only thing living in a frozen world of the dead.

That notion brought her father to mind. Had the last blast of that rifle struck him? Was he now dead? No, she told herself. Edoda had warned her about bounty hunters. Those men wanted to turn him in for money—they would need him alive to do that.

Forcing her mind to Unaka, she thought of the boy she prayed was waiting for her. Blonde, handsome Bryan. He would wrap his arms around her as she explained the trouble she was facing. He and his uncle would help her, for sure. They would take her to the police and they could all come back and save Edoda.

But from what? The police wouldn't do anything if the Snow Men were bounty hunters. They'd happily let them take Edoda back to Oklahoma. Then she'd have to go live with Grandpa Moon. She wanted to live

WHITE TREES CRIMSON SNOW

with Bryan, not some tottery old fart whose false teeth clacked every time he ate. Somehow, she needed to figure out what to do.

She hurried on, snowshoes crunching the frozen weeds, her ankle hot inside her boot. She'd just reached the banks of Paint Creek when she heard a snap and a groan behind her. Ducking behind a tree, she grabbed her hatchet, certain that the Rifleman had caught up with her. She peered into the darkness, listening for his raspy breathing, sniffing the air for the scent of cigarette smoke. But again, she found no trace of him.

Probably keeping his distance, she decided. Probably thinks he's got me cornered by this creek.

"No way," she whispered. This was her home turf; she knew where she was. One more high, ridge to climb and she would be at Unaka.

Quickly, she unstrapped her snowshoes and crossed the creek, jumping on her left leg from rock to icy rock, arms wind milling to keep her balance. When she reached the opposite bank, she charged up the ridge in her boots, using the end of one snowshoe as a kind of cane. Fewer brambles pulled at her coat here, but the snow was like glass under her feet. For every step forward she seemed to slide two steps back. Fifty feet up the ridge she heard a loud splash in the creek. Again terrified that the Rifleman was coming after her, she threw herself up the ridge, as some nearly hysterical part of her wanted to laugh—she must look like some cartoon character, gimpy legs churning but going nowhere.

Up she clambered, frosted tree limbs dumping snow on her head as her legs burned like fire. Finally, she crested the top of the ridge. Gasping for breath, she looked back the way she'd come, expecting to see the goggle-eyed monster charging up from below. But instead, she saw only trees and her own tracks through the snow.

"You're going crazy," she whispered. "There's nobody there."

After she leaned against a tree long enough to catch her breath, she slipped and slid her way down to the road that led to Unaka.

Making better time on the more even ground, she limped along, shining her flashlight on the snow, searching for any sign of Bryan. But she saw no tire tracks that indicated any kind of car or truck had passed.

"Maybe they're already at Unaka," she whispered, her heart swelling with hope as she rounded the last curve before the recycling center. His uncle might have pulled off there—the road was wider and the dumpsters offered a bit of shelter from the wind.

She hurried on. In the distance her flashlight revealed the Unaka bins, now just huge white humps of snow. Excited, she started to run, but she saw not a single tire tread marring the trackless field of white.

"He's not here," she whispered, her chin starting to quiver. She had counted on him being here! She was depending on him to help her.

"He'll be here in a little while," she told herself with a confidence she did not truly feel. "He probably just got bogged down in the snow." After all, he'd told her that she was beautiful and he loved her. People didn't say things like that and then just not show up.

CHAPTER 13

Sunday

Mary Crow lay sleeping in Victor's bed, curled up in his comforter instead of his arms. She was dreaming—not of Victor or weddings, but of searching for a red pickup truck that was careening through the Emory campus. She had just found the vehicle behind her old dorm when its horn started bleating like a siren. In her dream she jumped back; from beneath the comforter she jumped up. As the dream evaporated she realized that no honking red truck had startled her awake. It was her office cell phone, ringing.

She made a woozy grab for it, wondering if Victor was calling he work number. "Hello?" she croaked, her mouth dry from sleep.

She heard nothing but static. "Hello?" she repeated, hoping it wasn't JimAnn Ponder or some stupid robo call. "Victor? Annette?"

Abruptly, a young voice came on the line. "Mary Crow?"

Mary rubbed her eyes, wondering what girl would be calling her in the middle of the night. "This is Mary Crow."

"Mary, it's Lily. Lily Walkingstick."

Mary looked at Victor's beloved weather/clock/radio on the bedside table. Green lights proclaimed that it was 4:13 a.m. The temperature was 22˚. I'm still dreaming, she decided. I talked too much about Walkingstick last night.

"Mary? Are you there?"

Mary wasn't sure what to say. When she'd last spoken with Lily Walkingstick, she'd had the voice of a child. This caller sounded like a teenager on the verge of panic. "I'm here," Mary finally replied.

"I wouldn't have called you...but I'm in trouble."

"Oh?" Mary asked cautiously, remembering the DA's staff warning her about Teofilo Owle. *He's sly as a spider and his web stretches wide. Be very careful.* "What kind of trouble?" she asked.

"Bounty hunters came," the caller replied shakily. "With guns. They may have shot Daddy and now one of them is after me..."

Mary frowned. "They shot your father?"

"I'm not sure. I-I ran out the door."

"I'm sorry to hear that," Mary replied neutrally, thinking that the girl's spiel sounded a lot like the con where scammers called old people, claiming to be a grandchild who needed to get bailed out of jail.

"Daddy made me promise to call you," the girl went on, her voice cracking. "If I was ever in bad trouble."

"Well, that does sound like bad trouble," Mary agreed.

"Don't you believe me?" the girl sobbed.

"I don't know," said Mary. "I'm not sure I'm talking to the real Lily Walkingstick."

"My mother was Ruth Moon," the girl cried. "After she died my father and I lived with you at your farm, on Bear Wallow Road. I played soccer. I was in Mrs. Crawford's brownie troop, number 112."

True, thought Mary. But Teo Owle could have found those things out, if he'd plucked the right thread on his web of informants.

The girl continued. "My grandfather Fred Moon sued my dad for custody of me, in Oklahoma. Your friend Alex was our lawyer. We all stayed at the Holiday Inn. I had a bodyguard named Cecilia. We had a PlayStation in our suite."

As she went on Mary remembered the pouty anger that had been Lily's MO during that whole, horrible time. She also remembered that Holiday Inn. It was the last time she'd seen Jonathan Walkingstick.

"Oh, forget it," the girl finally cried. "I'll find some other way to help Edoda."

The word *Edoda* caught Mary's attention. It was Cherokee for father, not commonly known. Still, it was something the half-Cherokee Teo might know. "Wait a minute," she said. "If you're Lily, then what's your father's favorite junk food?"

"Ding Dongs," Lily replied with true adolescent disgust. "He loves working the *New York Times* crossword puzzles. He wears a knife called Ribtickler and drives an old red truck."

Her heart thudding, Mary again looked at Victor's clock. Now it was 4:16 a.m. Maybe she wasn't dreaming this at all.

"Okay, Lily," she finally said. "I can call 911 for you. Where are you?"

"I'm at Unaka," the girl began, but the call started to break up. Mary heard the words "dumpsters... snow... strangers with guns" before a storm of static killed the conversation for good.

"Hello? Lily? Are you there?" Mary jumped out of bed and rushed to the window, hoping to improve the connection, but the person claiming to be Lily was gone. She clicked on her phone log and punched redial. The number rang twice, then an automated voice came on. *Your call cannot be completed now. Please try again later.*

Mary stood there, head spinning, phone in hand, trying to figure out what had just happened. Though Teo Owle had plenty of snitches, she couldn't figure out how he could have learned that Jonathan Walking-stick was a crossword puzzler with a lifelong addiction to Ding Dongs.

Reeling from the phone call, she put on a pot of coffee and pulled a North Carolina atlas from Victor's bookcase.

"Unaka," she whispered. The Cherokee word for white, a name for hundreds of different places in the Southern Appalachians. But she'd heard it mentioned around Drusilla's office as somewhere akin to the end of the known world. She flipped to the correct page in the atlas and poured over the map. After several moments of squinting, she found it—a tiny speck in the Tsalagi County woods, an eyelash away from the Tennessee state line.

"All this time I thought he was in Mexico,"she said airily, as if she'd knocked the scab off a still tender wound. "And he's been just one county away."

Angry, she flung the atlas across the room. How dare they call her? What universe were the Walkingsticks living in, to think she'd help them now?

"He should have called the cops." But suddenly she remem-bered–Jonathan wasn't the one who'd called. Lily had. A kid she'd once loved. A kid who now sounded truly terrified, stammering about hunters and guns.

She poured coffee into one of Victor's SBI mugs and tried the girl's number again. When she still got no answer, she started imagining the worst. Lily hurt, Lily lost, Lily freezing to death while she tried to find someone to help her. Finally, she picked up her phone and dialed a new number—Sam Ray, the sheriff of Tsalagi County. She had not worked there long enough to have much of a relationship with him, but he was the only person she knew to call.

He answered on the second ring, alert and awake, probably having fielded emergency calls all night. Mary explained the situation—a teenager she knew had called from Unaka claiming she'd been attacked by men with guns.

"In the middle of a blizzard?" asked Sam, incredulous.

"I suspect bounty hunters," said Mary. "She's a minor in a tribal custody case. There's a reward for the father."

"You sound like you know something about this."

"It's an old case of mine," she replied.

"I wish I could help you, Ms. Crow. But we're covered up. I've got three cruisers in ditches and one doubling as an ambulance. I could no more send a squad up to Unaka than I could rise and fly."

Mary felt sick in the pit of her stomach. "There's nothing you can do?"

"Call Sheriff Dwight Toedter over in Monroe County, Tennessee. They're closer to Unaka, and they might be having better luck with this storm."

She then called the number Ray gave her. Toedter listened sympathetically, but offered no help. "The park service closes all those access roads after bear season. Bounty hunters would need major bolt cutters to get back in those woods. Are you sure somebody's not pulling your leg?"

"I wish they were, Sheriff," she replied, again wondering if Teo was setting a trap. "But I think this is for real."

Beyond Monroe County law the only other person she could think of to call was Victor. But to what end? He was three hundred miles away in Raleigh. He couldn't do anything. And what would she tell him? *Hey, Victor, guess what! The day after you asked me to marry you my old boyfriend's daughter just popped back into my life. How about that!*

She poured another cup of coffee and turned on the weather channel, where a very young meteorologist stood wide-eyed in front of a map. "The governor has just declared an emergency for all counties west of Charlotte, North Carolina." Reporting that a true Snowmageddon was fast approaching Dixie, he explained how one massive storm was pumping moisture up from the Gulf of Mexico while the jet stream had dipped low into Texas. "Stock up on food, water and batteries, folks. Bring your pets indoors and stay home. This storm is a killer!"

Mary switched off the TV and looked out the window again. Though two feet of snow now topped the railing on the balcony, several cars had left tracks in the snow while three other brave souls were scraping their windshields. Hartsville, at least, had not yet been totally paralyzed by the weather.

She turned away from the window and considered her options. She had, she thought, fulfilled all her moral obligations to Lily (if it even was Lily). She'd baked cookies and attended school plays and cheered at soccer games, playing stepmother as best she could. And Lily had loved her as a mother, until Fred Moon poisoned her young mind about what had happened the night her real mother died. Lies and conjecture, all of it, but it had changed Lily from a happy little girl into a seething furnace of hate, all directed at her.

"Give it up," she told herself, rubbing her arms. "Lily can call 911 as well as I can." But that answer made her feel ashamed. Though she owed the Walkingsticks nothing, could she really stay in this cozy apartment and ignore a call from a panicked kid trapped in a blizzard?

"Don't do this," she told herself, but an hour later she'd equipped her new Subaru for every conceivable emergency. Food, her new ski pants, Victor's old Kelty sleeping bag, her Glock 9 and two boxes of ammo. If the weatherman was right, she figured she had a small window of opportunity to find and grab Lily before the full force of the storm whirled in. She was halfway out the door when she remembered that she should let someone know where she was going, just in case Lily was really Teo, waiting to put a bullet in her head. Grabbing a yellow legal pad, she wrote Victor a note.

Sweetheart—It's 6:43, Sunday morning. I'm driving to a place called Unaka, over in Tsalagi County. I got a distress call from a terrified kid claiming to be Lily Walkingstick. Going to check it out. Don't worry! I'll be fine!

I love you, Mary.

She stuck the note on the refrigerator with a little soccer ball magnet. She knew she should call him, but she also knew he would probably read meanings into her actions that weren't there."I'm just going to find out what the hell's going on, Victor," she whispered, thinking that she could probably get back here and tear the note up, long before he even read it.

CHAPTER 14

Victor Galloway was trying hard to pay attention to the lecture on forensics. Though the subject was fascinating—an Australian guy was talking about viable human DNA remaining in blowfly feces for as long as two years post mortem, his thoughts were all on Mary Crow. Last night on the phone he knew she was moving closer to the big cosmic YES—he could hear it in her voice. The prospect made him feel as if he could do anything—run for president, play goalie for DC United, solve the coldest case in Carolina. As the forensic psychologist wound up his remarks about bodies and blowflies, Victor broke into a big grin.

"You must love this shit," said Joe McGann, a lanky, fiftyish detective who'd become Victor's new best pal from Richmond. "You look happy as a clam."

Victor laughed. "Actually I was thinking that two nights ago I asked my girlfriend to marry me."

"Aw, man, that's terrific." Joe shook Victor's hand as they headed toward the hospitality room. "Congratulations. When's the wedding?"

"Don't know," said Victor. "She hasn't officially said yes, yet."

"Cold feet about marrying a cop?"

"More like cautious feet about marriage," replied Victor. "An old boyfriend really did a number on her."

"This your first trip down the aisle?"

Victor nodded. "I've come close before, but managed to dodge the bullet."

"I'm on my second," said Joe. "First one didn't take."

"Because you were a cop?"

"Mostly because I was too young, too stupid." Joe poured a cup of coffee. "What does your girl do?"

Victor spoke with pride. "She's a prosecutor."

"Cool. She's law and you're order. That means she'll get it when you're working a case. My first wife thought a stakeout was really a poker game with the boys. I'd come home cramped up from sitting in a cold car for eight hours and there she'd be, ready to read me the riot act."

Victor asked, "Does your second wife get it any better?"

"Carolyn's amazing." Joe added a blueberry muffin to his paper plate. "Waits up for me with a cold beer and a back rub. Don't know what I'd do without her."

As Victor poured a cup of coffee, the notion of him and Mary not working out chilled him. He couldn't imagine it, but he guessed every other guy who'd put a ring on someone's finger felt the same way. He turned to McGann. "So have you got any advice for those of us about to take the plunge?"

"Buddy, if I did, I'd write a book and get rich." Joe took a bite of muffin. "But here's my take on it. Treat your wife just like you treat your best friend."

"Excuse me?" Victor's best friend was Tarek Ahmadi, the goalie on the

Growlers soccer team. Tarek had a long black beard and thighs like tree trunks.

"Really listen when she talks. If she does something great, tell her. But mostly, don't criticize stuff you don't know shit about."

"Gotcha," said Victor, relieved.

"For a guy, the best two words in a marriage are 'Yes, dear.' Unless the question is *do I look fat?* Then, the right answer is always and forever no. Even if she looks like ten pounds of flour in a five-pound sack, the answer's still no."

Victor laughed. He couldn't imagine Mary turning into Two Ton Tessie, but he wouldn't care if she did. He loved far more than just her body. He was about to grab the last blueberry muffin when Captain John Stanfield, the chief of the seminar, walked to the center of the room and gave a sharp whistle over the low din of the room.

"I've got an announcement, folks," said Stanfield, who looked vaguely ridiculous in a fluorescent orange vest and unfastened snow boots. "We're going to have to end this workshop right now. A monster storm is barreling in, and the governor's declared an emergency in all the counties west of Charlotte. If we don't bug out ASAP, we could be stuck here for the rest of the week."

Though Victor murmured his disappointment along with everyone else in the room, secretly he was glad. The faster he could get home to Mary, the faster he could close the wedding deal.

Stanfield continued. "Raleigh-Durham airport is shutting down at one this afternoon, so those who are flying out should get there now. Those who drove here, please use extreme caution on the way home—salt trucks are out there, but they're fighting a losing battle. Thanks for attending, and safe travel home."

Victor drained his coffee and turned to Joe McGann. "If you want a lift to the airport, I can drop you off there. I've got my car."

"Thanks, but I drove, too," said Joe. "I'll just hop back on 95 and head for home."

"I guess we'd better get going." Victor held out his hand. "Nice meeting you, Joe. Thanks for the pre-marriage counseling."

Joe grinned. "Be safe, Victor. I hope you'll be bringing your bride to Richmond."

Victor went back to his hotel room, threw his clothes in a suitcase, and headed west on I-40. Already it had narrowed to one lane, moving at a crawl. As he drove he gave Mary a quick call. Earlier he'd gotten only her voice mail, and even now her recorded voice still invited him to leave a message.

"Hey sweetheart, just checking in with you. Since you're not answering your phone, I'm guessing you're either working on Teo's case or avoiding your unhappy divorcee. They cancelled the rest of the seminar, so I'm headed home. See you tonight!"

Though he tried to sound unconcerned, doubt began to gnaw at him. He wondered—could she have changed her mind about him since last night? Had some stupid red truck come along and hijacked her back into ancient history? Or worse, had Teofilo Owle somehow made good on his threat?

He considered calling her at her office, but decided against it. "Get a grip," he said aloud. "Don't go all worried husband on her yet. She's probably out buying bread and milk and just didn't hear the phone. "

Telling himself that all was well, he drove on, his tires and wipers struggling against a dizzying, unremitting snow. With luck, he would be home by late afternoon. Then, he could relax in a warm apartment and an even warmer Mary Crow.

Farther west, another man was having difficulty with the snow. Jonathan Walkingstick sat among a jumble of cast-off Scrabble tiles, his wrists zip-tied together. The bounty hunter he called Handgun had finally ceased his inane chatter and had, apparently, given up playing Good Cop with him. A wise choice, Jonathan thought, since he was planning to rip the man's throat out the first chance he got.

His fury igniting again, he started struggling against the zip-ties. But the plastic rubbed painfully against his wrists each time he pulled against them, and soon his efforts re-lit the fire in his shoulder. As he smelled the coppery aroma of fresh blood, he knew from his Army medic days that the bullet had passed through him, but had chewed up a chunk of his clavicle along the way. What it had done to his rotator cuff he couldn't imagine, except that every time he moved it felt like someone had put a blowtorch to his shoulder. Not a bright future, he thought, for a guy who made his living with hand tools and long bows.

But his future did not concern him now. His immediate worry was Lily, who was somewhere in the middle of a snowstorm, running for her life. And Handgun, who kept pacing around like the town sheriff waiting for the outlaws to arrive.

"Sit the fuck down," Jonathan finally said as the man made yet another circuit of the cabin.

"I'm keeping track of the snow," Handgun replied. "It hasn't let up at all."

"Seen tuhdajee yet?"

Handgun turned away from the window. "Who?"

"Tuhdajee. The mountain lion," explained Jonathan. "Tracks as big as dinner plates."

"Does he come here a lot?"

"More than I'd like," said Jonathan. "In the summer, the fishermen leave their cleanings out for him. They get a kick out of hearing him scream."

"He screams?" Handgun rubbed his belly wound.

"Just like a baby," said Jonathan. "But a hundred pound baby with fangs and claws."

"Don't they hibernate in the winter?"

Jonathan laughed. "No. They just get hungrier. Hope your partner's good with that gun."

He sat back against the sofa, enjoying Handgun's unease as he hurried over to make sure the front door was locked. Jonathan still couldn't imagine how these Bird Dogs had found them. They seemed clumsy—the kind who usually sought the low hanging fruit of bail jumpers and alimony cheats. How these two had tracked him to a closed up fishing camp in the Nantahala Forest was a mystery. Still, Handgun had spoken knowledgeably about Fred Moon and had tracked them all the way to Maine.

Moon must have put them on retainer, he decided. Last time he checked, Moon was offering ten thousand for him, but nothing for Lily. Maybe the bastard had sweetened the pot with a reward for her, as well. That would explain why the other guy had gone after her.

Seemingly worried that the mountain lion might be planning to have him for dinner, Handgun resumed his circuits of the cabin. Jonathan would have laughed, except for the Ruger the man carried and the fact that Lily was out in the frigid darkness, trying to outrun a man with an assault rifle.

"She can do that," he said in a whisper. Kitchee Boudreaux had made her a fine pair of snowshoes, which she kept in her cache. She had those, her bow and her survival coat, plus that cell phone and five hundred in cash. She should be able to get to civilization and buy a bus ticket somewhere.

But where would she go? Oklahoma? Maine? She'd been talking about Kentucky when these freaks burst through the door. They'd never stuck a toe in Kentucky—why would she want to go there?

He reminded himself that wherever she went, she knew to send a card to Krisjean in Maine. Then Krisjean would let him know she was safe. But what if she forgot to send that card? What if he never heard from her again? He fought a wave of panic. What if his last memory of his daughter was her beautiful young face terrified, running away as Scrabble tiles flew through the air?

"Nobody out back," announced Handgun, returning from the kitchen. "Nothing screaming like a hundred pound baby."

"Nobody's out back, you moron!" Jonathan cried, again struggling against his handcuffs. "My girl's miles away by now. And Tuhdajee's probably eating your partner alive."

"Shut up!" Suddenly Handgun went into a shooter's stance, pointing the pistol at Jonathan's head. Jonathan thought the man was going to kill him right there, but abruptly Handgun lowered his weapon and continued his circuit of the cabin, holding his belly and muttering to himself.

Jonathan closed his eyes, his heart going a thousand miles an hour. He wanted to howl his rage and frustration, but as long as Handgun was scared and trigger-happy, he needed to keep calm, to plan. He took a deep breath as he suddenly remembered the very first thing he'd drilled into Lily's head, so long ago. *If you ever need help and I'm not there, call Mary Crow.*

For a moment that thought comforted him. Though he knew Lily hated Mary, on every birthday he'd made her give her most solemn promise to call Mary if she needed help. He'd even programmed the number into her emergency phone.

But if Lily called, what would Mary do? She had every right to hate him. He had treated her shamefully—disappearing on her, ripping apart a relationship they'd had since they were kids. Would Mary blame Lily for that, as well? Hate her enough to say sorry, kid, your problems are no longer my concern. He didn't think so. Even if Mary hated him, he didn't think she would hate Lily, too. However far apart they might have grown, their shared history of love and anguish would bind them together until the day they died.

"Hate me all you want, Mary," he whispered, his throat thickening. "Just please take care of my child."

CHAPTER 15

Lily Walkingstick stood on top of one Unaka recycling bin, staring into the snow. She'd stayed awake all night, huddled under her space blanket, listening for either Bryan or the Rifleman. At one point she thought she heard a rough, rasping cough. She bolted up, awake, ready to swing her axe with both hands, but again, it was just the monster lurking inside her own head. Now, in the dim morning light, she saw no tracks of any kind in the snow. Rifleman had not come, but neither had Bryan. She was alone. Suddenly, she felt like an idiot for calling Mary Crow. She wasn't going to come up here and bring her a gun. What had she been thinking? She shook her head, embarrassed by her own panic. She only hoped that their connection last night had been so garbled that the woman had heard only static.

"She probably chalked it up to a scam call, anyway," Lily told herself.

Forgetting about Mary Crow, she pulled out her phone and texted Bryan. When the message still would not go through she began to wonder if he had ever really planned to come, or if he was safe at home, laughing at the stupid fool who thought he would really drive through a snowstorm for her. No, she told herself, willing her tears away. Bryan loved her, called her beautiful. The snow had simply delayed him. Then a new thought assailed her. What if he'd had a wreck? What if Bryan was lying in the snow somewhere, hurt, in just as much danger as Edoda? She felt as if her life was breaking into pieces, just like the snowflakes falling from the sky.

She took a deep breath, trying to quell all thoughts of death and disaster. Bryan was fine, he would be here soon. And when he finally showed up, his uncle could drive her to Murphy and they could get the police to see about her father. But she needed to wait somewhere more hidden than the top of a garbage bin—the Rifleman could still be out there, tracking her.

She looked at the area around the trash bins. They stood at a wide spot in the road, placed there to accommodate the people who had summer homes in these woods. Behind them rose a small overhang. If she could stake out a place on the overhang, she could keep watch on the road. When Bryan came she could flag him down. If the Rifleman came back, she would at least see him first. And if the Snow Men drove by with her father, she would know that Edoda was on his way to jail.

She decided to build a campsite, partly to keep her ankle limber and partly to take her mind off Bryan. Climbing gingerly to the overhang, she found two white pine trees growing so close together that their soft-fronded branches formed a mostly snow-free island between them. They afforded cover from the Rifleman, but were near enough to the road so she could hear anyone approaching.

After pitching her tent beneath the trees, she emptied her backpack and headed to the nearby creek she'd forded last night. She filled her backpack with the smooth creek stones that lined the bank and returned to her little camp. Four long trips later, as her ankle began to throb again, she was ready to build a fire. All she had to do now was find something to burn.

The woods offered nothing— rime ice coated all the trees and even the underbrush was soggy with snow. Cursing as she realized she might have lugged all those rocks up here for nothing, she remembered the garbage bins. If one of them held anything dry enough to burn, she might be able to pull this off.

She picked her way down the little ridge and pushed up the lid of one bin. An eye-watering array of odors came forth, neglected garbage from the summer people who'd returned for Thanksgiving. She found decaying turkey carcasses, empty wine bottles, mashed down cartons of organic chicken stock. Slamming the lid back down, she moved to the next bin. This time she turned her head as she lifted the lid, but this bin emitted no odors–all the garbage inside was tied up in black plastic bags.

"Damn," she whispered. "Doesn't anybody up here read a newspaper?"

She moved down to the last bin and lifted the heavy lid. She held her breath, dreading more Thanksgiving trash, but to her great joy, the bin was full of torn Christmas wrapping paper and discarded gift boxes. Someone had even topped off the junk with an old oak rocking chair, broken into pieces. She took off a glove and felt the thing. It was cold, but dry. "Thank you, Santa Claus," she said, laughing. She could light quite a bonfire with all the stuff in here.

Freshly energized, she dragged the rocking chair and a backpack full of paper up to her little camp between the trees. She laid the creek stones out flat, covered them with crinkled silver wrapping paper and lit it with her emergency lighter. She fed that fire to a nice blaze, then added the woven seat of the old rocker. She knew if she got the fire hot enough, the pieces of the chair would burn and heat the stones for hours.

She sat at the edge of her tent, nursing the fire, listening both for the boy she loved and the tracker she feared. As she watched the small orange flames dance, she thought about her father. Yesterday she wanted nothing more than to escape his care. Today, all she could think about was how fast he'd grabbed his knife and how loudly that gunshot had rung out. But worse was that the Snow Men might be taking him to jail. That would kill him. Not the guards or the inmates, but the iron bars that would cage him like an animal. Edoda was Cherokee, too proud to live confined. Tearing up at the image of her father languishing in a prison cell, she realized she was stuck. If Bryan did show up and drove her to the sheriff in Murphy, it would do no good. The Snowmen would have papers, warrants for her father's arrest. Suddenly, she realized it was up to her. She was the only one who could free her father.

"I'm sorry, Edoda," she whispered. "But I cannot keep my Atli promise like you wanted. I cannot go away and leave you alone."

While Lily tended her fire, Mary was driving up a state road that twisted into the game lands beloved by hunters and fishermen. No sportsmen ventured forth today, though. The snow kept pummeling down, and with every switchback she climbed, the air grew colder, the road icier.

For miles, she had seen no one, passed no other traffic. She felt as if the world had been drained of color; the gold and russet trees of three months earlier were now lifeless black limbs, being slowly shrouded by white snow. She checked the atlas, wondering if she had taken a wrong turn, but the map and the compass on her dashboard read WNW–the right direction.

She drove higher, her windshield wipers doing double-time. As she crested a rise the road widened a bit, before leading even further up the mountain. Praying that this might be the elusive Unaka, she slowed to a crawl when a sudden movement caught her eye. A figure in a dark green coat lurched out from behind what looked like some snow-covered garbage bins. Remembering that this was Teo country, she reached for her Glock.

"Bryan?" she heard a young female voice call eagerly. "Is that you?"

Mary stopped her car. As the figure edged closer, she pulled back the hood of her coat. Though the features were now more of a teenager than a child, Mary immediately recognized the striking blend of Jonathan Walkingstick and Ruth Moon.

She rolled down her window. "Hello, Lily."

"Oh." Lily's tone was disappointment mixed with surprise. "It's you."

Mary didn't know what to say. When they parted so long ago, Lily had despised her. From the look on her face now, it seemed she still did. It wouldn't have surprised her if every snowflake that fell on Lily sizzled into a hot little bit of angry steam.

"I didn't think you'd come," the girl said flatly.

"I only heard pieces of your call. I took a guess you were talking about this Unaka." Mary stashed the Glock behind the driver's seat. "What's going on?"

For a moment, Lily's hard look of hate waivered. "Men with guns broke into our cabin. Bounty hunters, probably. My father pulled his knife and told me to leave. Then I heard a gunshot and one man chased me with a rifle."

"Up here?" asked Mary.

The girl nodded so matter-of-factly that Mary wondered if she was in shock.

"Did they shoot your father?"

"I don't know," she replied. "I ran away."

"Come get in the car," said Mary. "You can warm up and we can talk."

For a moment Lily did not move, then she limped over and flopped into the passenger seat. Mary left the motor running as Lily removed rabbit skin gloves and blew on her hands. The gesture was so Jonathan, Mary felt as if she were sitting with a ghost.

"Are you okay?" asked Mary. "Why are you limping?"

"The Rifleman tackled me. He grabbed my ankle but I got loose."

"Here." Mary offered her a PayDay candy bar. "Eat this and tell me exactly what's happened."

Between bites of candy, Lily fleshed out her story, beginning with their year at the fishing camp, ending with her terror at being chased by the man with the rifle. "That's when I called you."

"Why me?" asked Mary, wondering how her lucky number had turned up.

Lily held up an older model iPhone. "Every year Edoda makes me promise that if I ever get in real trouble, I'll call you. But when I called last night I was just freaking out with the snow and the cold. I really don't need you."

Mary gazed at her windshield, fast becoming a field of white. After all this time, after all the silence and the distance and the not knowing, Jonathan still trusted her with Lily. She didn't know whether to feel flattered or furious. She decided not to feel anything and just deal with the problem at hand.

"Okay," she said, shifting the little Subaru into reverse. "We'll beat it back to Murphy and call Sheriff Ray."

"No!" Lily grabbed her hand. "Those men will have warrants. The sheriff will read them and let those men take Edoda back to Oklahoma. They'll send him to prison."

Mary snatched her hand out of Lily's grasp. "What do you want me to do, then?"

"Did you bring your gun? Just give it to me and I'll take care of everything," she said, her chin quivering.

"I didn't bring a gun, Lily," Mary lied, looking into eyes as dark as Jonathan's. "Even if I had I wouldn't give it to you."

"Then just go home," Lily said, her mouth curling in an ugly snarl. "I only called you because Edoda made me promise." She grabbed her gloves and flung open the car door. "Sorry you came up here for nothing."

She slammed the door so hard the Subaru rocked. Before Mary could say another word, Lily was a dark blur, quickly vanishing into the wind and snow.

"Wait, Lily!" she called. "This is crazy dangerous!"

The girl flung an inaudible curse over her shoulder. Her words were hot with anger, but they came softly, from a distance, muffled by the snow.

"What the hell does she want?" Mary cried. Going back to town and calling Pete Ray was the sensible thing. But she barely knew where she was, much less the location of Jonathan's fishing camp. She grabbed her cell phone and punched in 911. The only thing that came on the screen was a "No Service Available" message.

"Damn it," she whispered. "Damn the Walkingsticks and damn this snow." Clenching the steering wheel, she tried to calm down with several deep breaths. "You're the adult here," she told herself. "Figure this out."

She considered what Lily had told her. Two skip chasers had apparently tracked Jonathan up here and grabbed him in the middle of a blizzard. Both were armed and one had pursued Lily. Had they shot Jonathan? If so, what were they doing now? Trying to drive out of the mountains?

"Or maybe waiting for Lily to come back," she whispered, remembering Fred Moon's fierce determination to win custody of his grandchild. "Maybe they've baited a trap for Lily with Jonathan."

Of course the girl would want to go back and free her father. Lily was smart and brave. The forest held no terror for her. But a teenaged girl with a bow and arrows going up against at least two men with rifles? It was madness, without question.

Mary got out of the car and started walking in the direction Lily had taken. If she could catch up with the girl, she would drag her back to the car if she had to. Saving Lily came first. Jonathan would have to take care of himself.

All at once, a boom like a cannon thundered through the forest. Mary plunged to the ground, thinking that the bounty hunter must now be firing at her. But after the single, bone-jarring report, the woods returned to snowy silence. Trembling, she looked around and gasped. Thirty feet away a massive pine tree had fallen, its trunk crushing her Subaru like a tin can. Had she lingered in her car a moment longer, she would be dead.

She lay there stunned, gazing at the tree and the snow—deep now, and growing deeper. As fingers of icy cold plunged down the collar of her coat, she realized she was alone, miles deep in a strange forest, her shelter gone and no way to call out. For the first time in her life, Mary Crow was afraid in the woods.

CHAPTER 16

Lily bolted upright in het tent, terrified, figuring that the Rifleman had just killed Mary Crow. Grabbing her bow and quiver, she crept to the edge of the little overhang, fulling expecting to see the camouflaged monster standing over a bloody corpse. Instead, she saw only Mary, gaping at the remains of her flattened car.

"Holy shit," she whispered. Not five minutes earlier, they had both been sitting exactly where that tree had landed.

She watched, waiting to see what Mary would do. At first she just stared at the car in disbelief. Then she started tugging hard on the unyielding doors, finally managing to pry open the trunk. Crawling inside, she wormed her way into the backseat, extricating a hiker's backpack, complete with a bright orange sleeping bag. Impressed at the array of her equipment, Lily remembered one of Mary Crow's cardinal rules–*never go into the woods unprepared.*

Now, though, the famous Mary Crow was stuck in the forest only marginally prepared, with a useless car and a cold wind blowing in like a freight train.

"Serves her right," muttered Lily. Mary Crow had killed her mother—freezing to death up here would be a better fate than she deserved. Lily started to back away and return to her tent, but she remembered her father's cardinal rule. *Feed your good wolf.* Which meant, as best she understood it, to do good things instead of bad. Leaving Mary Crow alone and shivering in a snowstorm would not be feeding her good wolf at all. And as much as she hated to admit it, when Mary Crow had pulled up a few minutes ago, she'd been glad to see her. Mary wasn't Bryan, but at least she was another warm human being.

"Okay," she whispered, her good wolf nipping at her guilt. "This is for you, Edoda."

Mindful that she might be giving her position away to the Rifleman, she stood up, cupped her mouth and yelled as loudly as she dared. "Come up here! I've got a fire."

Mary turned, squinted up at her through the falling snow. Lily pointed to the path she'd worn in setting up her camp. Shouldering her gear, Mary followed Lily's directions. A few moments later, she reached the top of the ridge, breathing hard and heavy.

"I've got a tent over here," said Lily. "You can warm up."

"Thanks," gasped Mary, her breath like smoke.

Lily led her over to the tent. Warmth now radiated from the hot stones she'd moved inside, while space blankets made a bright silver quilt.

Mary entered the tent and sat near the stones. Lily was surprised at how little she'd changed—she was still slender, still wore her dark hair just touching her shoulders. She probably looks a lot like my mom would have, Lily thought. If my mom were still alive.

"Here," said Lily filling a thermos cup with tea. "Hold this with both hands. It'll warm you up."

Clutching the cup, Mary looked around at the blankets and tiny stove.

"You've done this well," she said. "Not many people could camp so comfortably in snow."

"I learned in Maine. We camped a lot up there."

Mary breathed in the steam rising from the tea. "How long were you in Maine?"

"A while." Lily said, adding nothing more. Her Maine memories were precious to her; she didn't want Mary Crow's fingerprints on any of them. "Too bad about your car."

"Yeah. I just bought it last summer. Now I can't even crawl in the front seat."

"That tree would have killed you."

"That tree would have killed us both." Mary gave a weak laugh. "I guess the Old Men were looking out for us."

"The Old Men?"

"*Dodahluh*," Mary replied. "The mountains."

Lily frowned, remembering that Mary Crow probably knew as many Cherokee words as Edoda. "I wish the Old Men would make the snow melt."

"Their wishes aren't ours." Mary turned to the girl. "Tell me again about these bounty hunters. Don't leave anything out."

Lily repeated the story. Mary questioned her as if she were in court—how many men were there? Were they both wearing camo? What kind of weapons did they carry? Which one shot your father?

Lily shook her head. "I don't know. He drew his knife, and made me run out the back door. He calls it *Atli*. He's always made me promise to run away if anything bad happened." As Lily gazed at the orange coals that lay on the stones, her tough, adult façade cracked. "It was really scary," she whispered. "I had to sneak to my deer blind and get my sup-

WHITE TREES CRIMSON SNOW

plies." She looked at Mary, again trying not to cry. "You can stay here tonight, if you want. You'll have plenty of room after I leave."

"Still going back to the cabin?"

She nodded.

"What if your tracker finds you?"

"I've got an axe," said Lily. "And a bow with twelve arrows. Man killers, Edoda calls them."

"That's something, I guess." Frowning, Mary paused for a long moment. "Could I offer another suggestion?"

"I suppose," Lily said unenthusiastically.

"You said you stayed awake all last night. Why not hunker down here overnight and go back in the morning? We can sleep in shifts and keep watch. Tomorrow, the snow might stop and you'll be a lot fresher."

"But what if they leave with him before I get there?"

"Is this road the quickest way to civilization?" asked Mary.

Lily shrugged. "I guess so. It's the only one we ever take."

"Until they clear away the tree that just totaled my car, nobody's going anywhere on this road for quite a while."

Victor Galloway pounded his steering wheel in frustration. He'd expected a challenging drive home from Raleigh. What he hadn't imagined was a skidding, sliding crawl along the ice rink formerly known as Interstate 40. Everything Northerners complained about Southerners and snow had proved true—people didn't know how to drive in it, cops didn't know how to manage traffic in it, and snow plows were as non-existent as dodo birds. In eight hours he'd traveled a hundred miles, only now nearing the little town of Old Fort, where the foothills ended and the true Appalachians began.

Before the real fun started, he pulled off at a gas station. A full tank would put more weight on his back wheels and anyway, he wanted to try Mary again. All day he'd called; not once had she answered. He knew she had a lot on her mind, between marrying him and prosecuting Teo Owle, but this was nuts. He punched in her number and again, got her voice mail. This time he didn't bother to leave a message. This time he hung up and called Ginger Cochran.

Her phone rang almost as long as Mary's had, but to his great relief, Ginger finally answered—a living, breathing person on the end of the line. He wasted no words.

"Hi, Ginger. This is Victor. Have you seen Mary today?"

"No, we're totally snowed in. Haven't you seen her?"

"I've been in Raleigh. I've been calling her for hours and all I get is voice mail."

"Our power's been on and off all day. The phone lines might be down–Jerry's calling me on his police line," said Ginger. "By the way, Mary showed me her ring last night at dinner–it's gorgeous!"

He perked up. Mary showing Ginger her ring was a good sign. "Did she say anything about, you know, getting married?"

"She said quite a lot. We even looked at spring gowns in Tarcila Moreno's dress shop."

The tightness in his neck eased a bit. Maybe a red pickup hadn't rolled up and driven Mary out of his life. He decided to risk the most important question of all. "So do you think she might say yes?"

"I told her she'd be crazy not to," said Ginger.

"But she's got all that Walkingstick baggage."

"I know. But I think your luck's looking very good. Buy me a lottery ticket on your way home. I'll split the power ball with you."

He laughed, looking at the crowded gas station. Lottery tickets were not a priority tonight–people were stocking up on the true necessities—beer and cigarettes. "I'm in Old Fort now. I might make it home by spring."

"You be careful, Victor. Jerry's worked out of the cruiser for twenty hours straight, just on traffic calls. And it's not supposed to get better until the middle of next week."

He thought of asking Ginger if she would have Jerry check in on Mary, but decided against it. Cops were always slammed when the weather went crazy, and he didn't want Mary to think he was keeping tabs on her.

"Thanks for the update, Ginger. I'll see you guys soon." And Mary sooner, he thought hopefully as he clicked off his phone and headed back out onto the ice-covered interstate.

CHAPTER 17

Monday

While Victor was making slow progress along I-40, Mary Crow was struggling up from a coma-like sleep. At first she felt only deep and unremitting cold, her face waxen, her arms and legs cold as stumps. Then her brain, or at least her memory, thawed and she remembered Victor proposing, Ginger making her look at dresses, finally a phone call from Lily Walkingstick that had pulled her from a warm bed into the teeth of a blizzard that had crushed her little car like an empty beer can.

Mary sat up and opened her eyes. To her surprise, Lily was gone, her bedroll empty. She crawled out of her sleeping bag, blew her hands and stuck her head out of the tent flaps. It was still snowing but Lily was crouched on the edge of the overhang, a dark figure in a swirl of white.

"Lily?" Mary called. "Are you okay?"

She jumped, startled. "Yeah. Just keeping watch."

Mary struggled out of the tent, her joints seemingly welded in place. Amazingly, the snow still came down. A good fifteen inches surrounded their tent-between-the-trees. She put her boots on and joined Lily at the overhang.

"Any sign of your tracker?"

"No sign of anyone," she replied glumly, as if she'd been expecting a carload of her buddies to drive up for a joy ride.

"How's your ankle?" asked Mary.

"A little better," Lily replied. "Walking should help it limber up."

"Still going back to the camp?"

She nodded. "I can't let them take Edoda."

Mary gave an inward cringe at the craziness of it. She'd hoped that shivering through a night in an icy blizzard might have changed the girl's mind, but Lily remained determined. Truly Jonathan's child, thought Mary. But she still decided to try reasoning with her.

"You know, going back might be pointless. Bounty hunters usually go in, grab their guy, and get out fast. Maybe they're already gone. Maybe they came by these bins before you got here. Or maybe they knew another road, through Tennessee."

Lily looked at her. "Did you pass anybody on your way up here?"

Mary thought back. She couldn't remember anyone crazy enough to be out driving yesterday. "No, I didn't."

"Then they must still be there," the girl said. "The road to Tennessee is crazier than this one."

"Okay. But even if you went back to the camp it would still be your bow against their guns."

"Doesn't matter," she replied. "I can shoot from the cover of the trees."

Mary frowned, growing frustrated. "Okay, let's say you get a kill shot on one. That leaves the other, or maybe the *others*. If they don't shoot you right off, they could use your father as a hostage."

"And come after me." Lily finished Mary's sentence in a mocking, singsong voice.

"Absolutely," said Mary. "Use your father to set a trap for you. You blunder into it, and they drive away with both of you. Your dad goes to jail, and you go live with Grandpa Moon."

For a long moment, Lily stared down at the snow covered road. Finally, she spoke. "It doesn't matter," she said. "I can't leave Edoda up there. He'll either fight to get away and they'll kill him. Or they'll take him to jail, which would kill him in a different way."

Mary knew Lily was right about that. She couldn't see any good outcome for Jonathan, whichever way you cut it. He'd blown his standing with the court when he took Lily in the first place. If the bounty hunters returned him to Oklahoma, he'd likely be looking at some serious time. Still, she pressed on.

"Well, if you won't come back with me and fight for your dad through legal channels, then let me go with you, back to the camp."

"No," Lily said flatly. "It's a hard hike. You'd only slow me down."

"Probably." Mary ceded Lily that point. "I have lately spent more time in the courtroom than in the deep woods."

"That's what I mean. You can't even—"

"But that's taught me a lot," Mary continued. "About criminals and skip chasers and how they think. Which isn't one bit like you and me."

Lily frowned. Mary had seen the same weighing-my-options look on Jonathan's face many times before. She decided to play her ace in the hole.

"And here's one other thing to consider, Lily. As old and decrepit as I might be, I've got two good ankles and this." She reached inside her jacket and pulled the Glock from her shoulder holster. "Surprise. I brought a gun after all."

Lily gaped at the pistol, wide-eyed at its dark, gleaming lethality. She swallowed hard, wavering. Mary moved to close the deal.

"Listen—I think your plan is very dangerous. But if you're determined to do it, then I'm willing to take this gun and level the playing field. If you'd still rather go limping on alone, I'll thank you for your hospitality and hike back to town."

Lily gave a snide little laugh. "You really think you can hike fast for hours? Up ridges, in the snow?"

Mary shot Lily an angry glare. "Honey, I survived the camping trip from hell before you were born. No food, no weapons, and no clothes, all while tracking a rapist. A cold hike to a fish camp is nothing."

Lily sat there in the dim light, looking like both a brave young woman and a frightened little girl. The seconds seemed to drip like hours. Finally, she spoke.

"You won't send him to prison?"

Mary almost laughed. Was that the deal-breaker here? Turning Jonathan into the authorities? "No. I would doing anything in my power to keep your father from going to prison."

"But you're a lawyer. Aren't you supposed to uphold the law?"

"I've sworn an oath to do that."

"So you'd break the law for him?"

"There are two people on earth I'd break the law for. One is your father."

Lily cocked her head. "Who's the other?"

"You."

The same cold, white morning found Leroy still making his rounds inside the Indian's cabin. He'd waited for Chet and Kimmeegirl all night, long after the Indian had slumped over in a restless sleep. Around six he thought he heard the back door creaking open. Pulling his pistol, he crept into the dark kitchen, hoping Kimmeegirl might be sneaking in. But all he found was the screen door, rattling on its hinges.

Nonetheless, he stepped out on the back porch and aimed one of the Indian's flashlights into the darkness. The beam revealed a trackless field of white that ended in the hulk of the snow-covered truck.

With a deep, frustrated sigh, he realized this cutie hunt had gone badly off the rails. The prospect of his enjoying the unsullied Kimmeegirl was growing dimmer by the minute, and God only knew what had happened to Chet. He could be lost, frozen to death or eaten by the cougar. Conversely, he could be lying in their camper, diddling Kimmeegirl and having a good laugh at him.

Sourly, Leroy went back into the cabin and brewed a pot of coffee, wondering what he should do. It seemed silly to stay here with the Indian, and if Chet had died, he would be a sitting duck if Kimmeegirl came back with the cops. But his wound had throbbed like a bad tooth all night and when he lifted his shirt to examine it, it looked red and swollen to twice its size.

"So much for that Midol shit," he whispered. "I need some of Chet's pain pills."

Returning to the camper finally seemed the best thing to do, so Leroy threw a box of Daisy Fresh pads, the Indian's wallet and some extra flashlight batteries in an old knapsack. He considered driving the both of them back to the camper in the Indian's truck, but digging the thing out of the snow would only make his belly hurt worse. After letting the Indian piss in the toilet, they trudged up the driveway, his pistol pointed at the back of the Indian's head. Half an hour later, sweaty and breathless, they reached the camper. It looked like a loaf cake iced in thick frosting, snow covering the roof and hood, drifting halfway up the tires. If Chet and the girl had left tracks around the thing, the snow had long since covered them up.

Shit, thought Leroy, staring at the camper in disbelief. He'd been so sure that Chet would be in there with Kimmeegirl that he'd spent the long trek up here rehearsing the accusations he was going to level at him. But his wrath stalled; Chet was not there.

The Indian turned and glared at him. "Well? Are we going inside? Or just enjoying the view?"

Leroy brushed the snow from the side of the vehicle and unlocked the door. He pushed the Indian up the steps and followed him inside. The thermometer in the galley read 51°. Warm by outdoor standards; chilly for a man enjoying a young girl. Just to make sure, Leroy stepped over and banged on wooden panel that closed off an upper berth nudged over the cab of the truck.

"Anybody home?"

Leroy pulled his ski mask up and listened, but heard nothing. He banged again. "Are you in there?"

Again, he heard only a silence that was broken when the Indian started to laugh.

"Tuhdajee probably got him."

The Indian's levity enraged Leroy. He lifted his pistol and brought the butt hard down on the Indian's torn shoulder. The man groaned as he crumpled to his knees.

"Shut up," Leroy snarled. "Or you'll wish Tuhdajee got you."

He opened the panel that enclosed the upper berth. Cold, stale smelling air rushed out of a room that was dark as a cave. He grabbed the Indian by his coat collar and lifted him to the ladder that accessed the place.

"Get in there," said Leroy, shoving the muzzle of the gun between his shoulder blades. "I'll let you out when we get to Oklahoma. I'm sure old man Moon will be the first to say hello."

CHAPTER 18

Jonathan climbed up into a fetid darkness. For a long time he sat still, waiting for his eyes to adjust to the non-light. When they finally did, he got a slightly better sense of his surroundings. The upper berth of a camper, about the size of a double bed, with rough, greasy carpeting covering the floor and walls. Every surface smelled sour, as if the sweat and gush of a hundred sex acts had dried and never been cleaned up. Still, the trip up here from the cabin had told him a lot. The bird dogs had hunted him from a two bedroom camper with a galley and a dinette. Normal people would have driven such a vehicle to see the Grand Canyon or Mount Rushmore. These men used it for a darker purpose. Still, the most telling detail made him weak with joy. Lily was not here.

"Good girl," he whispered. She'd done Atli perfectly. Run like jula and never look back. As long as she was safe, he could deal with anything these guys dished out.

He guessed if the one named Chet ever showed back up, they would take him back to Oklahoma and collect the ten grand from Fred Moon. As bird dogs went, though, they were a pretty pathetic pair. Though they'd mangled his left shoulder and cuffed his hands, Handgun had not taken his belt and shoes, or even searched the pockets of his coat. He didn't know that Jonathan had a half a pack of crackers that Lily hadn't wanted, the keys to his truck, and a small Swiss Army knife complete with toothpick and tweezers. He doubted he could kill anyone with it, but thrust into an eye or a jugular vein, the little blade could do some damage.

He ate one of the stale crackers, wondering if he could find a way out of here. He knew that campers like this usually had windows that looked out over the hood of the vehicle. Twisting his legs out straight, he dug the little knife from his pocket and flopped over to face the front of the camper. If he could pry or cut some carpeting loose from that window, he might be able to see what was going on.

Holding the knife in his teeth, he pressed one hand against the carpeted wall. Soon he felt the oblong shape of a window frame. Careful of his throbbing shoulder, he lay down and started at the bottom corner of the window, plunging the tiny knife into the carpet and sawing away. He worked, fumbling with his right hand, careful not cut out more than he could quickly cover up. After a while he'd removed a strip the length of his index finger. As an annoying lump beneath the floor carpeting dug into his side, he was finally able to look outside.

The snow stood over a foot deep on the hood of the truck, with more flakes peppering down. The world had become monochromatic, with white snow, black tree trunks, and everything else in varying shades of gray. Still, he recognized the road that passed by the fish camp. Park Rangers had closed it off in early January, after bear season. Only he and Enoch Stiles, the owner of the camp, had keys to unlock the barricade.

"Unless you had a bolt cutter and a big check from Fred Moon waiting for you," he whispered.

Since he had nothing more interesting to watch than falling snow, he tucked the strip of carpeting back in place and rolled over on his side. Avoiding all pressure on his shoulder, he nestled his head on his right arm and closed his eyes. Sleep, he told himself. Sleep and you might come up with a way to get out of here.

But sleep did not come. Handgun kept stomping around as the wind swayed the camper like a boat on the lake. With the under-the-carpet lump digging into his side, he twisted and turned, desperate to find a comfortable position.

Slowly, his frustration heated from a simmer to a boil, and he sat up. He jerked the cover from his peephole for light, and with his miniscule knife, started cutting out the maddening lump in the carpet.

He assumed it was a bad wrinkle in the backing or insulation, nothing more than a crappy installation job. But when he reached under the carpeting to smooth it out, he felt material much softer than commercial pile nylon. He grasped it, and pulled. To his amazement, a small white bra emerged, cups generously padded with thick foam.

"What the hell?" He frowned, wondering how such a thing could have gotten under this carpet. Holding it up to the peephole, he saw that someone had written inside one lacy cup, in one of those electric blue markers Lily once loved. As he held the thing up in the sliver of light, he grew sick inside.

Dear Mama, someone had scrawled in twisty, uneven letters. *I am so scared. I...*

After that, either the writer or the marker ran dry. He felt the hair lift on the back of his neck. Though the light was dim and the letters blurry, he knew that he'd just read a note from someone who'd once huddled in the same camper that now held him. He gulped, wondering if these men were bird dogs at all. The little bra made him think they might be something far worse.

Twenty hours after leaving the seminar, Victor Galloway rolled into Hartsville. On the way he'd had two fender-benders, helped one shivering old woman change a flat tire, and fought a fierce headwind that wanted to push him all the way back to Raleigh. But his little Mustang, chugging along to satellite radio, had gotten him through. Though he reached Main Street at eight a.m., he found the town deserted, covered by a thick blanket of white.

"Power's still out," he said, stopping at a dead traffic light that swayed in the wind. He drove by Mary's office, wondering if he should stop and see if she was working by flashlight, but decided no. Mary was dedicated, but not crazy. She'd probably returned to his apartment hours ago.

"Then why won't she answer my calls?" he said, voicing his concern over the countless calls that had gone unanswered. Ginger had reassured him that Mary had just submerged herself in the Teo Owle case, but what if Teo Owle had acted on the threat he'd made in the courtroom? The timing would have been perfect—a blizzard knocking out power, stopping traffic, hampering police response.

Calm down, Victor told himself again. You're going to feel like a real Nellie when you go home and find her cuddled down under warm blankets.

Hurrying, he drove past her office and headed to his apartment. It looked as frozen as the town—no lights on, every car in the parking lot just a lump of snow. Unable to tell where Mary's car was, he slid into his regular spot, the only snow-free automobile in the whole lot.

He grabbed his bag and hurried across the snow, slipping and cursing. No kids had built snowmen, nor did he see any tracks of cross-country skis or snowboards. Just too frigging cold, he thought, shivering as he struggled up the stairs to his apartment.

He unlocked the door and stepped inside. With no power, it was dark and cold. Dropping his bag, he headed to the bedroom. "Mary?" he called. "It's me. I'm back!"

He grinned, excited, hoping to see her in bed, peeking from beneath every blanket he owned. But his smile vanished when he found his bed neatly made, the down comforter folded at one end.

He went to the room they used as a study, thinking maybe she'd curled up on the couch. Though pages of her case file were spread out on the desk, the room was as cold and empty as the bedroom. He checked the living room, bathroom, kitchen. Empty.

She must have gone to her place, he decided. To turn the water on to keep the pipes from bursting. He walked to the kitchen, thinking he should take that precaution himself. He was reaching for the faucet when he noticed a sheet of yellow legal pad attached to the refrigerator door. A note in blue ink, in Mary's handwriting, underneath a soccer ball magnet.

He read it three times, his blood going as cold as the wind outside. Mary hadn't been here since yesterday morning. She'd gone on some rescue mission for Lily Walkingstick.

"Bullshit," he whispered. "This isn't Lily Walkingstick. This is Teofilo Owle." He knew that Teo had taken it personally when Victor, a fellow Latino he called *compadre*, had shown up at his trailer and questioned him about Drusilla Smith's murder. Given Teo's reputation, the little bastard had probably done his own digging, and found that Victor and Mary Crow were much more than friends.

He shoved the note in his back pocket, grabbed his phone and managed to get the SBI switchboard to patch him through to Sheriff Ray in Tsalagi County. When the harried sounding Ray finally answered, Victor explained that Mary Crow had been missing two days, quite possibly the victim of Teofilo Owle.

"She called me yesterday," said Ray. "Something about a kid in a custody battle. I couldn't help her then and I can't help her now. I got a high school basketball team stranded in the gorge. School bus slid off the road."

"You don't have anybody else?" asked Victor, incredulous.

"Not till tomorrow. Maybe not even then."

"But Mary Crow is your acting DA!"

"She's one woman, Galloway. I've got a busload of kids freezing in sweat suits and basketball shoes."

Begrudgingly, Victor saw the sheriff's logic. He pulled Mary's note from his pocket and reread it. "Do you know a place called Unaka?"

"It's a little nothing of a spot up near the Tennessee line. Trash bins for Floridians, mostly. Why?"

"I think that's where she's gone."

"Unaka's a far piece on a twisting road. I doubt you could even get up there in this weather."

Maybe you couldn't, thought Victor. But I'm sure going to try.

CHAPTER 19

An hour after Victor pulled into his apartment parking lot, he pulled out again. After talking with Sheriff Ray, he gathered his camping gear, his service pistol and enough ammunition to kill Teo Owle a hundred times over. On his way out of town he made one last call, to Spencer, his boss at SBI.

"Where the hell have you been, Galloway?" Spencer demanded before Victor could get a word out of his mouth. "We need all hands on deck, working this storm. You were supposed to check in yesterday."

"I was at the forensic conference, in Raleigh," Victor reminded him. "I'm now proceeding into the Nantahala Forest on a possible abduction."

"On a what?"

"Teofilo Owle verbally threatened acting DA Mary Crow in court three days ago," reported Victor. "Owle was not remanded. I think he is acting on that threat."

"What makes you think that?" asked Spencer.

Victor could hardly say that the note on his refrigerator was the reason for his suspicions. "Owle has a history of witness intimidation. The last DA who prosecuted him died under unusual circumstances."

"Galloway, isn't this Mary Crow your girlfriend?"

Victor dodged his question. "We worked the Teo Owle case together."

"Then is it possible Ms.Crow might have just skidded into a ditch? That Owle abducting her in the middle of a blizzard could be just another of your loose cannon conclusions?"

"No, sir."

"Agent Galloway. You are needed for emergency services at the Hartsville office immediately. Fail to report and I will personally make sure that this will be your last day in law enforcement."

Victor flinched, but did not change his mind. He knew this confrontation with Spencer had been coming for a long time. "As I said earlier, sir," he replied. "I'll be in the Nantahala Forest, investigating the possible abduction of Mary Crow."

On the way out of town Victor found one small convenience store still open. Though the shelves had long since been emptied of bread and milk, he bought a large coffee, a dozen energy bars and the last half of a dry, overcooked pizza.

After that he headed up into the mountains. He'd visited Teo's trailer before, and knew that he lived at the end of a narrow, twisting two lane. A treacherous mix of ice and snow covered the road, but his old green Mustang rode low to the ground and managed not to slide into any ravines. In two hours he made it to Lickspittle Road; half an hour later he turned at a battered, bird-shot mailbox that had a serape-clad skeleton doll dangling from it. Teo must have celebrated Dia De Muertos last year, thought Victor, staring at the snow-covered decoration.

"Teo, if you've done anything to Mary Crow, today will be your dia de muerte," he muttered. "And it won't be quick or painless."

He got out of the car, pulled on his Kevlar vest, and walked up the rutted driveway, now just an indentation in the snow. As he neared the front stoop of Teo's trailer, he noticed the faintest of tracks leading down the porch steps, across the front yard to a slightly less snow-filled rectangle where some vehicle had been parked. Mary, he thought with a sick feeling in the pit of his stomach. Had Teo driven Mary into the woods and left her there to freeze? Or just killed her right off? What had he done with her car?

He took the safety off his pistol and crept up on the porch. Pressing one ear against the front door, he heard faint music playing. He grabbed the door knob, tested it to see if it moved. To his astonishment, it was unlocked. Slowly, he turned the knob and eased the door open. Inside, the trailer smelled of coffee and cigarettes. Minimal warmth issued from an old electric heater while Rascal Flats blared from a tinny radio. Teo sat in a rocking chair, curled in front of the heater, a thick wool blanket pulled over his head.

He crept closer, careful not to make a sound. Just behind the rocker he stopped, lifted his pistol and pressed it against the back of Teo's skull.

"It's 11:33, Monday, Martin Luther King Day," he said softly. "Raise your hands high if you want to live to see 11:34."

Teo jumped, lifting his hands from beneath the blanket. Victor blinked. Where he'd expected to see stubby hands with spider tattoos creeping across the knuckles, the hands that lifted were small and delicate, with black polished nails bitten down to the quick.

"What you want me to do?" said a husky female voice that sounded more surprised than scared.

"Stand up and turn around."

The suspect obeyed. The blanket fell to the floor, revealing a thin woman in black yoga pants and a blue hoodie. Though she had bright orange hair sprouting from very black roots, she still might have been pretty, if she hadn't looked like she'd gone three rounds with Ronda Rousey. Her left eye was eggplant purple and swollen shut.

"Who are you?" asked Victor, noting her bare feet and black-painted toenails.

"Coza Lambert. Who are you?"

"SBI." Victor flashed his badge and dug in his pocket for one of his cards. He put it in the woman's still raised left hand. She lowered it, read the card.

"Teo's not here," she said quickly. "He's gone squirrel hunting."

"Yeah, right. White squirrel hunting, no doubt." Victor grasped her shoulder and turned her around. "Let's take a little tour of this trailer."

Keeping his gun drawn, he walked her around the trailer. With her bare feet slapping on the floor, they went through the bedroom, the kitchen and the bath, finding only dirty dishes, a rumpled bed, and a shower with long orange-and-black hairs curling around the drain. Beyond that, nothing. No Teo, no other accomplices, and most important, no Mary.

Victor pushed the woman back into the living room, into the chair in front of the heater.

"Look," said Victor. "We both know nobody hunts squirrels in a blizzard, so I'm going to give you one more chance to be straight with me. Where is Teo? Is he with a woman named Mary Crow?"

The woman's good eye widened. "I don't know who you're talking about."

"Yeah, you do. Mary Crow. The DA. The woman who revealed your boyfriend's secret escape routes in court."

The woman shrugged, all innocence. Victor went on.

"Friday, Teo threatened Mary Crow in court. Now no one's seen her in days. And I notice there's been some recent traffic in your front yard."

"Neighbors came," she said. "A little while ago. They wanted some cigarettes."

"Who were they? Where do they live?"

She shrugged again. "Down the road. I don't know their names."

"Put your shoes on," said Victor. "Let's go."

"Where?"

"Jail."

"Why?" she cried.

"Aiding and abetting. I think you know where Mary Crow is and nothing jogs the memory quite like jail."

She frowned, as if deciding whether jail might be a better alternative to riding out a blizzard in this tin can of a trailer. Then she said, "I might know where Teo is. But I swear I don't know anything about Mary Crow."

"You've got sixty seconds," said Victor.

She told him that two days ago, before the snow, a family of Mexicans had knocked on the door. "They gave Teo a pile of money to help them get to Washington, D.C. They said some grubs were after them."

"Grubs?"

"White assholes who roam the mountains, hunting illegals."

"And Teo took these people to DC?"

"No, to Del Rio, Tennessee. He knows the cock fighting people there. If the money's right, they'll help illegals. Teo probably got stuck over there by the snowstorm. It's always worse on the west side of the mountains."

At first he thought she was bullshitting him, but when he pressed her for details, she came up with them easily. The fleeing couple claimed to work at the casino in Murphy. The mother was a maid, the father a maintenance man. One baby was crying with an earache; two scared little boys hid behind their father's coat. Finally Victor decided this woman was either telling the truth or she was the most inventive liar on the planet.

"If I find out you're lying," he began.

"I know, I know. You'll take me to jail." Abruptly, she fingered her swollen eye. "Look, I need to take some aspirin, okay? You can hook me up to your lie detector in the kitchen."

He followed her into the kitchen. She poured two mugs of coffee and grabbed a giant-sized bottle of aspirin from one cabinet.

"Have a seat," she invited, pulling a chair out from a small table beside the refrigerator. He sat down across from her, watching as she washed four aspirin down with a slug of coffee.

"Run into a door?" he asked, repeating the usual excuse battered women used to explain their injuries.

She shrugged. "A little good-bye pop from Teo. He didn't want me going out while he was gone."

"You could swear out a warrant," said Victor.

"Honey, Teo lights the stove with warrants." She reached for a pack of cigarettes on the kitchen counter and changed the subject."So who's this woman you're looking for?"

"Mary Crow. The acting DA of Tsalagi County. She took over the case against Teo, after Drusilla Smith drowned."

Coza lit a cigarette, blew a plume of smoke up at the ceiling. "Come to think of it, I might have heard Teo mention that name."

No shit, thought Victor.

"Cherokee girl, right? Big deal prosecutor."

"That would be the one."

She frowned, as if slowly recovering a distant memory. "Yeah, Teo was carrying on about her right before the Mexicans showed up. He said she was a witch and he was going to need a lot of money to fight her in court."

"And that's why he took those Mexicans?"

"He wouldn't do it out of the goodness of his heart. Teo doesn't have any heart." She took another drag off her cigarette. "So why you are so worried about Mary Crow? Couple of days isn't that long. Maybe she ditched the snow and went to Florida."

"She's my fiancé," Victor said, nudging the truth a bit. "That's why I'm worried."

"Maybe she needed some alone time. You're a pretty intense dude."

Victor pulled Mary's note from his pocket, handed it to her. She read it slowly, then lifted one brow. "Who's Lily Walkingstick? And why the hell would either of them be up at Unaka now?"

"You know Unaka?"

She nodded. "High class garbage dump. I've gone up there lots with Teo."

"What for?"

Her good eye narrowed, suspicious. "Off your official arrest record?"

"Okay."

"Summer people up from Florida buy their drugs there. Weed, opies, whatever. Teo and I load up and go."

"So you're his little drug mule?"

She lit another cigarette off the butt of her first one. "I'm lots of things, SBI. To lots of people."

"So where is this Unaka?" he asked.

"Middle of nowhere."

"Could you draw me a map?"

SALLIE BISSELL

"From here, it would take you most of a day to get there in a car. Teo and I always hike."

"Draw me a map anyway."

She got up and rummaged in a drawer. She came back to the table with a black marker and a paper towel. Frowning like a kid learning to write the alphabet, she lettered the word UNAKA at the top of the page and proceeded to draw a bunch of squiggles and two big X's. When she finished, she shoved it to him across the table. It made no sense at all.

"If you're good in the woods, you could get there by mid-afternoon," she said. "If you're not, you'd probably get lost and freeze to death."

"I'm good enough," he said, annoyed at her implications about his hiking abilities. "I've hiked the Merlos, in Argentina."

She gave a husky laugh. "Plus you've got your love to keep your warm, huh?"

"You could say that."

She sat back and regarded him closely, as if calculating the odds on some wildly unlikely venture. "You know, SBI, these woods aren't for rookies even in good weather. Snow makes 'em twice as bad. How about I make a deal with you?"

"What?"

"I'll take you to Unaka, if you'll get me to an airport."

"Why do you want to go to an airport?"

She put down her smoke, touched her swollen eye. "Because this isn't the first one of these I've gotten, and it won't be the last. All morning that radio's played nothing but songs about getting on the road. Faith Hill's going to Vegas, LeAnn Rimes is buying a one-way ticket on a westbound plane. That's what I want to do."

He wondered if this was some kind of trap, where she protected Teo and made short work of cops who came nosing around. She sat across the

128

table, jiggling her leg and starting to bite one nail. She seemed like some-one desperately trying to hide their desperation.

"Any outstanding warrants on you? Don't lie, because I'm going to check."

"No."

"Planes cost money," he said. "You'll need ID's."

"I've got money. I've even got one of those new, fancy ID's. The only thing I haven't got is a damn ride to a frigging airport."

Victor sat there, considering everything she'd said. Taking her to jail in Murphy would cost him the better part of a day, and at the end of that day he would be no closer to finding Mary. But could he trust this beaten up, pumpkin-haired freak to get him to Unaka? He was in good shape and he could read a compass well enough not to let her lead him in circles. But still—she was Teo Owle's girlfriend.

"I've got a few conditions," he finally said.

"Such as?"

"You can't carry and you can't drink. Or do any drugs."

"Teo took my gun and the only drug I do now is nicotine," she replied, perking up like a child promising to behave.

He knew she would claim to meet whatever conditions he could come up with. Peeking out from the faded yellow curtains that hung at the kitchen window, he saw only more snow. His getting to Unaka was unlikely without her. Though no cop in their right mind would dream of doing such a thing, going with this Coza person might be his best shot at finding Mary.

He looked at her. Still wondering if she was God's own liar and he was God's own fool, he said, "Ok. Get your things and we'll go."

CHAPTER 20

———

Miles away, Lily turned to Mary, her eyes hard. They'd set off on their trek to the fish camp, Lily favoring her right leg on snowshoes while Mary walked a few paces behind. "Do you know what a blaze is?" the girl asked.

"A mark cut into a tree that indicates a trail," Mary replied. "Your father always used the Cherokee letter *hu*, from the syllabary." She leaned over and drew a backwards seven in the snow.

"Right," Lily said begrudgingly, sounding irked that Mary had known her father's blaze. "I'm going to start walking faster, so let's split up. If we get separated, just look for that blaze. I marked the trail here last night."

"Okay." Though Mary had assumed they would make this trip together, maybe going separately was not a bad idea. Lily wouldn't be saddled with an adult slowpoke and she would no longer have to endure a sullen teenager.

As Mary adjusted her pack, Lily pulled a cell phone from her coat and held it up to the sky. A few moments later she lowered the thing, glanced at the screen and returned it to her pocket, obviously disappointed.

———

"I'm going on," she called as she headed deeper into the woods. "Watch for the blazes. And the Rifleman."

"Who looks like what?"

"Big guy in snow camouflage and goggles. Carrying a commando rifle."

The girl strode off, her bad ankle apparently less of an issue. Mary followed, wondering what message the girl had hoped to receive from cyberspace. Then she remembered when she'd first driven up, she thought she heard Lily call the name *Bryan*. Did she have a boyfriend up here? Some white knight she'd expected to come to her rescue?

If so, she's as delusional as her father, Mary decided, recalling how Jonathan had smeared his face with war paint and searched for her mother's killer. He and Billy Swimmer had stalked the woods for days, full of fire and outrage, convinced they could find the murderer. Jonathan had wept when they came home empty handed.

"It's always one of us in the woods, Jonathan," she whispered as she followed Lily. "Either the real woods, or woods of our own making."

Hoping that Lily's tracker had given up, Mary made her way through the snow. Soon Lily's prints changed from wide hatch-marks into deep boot prints, in the old single-file Cherokee fashion. From the length of the stride Mary could tell she was hurrying. Scared, probably. And mad. No doubt hating to be stuck with her, the evil old bitch she despised.

"Pretty little Lily," she whispered. "A war party of one."

Mary picked through snow-frosted gorse and laurel. With her thighs burning at every step, she realized that she was not going to get back in time to tear up the note she'd left for Victor. Possibly he'd already read it by now. What would he think? Would he be hurt? Furious? Frantic? All those things, she decided glumly. She wished she'd explained that she'd called the sheriff, tried to go through official channels, but the snowstorm had paralyzed everything. Though she knew it was pointless, she opened her own phone, took off her gloves and recorded a message for Victor.

"Hi Sweetheart. I'm in the woods, going north from Unaka, North Carolina, following Lily Walkingstick," she said. "I had no choice. The girl is in trouble, and I couldn't get anybody else to come. I love you and I'll explain everything later."

She almost said *if there is a later*, but decided against it. Of course there'll be a later, she told herself. Pressing *send*, she put the phone back in her pocket. If she was lucky, he would get that. If she wasn't so lucky and wound up frozen to death, maybe someone would find her phone and give it to him. Then, at least, he could listen the message and know that she loved him.

For hours Mary followed Lily. The snow continued, now joined by a swirling mix of fog and sleet. She felt as if she'd fallen into a snow globe, where some invisible hand was shaking the world. By mid-afternoon she was even wishing for Lily; even a brooding, quarrelsome girl would have been company in this hard-edged forest of frost and ice.

At a delicate growth of tall, willowy cane, Lily's tracks changed again. No longer were they single-file boot prints. She'd gone back to the snowshoes. "Her ankle must hurt," Mary whispered, tracing the basket-weave track with a gloved finger.

A quarter mile later, she realized that Lily's ankle was not the reason for the snowshoes. She'd decided to scale an amazingly steep ridge, ignoring the blazed switchbacks and going straight up. It was a dangerous climb—one misstep could send you plunging downward in a neck-breaking fall. Still, Mary was determined to keep up with the girl. Taking a deep breath, she turned and began climbing side-stepping up the incline. She knew that looking down would induce vertigo, so she kept her eyes straight ahead, focusing on each tree that she passed. With sweat dripping in her eyes, she finally reached the top of the ridge. Thirty feet away she saw Lily, again lifting her cell phone to the sky.

"Getting any signal?" Mary called.

Lily looked up, surprised. "I thought you were following the blazes."

"No," gasped Mary. "Following you. Any luck with the phone?" she repeated, longing to talk to Victor.

"No. The best place for cell phones is Shagbark Ridge, but it's on the other side of the fish camp."

"Any sign of the Rifleman?" Mary asked, still breathless and dizzy in the freezing temperature.

"I thought I heard something a few minutes ago," said Lily. "But it could have been an animal. Anyway, the fish camp's over the next ridge. If the Snowmen are waiting out the weather, they're probably still there."

"Okay." Mary pressed her left arm against her body, comforted by the weight of the Glock in its holster. "Lead on, but cut new blazes, in case we get separated."

Lily stuffed her snowshoes behind her backpack and plodded ahead. Mary noticed that she was not walking with her earlier bravado. Though she blazed the trees every thirty yards or so, she stuck closer to Mary, tilting her head at certain sounds, once taking a deep whiff of the wind, as if trying to detect the scent of strangers. Quietly, Mary drew her pistol. She'd seen not a trace of anyone, but she didn't want to be surprised if the Rifleman materialized out of the whiteness.

They reached the fish camp from the backside, circling a wide lake that sported a boathouse and a dock. Thick white ice splintered around the dock pilings, while the middle of the lake remained a slushy dull gray. For a moment Mary was surprised that Jonathan had forsaken guiding hunters for a fish camp job, but then she remembered that he'd spent most of his life on the Little Tennessee River. Fishing, rafting, swimming naked with her while a huge summer moon shimmered on the surface of the water.

"Follow me," said Lily. "If they're keeping watch they won't see us if we stick to the cover of these trees."

Keeping the lake on their right, Lily threaded through trees that in summer would have shaded a narrow walking path. For a moment the snow quit, but soon another bank of thick clouds rolled in. They reached the camp's woodshed as a new round of flurries began.

Peeking around the corner of the shed, Mary studied the cabin. It was small, no doubt built for the caretaker of the camp. No lights shone from the windows, nor did any smoke rise from the chimney. If the Snowmen were there, they certainly weren't availing themselves of the comforts of home.

"Tell me the layout inside the cabin," she whispered to Lily as she flipped the safety off her Glock.

"We're looking at the back porch and kitchen," the girl replied. "Two bedrooms open off a hall, to the right. Living room's in front."

"How many windows?"

"One in each bedroom. A big one in the living room. Two on either side of the chimney."

"Okay," said Mary, taking command of the mission. "Give me your flashlight and I'll go check it out."

Immediately, the girl began to protest. "But—"

"Hard lesson number one, Lily. Whoever's got the gun, makes the rules. You stay here until I signal you. If you hear any gunshots, turn around and get the hell out of here. That is what your Edoda would want."

Lily gave a disgusted sigh, but produced a small flashlight from the pocket of her coat.

Mary took several deep breaths, and tried to sprint through the knee-deep snow. She reached the shadows of the cabin's back porch, where a screen door flapped in the wind. Dodging Jonathan's snow-covered truck, she kept her gun low, and crept along the side of the cabin, toward the living room. She saw no other vehicle beyond the truck and no tire tracks broke the smooth silk of the snow.

Nobody here, she decided. But what will I do if Jonathan's in there dead? Eyes wide, mouth gaping open in cadaverous surprise. Her stomach clenched. Years before she'd seen her mother like that; it still made her sick to think about it.

Gun in hand, she ducked beneath the first window and pressed her cheek against the chimney. The stones were icy cold; no fire had burned there lately. She lifted the Glock, crept to the edge of the second window, and risked a peek inside the cabin. But the window panes were a glittering collage of ice and snowflakes, and she could see nothing but frosted glass.

Summoning her courage, she headed toward the porch. A muddle of churned-up snow surrounded the front door, which stood wide open. Cautiously, she stepped inside, directing her flashlight beam around the room. It was a wreck of overturned chairs, a rustic looking sofa, a coffee table with its legs in the air.

She closed the door, and smelled a pungent, coppery odor. She recognized it immediately, from her days in Atlanta. It was blood. Quickly, she stole down the hall, peering in the bedrooms, readying herself to see Jonathan dead. But it wasn't until she reached the bathroom that her heart stopped. The room looked like the scene of an axe murder. She turned on the light to find dark, clotted blood drenching the sink and around the toilet, while cotton swabs, gauze and menstrual pads lay strewn all over the floor.

"What the hell?" whispered Mary. "Was a woman involved in this too?"

Trembling, she hurried to the kitchen, the only room remaining, wondering if Jonathan had crawled in here to die. But she found no body; just a stove, a refrigerator, and a sinkful of dirty dishes.

She leaned against the refrigerator and started to cry. Tears of relief, of anger, confusion and an emotion she had no name for. She had been so scared; she was still so scared. Just because Jonathan wasn't dead here, didn't mean he wasn't dead somewhere in a bank of snow or even in the middle of that lake.

For a moment she couldn't move. Then she looked out the kitchen window and saw Lily, huddled in the distant trees. "Get her inside," she told herself. "She'll be safe here. We can clean up the mess, and then decide what the hell to do next."

CHAPTER 21

All afternoon Coza Lambert had led Victor Galloway up into the woods, unbelieving of her good fortune. At the trailer, when she felt that gun digging into the back of her head, she first thought ICE had followed those Mexicans to the house and had come to raid the property. But when she learned it was a lovesick SBI agent, her heart soared. This guy was her ticket out—out of the trailer, out of the woods, out of the web Teo had trapped her in. Even better was the fact this guy was good looking and hadn't taken a swipe at her, once.

She'd led the way at a steady pace, aware of the cop's heavy breathing behind her. She knew he was keeping an eye on her, his hand on a big Smith & Wesson, in case she decided to get cute. But she also knew that she could easily kill him if he got any ideas. She could lose him in the forest, send him tumbling down an icy ledge, or push him over a water-fall. Teo had shown her several ways to kill people in the woods, and not one was provable in court.

Halfway to Unaka, she realized she didn't know what to call the guy. "Hey, what's your name? I left your card in the trailer."

"Victor Galloway."

She smiled. "You're keeping up pretty good. Where did you say you'd hiked? Brazil?"

"Argentina."

"World traveler, eh?"

"I have family there."

"Galloway doesn't sound very Spanish to me."

"My dad's Irish. My mother's Argentine."

"My mother's from Georgia," she offered. "Or maybe Florida."

"You don't know?"

She shook her head. "She dumped me early on. I'm a foster kid."

"What was that like?"

"Depends on who they put you with. Sometimes it was okay. Other times it was shitty."

She took him higher, struggling through deep snow. He followed close on her heels, like a car tailgating on the highway. Juiced on love, she decided. SBI must have a real jones for this Mary. She tried to recall if she'd ever wanted anyone that badly. Maybe cute Darryl Young, back when she was in junior high. Ever since then she'd flipped from man to man, like the silver ball in a pinball game.

They stopped only once—to eat, to pee and for her to have a smoke. Then they went on, until the trail ended above a narrow swath of relatively even ground. She jumped down onto the flat area; SBI followed.

"The road to Unaka." She held her arms out with a flourish.

"How much farther is it?" He asked, looking worried.

"Not far. A mile or two."

They went on, ascending two coiling switchbacks. As they rounded a third one, Coza gave a yelp of surprise. There, in the middle of the road, sat a small Subaru, mashed flat by a monstrous pine tree. Instinctively, she backed away. She'd seen lots of people die from overdoses and bullet wounds. But the gore of car crashes made her stomach churn.

"Oh, Jesus," she heard SBI whisper behind her. He threw down his pack and rushed forward, diving into the branches of the fallen tree. "Mary?" he cried, fighting his way to the car. "Mary, are you in there?"

No one answered. SBI wiggled his way to the door, grabbed it and pulled. Coza closed her eyes, not wanting to see some bloody dead woman fall out of the driver's seat. But she only heard SBI scrambling around the branches. She looked to see him trying the other doors. None of them worked, so he finally had to enter the car through the open trunk. A moment later, he called out, his voice buoyant with relief.

"She's not here!"

Equally relieved, Coza moved closer as SBI squeezed into the driver's seat and examined the inside of the car.

"I don't see any blood," he called. "She must have gotten out before the tree fell. She must still be okay."

Coza thought that this Mary Crow had probably just crawled off to die somewhere else, but she kept her mouth shut. SBI would really freak out over that.

"She has to be up here somewhere," said Victor, emerging from the car. He hurried up the road, cupping his hands around his mouth and calling "Mary!"

Coza grabbed his pack and followed him. Teo had also taught her how to track people through the woods, and she'd gotten pretty good at it. While SBI yelled for his beloved, she saw faint indentations in the snow; footprints leading across the road and up to the top of the embankment above the recycle bins. In his crazed hurry to find his girlfriend, Galloway had tromped right through them.

"Hey, SBI," she yelled. "Tracks over here."

He was halfway to the next switchback, but he turned and ran back. "Where?" he asked, out of breath.

"There." She pointed to the barely visible line of depressions in the snow. "Going up that little hill."

He threw himself, slipping and sliding, up the embankment. She followed, figuring now they'd find his precious Mary frozen like a popsicle. But when they reached the top they didn't find anybody—only more vague tracks leading to two pine trees and an odd circle of snow-free earth.

They walked over to the trees. Several flat river rocks lay between them, covered with ashes, barely dusted with snow.

"Somebody made a fire here," Coza said, kneeling to touch the rocks. "Heated these stones to keep warm. Teo and I once saw Mohawks do that at a pow-wow." She squinted up at him. "Your girl know how to do this?"

He shrugged. "I don't know. Maybe. She's part Cherokee."

"Well, it's crazy to let it go to waste."

"What do you mean?

"I mean we've got about hour left before dark. We're gonna have to camp, either up here or in the back of that car."

He shook his head. "We need to look for more tracks now."

She sighed, knowing if they waited until dark they'd have to sleep in that flattened can of a car. "How about we cut another deal? I'll look for more tracks while you build a fire on these rocks."

"With what wood?"

"Try the dumpsters," she said. "The Florida people throw all kinds of shit in those things. Teo and I once found a whole case of perfectly good wine."

"And we'll camp here? Underneath those trees?"

"We'll have more room there than in that squashed car."

"I guess so," he said, shifting the backpack on his shoulders.

"Then go look for something to burn and I'll go see where your girl-friend went."

She followed the road north, calling Mary's name every twenty yards. She felt stupid yelling for a woman, and was tempted to blow SBI off, telling him she'd seen nothing and his girlfriend was probably dead. But there was a sweetness about him that touched her. He loved this Mary, pure and simple. And he would do anything to save her. She'd never seen any man act like that before. After she walked up the next switchback, she turned around and headed back to the bins. Nobody had answered her calls and not a single print of bird or beast disturbed the smooth blanket of snow.

When she neared the bins she smelled wood smoke, so she figured SBI must have found something to burn. But instead of going up the embankment to report she'd seen no tracks, she turned left, into the woods. It was the only direction that now made sense—had this Mary walked south along the road or gone west past the campsite, she would have seen footprints. East was the only direction left.

She headed off the road, fighting her way through some gorse to a small, narrow path that led into a wide swath of dark pine trees. There, under the pines, where the snow was not so deep, she saw them. Crisper than the ones on the road, she saw two sets—one hatch-marked snowshoe prints, the other a lug-soled boot. Proud of her expertise as a tracker, she started to yell.

"SBI! I found something!"

Hearing a faint reply, she waited. In a few minutes she saw him, looking for her alongside the road.

"Down here!" she called. "Under these trees."

He saw her, and plunged headlong into the woods, running like his hair was on fire. "Did you find her?" he called, breathless.

"No, but I found these." Coza pointed at the marks in the snow. "I think the wide ones must be snowshoes, but the narrower ones are boots." She looked at Victor. "Your girl have a pair of snowshoes?"

"Not that I know of," he replied. "But we both bought new boots, back in October."

"Then she's well enough to walk and follow somebody who's spent some time up north. Southerners don't snowshoe."

"How about Teo?"

"I've never seen him with snowshoes. But that's not saying he can't."

Victor looked through the towering trees, still puzzled. "But where would these tracks be going, though? Is there a town near here?"

"Nope. Just summer cabins, closed up for the winter."

He said, "Maybe they went to one of those."

"Maybe so. We can head up that way tomorrow."

He shook his head. "But we need to—

She cut him off. "Look—we're about to lose what light we've got. If you want to try and follow these tracks tonight, you go ahead. But I'm going up to that campsite and pitch my tent by whatever fire you've got going."

She turned and strode back to the bins. She didn't care what he did about his stupid fiancé. She was cold, tired and she needed a cigarette. When she scrambled to the top of the embankment, she saw that he'd not only built a huge fire on the rocks but had already pitched her tent beside it. She unfolded her sleeping bag in one side of the tent and dug out a can of Vienna sausages from her backpack. She was eating the last one when SBI appeared on the other side of the campfire.

"I tried to follow those tracks," he said. "But you were right about the light."

She looked at him, shocked. Never had a man given her credit for being right about anything. Her earlier anger dissipating, she held the flap open for him. "This is a two person tent. We'll stay a lot warmer if we both sleep in here."

For a moment he hesitated, then again, he acquiesced to her greater experience in the Appalachian Mountains. He untied his sleeping bag from his pack and spread it out on the opposite side of the tent.

"You did a good job with the fire, SBI," she said.

"I found an old Ikea bookcase behind one of the bins," he said, digging some energy bars from his pack. "The dry parts should burn for a while."

He ate one bar and looked at her. "You think we'll be able to read those tracks tomorrow?"

"If they kept walking under those trees."

"But what if it keeps snowing? Covers the tracks?"

"I don't know." She pulled up her pants leg and reached deep into a wool sock, pulling out a joint. "I know you said no drugs, but this helps me sleep. Want to share it? Or does weed go against the SBI code of honor?"

"You enjoy it," he said. "I don't think anything would help me sleep."

"Too worried about your girl?"

"Yeah," he said, his voice hoarse as he curled up in his sleeping bag. "Something like that."

CHAPTER 22

————

"Would you just shut the hell up!" Leroy shrieked, bolting up from the bed. After he locked the Indian in the cave, he flopped down in the bedroom, exhausted. He'd taken their album with him, intending to pleasure himself while looking at the pictures. But neither the photos nor his fingers brought him any comfort; all he could think about was the hot pain in his gut and his brother. Chet enjoying his Kimmeegirl, Chet as the cougar's midnight snack, finally Chet lost and frozen, leaving him to deal with the Indian all alone. Then, as he began to drift off to sleep, the Indian started to kick his way out of the cave. Fast kicks followed by a long pause; followed by thunderous kicks that rattled the camper. Driven to a homicidal fury, Leroy zipped his pants, grabbed his pistol and stormed to the front of the camper.

"One more kick," he screamed, hammering on the cave door with the butt of the gun, "and I'm putting bullets in both your knees!"

He stood there livid, eager to empty nine rounds into the Indian's legs when he heard a muffled voice outside the door. "Open the goddamn door, Leroy! I'm fucking freezing out here!"

————

Leroy jumped, whirling around to turn on the outside light. To his amazement, Chet stood at the door, wild-eyed, his breath making angry wisps of smoke.

Weak with relief, Leroy unlocked the door.

"What the fuck were you doing?" cried Chet, climbing the steps and pushing past him. "I've been pounding on the door for half an hour."

"I fell asleep," Leroy lied, not wanting to admit he'd mistaken Chet's pounding for some nonsense the Indian had dreamed up. He blinked as Chet pulled off his balaclava. The skin around his eyes was a rosy mask of snow-burned flesh. "Where have you been?"

"Tracking the cutie."

"Did you find her?" Leroy held his breath. If Chet had killed Kimmee-girl he would plug him with the nine rounds he'd just earmarked for the Indian.

"Are you kidding? You'd have to be an Eskimo to find that one."

Secretly relieved, Leroy hid his smile. "What happened?"

"That first night she crossed a creek and vanished, so I went back up to the road and hiked to those garbage bins. Made a hell of a lot better time on foot than we did driving, too."

"And?"

"I knew she was expecting her fake boyfriend, so I waited for her up there." He took off his coat. "That's when things got weird."

"What do you mean?" The look in his brother's eyes made the hair lift on the back of Leroy's neck.

Chet shook his head. "Something was tracking me, Leroy. Never could see it, but it was big. And it was after me."

Leroy thought of the Indian's mountain lion. "An animal?"

"Yeah, but wIith all the snow, I never got a good look at it. Whatever it was, it creeped the shit out of me."

"What did you do?"

"Got the hell out of there. Then I took a wrong turn and wound up in a tangle of bushes you wouldn't believe."

"And it took you this long to get here?" Leroy wondered if Chet hadn't really found Kimmeegirl and was lying to cover it up.

"You go wander around these mountains in a fucking blizzard and see how well you do." He rubbed his hands together. "We got any hot coffee?"

"I can make some," said Leroy.

While Leroy put the coffee on, Chet constructed what he called an Elvis special—three bologna sandwiches stacked up together, with mayonnaise and pickle relish in between the layers. He sat down at the dinette and began to eat.

"So did you off the Indian?" he asked, as he crammed one bite of the sandwich in his mouth.

"No," said Leroy. "The Indian's in the cave."

"The cave?" Chet stopped chewing, astonished. "What the fuck for?"

"Read this." Leroy pulled the news clipping from his back pocket.

Chet scanned the article quickly, then looked, wide-eyed, at his brother. "Crazy Horse is worth ten grand?"

"I think so."

"Damn, Leroy!"

"Since we've lost out on Kimmeegirl, I figure we can drive him to Oklahoma and collect the money. That way the trip won't be a total loss."

"If we can get to Oklahoma," said Chet, licking his fingers. "Snow's halfway up the wheels. We'll have to dig out."

Leroy pressed his hand against his wounded stomach. "I don't think I'd better dig any snow."

"Why not?"

"I can't get my gut to quit hurting."

Chet took a slurp of coffee. "Let me see."

Leroy lifted his shirt, revealing a menstrual pad secured by Band-Aids. Chet took one look and spewed coffee all over the table, braying with laughter.

"Are you fucking kidding me? You're wearing a girl's rag?"

"It was all the bastard Indian had," said Leroy, glad he hadn't revealed that he'd also taken some Midol.

Chet wiped tears of laughter from his eyes. "Lift up the biscuit. Let's see what your belly looks like."

Leroy peeled off the Band-Aids. Underneath the bloody pad, the wound had abscessed. It had swollen badly, and the red streaks surrounding it made it look like a little starburst of infection.

"Jeez, Leroy." Chet leaned back, wrinkling his nose. "It really stinks."

"I know," said Leroy, carefully reapplying the pad. "I don't want to start it bleeding again."

"Well, shit," said Chet. "You've got a hot poker in your belly and I'm dead on my feet. Doesn't look too good for a trip to Oklahoma."

"You really don't think we can just drive out?"

"Not without some serious shoveling." Chet stared at his coffee, brows knitted, when he looked up. "Why don't we do this—I'll get some rest while you go back to the cabin and see if Crazy Horse has any rock salt or ice melt. First light tomorrow, maybe we can melt the snow off the back tires and get the hell out of here."

Leroy frowned, remembering the long, dark walk back to the cabin and the cougar that squalled like a hundred pound baby. "Couldn't we just ask him if he has any ice melt?"

"Leroy, I don't think he's gonna help us take him back to Oklahoma.

Take my bullpup if you're scared," offered Chet. "And my night vision goggles. I'll stay here and keep an eye on him."

"I'm not scared," snapped Leroy, though he was actually very scared. But if a solo hike back to that cabin got them out of this cold hell any faster, he'd do it.

Leroy fixed his own bologna sandwich, put on Chet's gear and set out for the cabin. The night vision goggles turned the snow a sickly green, the towering pine trees a dusty black. He now heard only the crunch of his own footsteps, isolated and amplified by the silence of the forest. Soon his mind wandered back to the other part of Chet's story—the unknown creature he claimed had tracked him. Had that been the cougar? Was it right now hiding these woods, hungry and waiting to pounce?

He walked faster, keeping one ear on the surrounding woods. When he reached the cabin, at first it looked like the same little place he'd left hours ago. But as he drew closer, he noticed that the truck that had earlier been just a mound of white, had been brushed clean of snow.

"What the fuck?" He pulled up the night vision goggles and looked again. Was he also seeing a faint glow of light from the front window?

Quickly, he knelt down. Who the hell was in there? The cops? Kimmeegirl? Or some new person he hadn't figured on? His first impulse was to hurry back to Chet and the camper. But what if it was Kimmeegirl, in there all alone? If that was the case, he could have that luscious young flesh all to himself and Chet would never be the wiser.

"Ok," he whispered, enjoying a sudden rush of courage. "Let's go check it out." He crept across the road and slipped into the trees that grew near the cabin. Holding the bullpup awkwardly, he crawled toward the front porch. If he could reach the front window undetected, he could get a clear view of the living room.

He reached the corner of the cabin and eased onto the porch. Slowly, he crept over to the window and risked a peek over the sill. To his utter astonishment, the room looked normal. The overturned chairs had been righted; the Scrabble tiles were no longer scattered across the floor. The only thing unusual was the small fire glowing in the fireplace and the two women sitting on a mattress in front of it.

Kimmeegirl he recognized immediately. The second woman was older and resembled the photo he'd seen in Crazy Horse's bedroom. What the fuck was going on? Did Kimmeegirl's mother live up here, too? Had she come to the girl's rescue?

His heart beating wildly, he sank down below the window. He could kill the older woman, do Kimmeegirl, and get back to the camper before Chet got suspicious. But why kill the older woman just yet? She was pretty, too. He and Chet could come back here and have fun with both women—take turns and trade off. Two cuties at once was something they'd dreamed of for years.

The possibilities excited him, but first he needed to find out if there were any other people there. He crept off the porch and keeping well beneath the windows, circled the cabin. A lantern flickered dimly in the kitchen, but the rest of the rooms were dark. He decided that the only occupants were the two women in front of the fire, who were probably planning on driving out in that truck, tomorrow. He had to make sure that would not happen.

Carefully, he slinked around the back of the cabin. After taking several deep breaths, he shouldered the rifle and hurled himself across the white expanse of snow between the cabin and truck.

He hadn't gone twenty feet before something caught his right foot and sent him sprawling. He hit the ground hard, his nose smashing against the barrel of the bullpup. Warm blood gushed down his upper lip as he struggled to get up, but his legs found little traction in the snow. After flailing miserably for what seemed like hours, he finally managed to get to his feet and stumble to the far side of the truck.

He clutched the rifle shaking, terrified that the women had heard him. Seconds ticked by as he waited for the squeak of a screen door or the glare of a porch light, but nothing happened. Though it seemed to him that he'd wallowed in the snow like a walrus, Kimmeegirl and her friend had apparently not heard a thing.

"Okay," he whispered. "Let's do this."

He took off his gloves and reached for the hunting knife that he kept strapped against his calf. With his nose still spurting blood, he rose to his knees, and with one motion, buried the knife deep in the top of the rear tire. Warm, rubbery-smelling air came out in a gush. After that, he moved to the front tire. As he slashed that one, he laughed. Kimmeegirl would not be going anywhere in this crate.

When both tires had flattened, he made a bumbling run back to the tree line. He couldn't wait to tell Chet to forget the snow melt—he had not one, but two women, all alone, trapped, and ripe for the picking.

CHAPTER 23

"Where did you get that ring?" Lily asked as she stared at Mary's hand, her question artless and callow.

Mary looked at her left hand. Even in the dim, amber glow of the fire, the ring glittered fiercely. Smiling, she thought back to when Victor put it on her finger. Just two nights ago! It felt like two lifetimes ago. "A man gave it to me," she replied.

Lily frowned. "Are you, like, engaged?"

Good question, thought Mary. Was she engaged? Being with Lily had resurrected so many memories that she didn't know what to say. Sometimes, she remembered Jonathan so keenly that it seemed like no time had passed at all. Other times, Walkingstick seemed more like a ghost, a stranger she no longer knew. "I'm not sure," she finally answered. "I haven't decided yet."

An unreadable look flashed across Lily's face. "Who is he? A cop?"

Mary smiled. "He's an SBI agent. He plays soccer, like you." She was about to go on, and tell her that Victor was handsome and funny and didn't mind evidence files on the dining room table, but Lily gave a dismissive grunt and turned back toward the fire.

Returning her gaze to the ring, Mary huddled closer to the warmth the lone maple log produced. Lily had wanted a big fire, but Mary dissuaded her. This cabin scared her. It stank of blood and death. She felt safer using lanterns instead of the generator, sleeping close together by the fire, instead of in the bedrooms. Lily had grumbled but Mary didn't care. Keeping Lily close kept Lily safe. Lily had already swept off the truck. Tomorrow, they would take it and attempt the trek back to civilization, on that crappy road to Tennessee.

Mary rose from the mattress, took a candle and went to the bathroom. She'd tried to clean the room up before Lily saw it, but the girl had come in, needing to use the toilet. She'd screamed when saw Mary washing the blood stains away.

"What happened in here?" she'd cried, tears streaming down her face. "Why are Poise pads all over the place? Is there a woman with them?"

"I don't know," Mary told her honestly. "It looks like they might have doctored a wound in here—didn't you say that your father threw his knife at one of them?"

She nodded, her eyes wide. "It was the last thing I saw him do."

"I think all this blood might be from that," said Mary. "Knife wounds bleed a lot." *And dead men don't bleed much at all*, she thought.

"But you don't know for sure that is wasn't Edoda," Lily pressed.

Mary sighed. "No. I don't."

That was hours ago. Now she sat on the toilet, her candle making the remaining bloodstains on the wall move in a macabre dance. Holding her breath against the smell, she peed and tried to muster an air of confidence as she returned to the living room. Lily sat gazing into a fire that had burned down to glowing orange embers. "Looks like we need another log," said Mary.

"I can get another one from the shed," the girl volunteered.

"I'll go," Mary said quickly, not wanting Lily to leave the safety of the cabin. "You stay here and keep off your ankle."

She put her parka back on and grabbed a flashlight. Unlocking the kitchen door, she listened to the night. No owls hooted; no foxes yipped. Only the eerie groans of ice shifting on the lake broke the snow-filled silence.

She headed for the woodshed, where Jonathan arranged his wood by burn order—soft pine and spruce kindling at one end, slow-burning ash and maple at the other. Mary grabbed a couple of pine splits and moved down to retrieve the thickest maple log she could carry. She'd just started back to the cabin when something caught her eye. To her left, she saw a wide mangle of thrashed snow that had not been there earlier. It looked like two animals had either furiously mated or fought to the death.

Curious, she walked over to have a closer look. She beamed her flashlight on the snow, half-expecting to see a dead mink or marten. Instead, she saw splotches of blood making an erratic path to Jonathan's truck.

She followed them, walking where something had seemingly dog-paddled through the snow. The bloodstains dribbled behind the truck, to the rear bumper on the driver's side. There the drops had formed a larger stain, as if something had lingered by the back tire. Kneeling down, she scraped some snow away and flashed her light beneath the truck, again expecting to find some dead or dying animal. But the only thing she saw was a rectangle of dry grass, free of snow and wildlife. Deciding that whatever had bled had scampered away, she stood up. As she did, her flashlight shone across the back tire. To her horror, she saw that the studded snow tire that she'd earlier thanked God for, now sat flat on the wheel rim.

"What the hell?" Incredulous, she examined the tire more closely. Though the treads still looked crisp and new, in one side wall was a single deep slit that had drained all the air. Quickly, she checked the other tires. The passenger side tires were still good, but both tires on the driver's side were totally flat.

"Shit!" she whispered, realizing what had happened. "The tracker's found us."

She dropped the logs and started to run, making no effort to hide herself. Through the backyard, onto the porch, into the kitchen.

"Lily," she called, breathless. "Grab your pack. We need to leave!"

The girl met her, wide-eyed, in the hall. "What?"

"Somebody's slit two of the truck tires," Mary said, pushing her backwards, towards her bedroom. "Get your stuff. We need to get out of here now!"

Lily ran to her bedroom. What should she take? What would she need? She grabbed a hairbrush, a photo of her mother Ruth, then she ran to the closet, where she'd hidden the backpack for her escape. To her horror, the thing was lying on its side, clothes spilling out. Who had opened it?

She didn't know; she didn't care. All she wanted was the picture of Bryan she'd secretly printed off. She'd left it on top, so it wouldn't get wrinkled, but when she dug down into the pack, she felt only the clothes she planned to take.

"Lily!" Mary appeared in the doorway, ready to go. "Come on!"

Lily hurried, wanting to grab more pictures, her diary, some memento of her last five years. But there was no time. The tracker had slit their tires. Someone had gone through her stuff.

She ran to the living room, dived into her army coat and shouldered her pack while Mary kept watch out the front window, pistol in hand.

"How far is that deer blind that your father rigged up for you?" asked Mary.

"Not far. You can see the top of it from the back porch, if you know where to look."

"How long would it take us to get there?"

"Half an hour, going like jula."

Mary frowned. "Jula?"

"The fox. You know, go in the opposite direction, to lead them away from your den."

"Have you packed everything you want to take?" asked Mary.

She longed for two more minutes to grab what was left of her life, but then she saw the look on Mary Crow's face, "I've got everything," she whispered.

"Okay. You lead the way. I'll stick close. If you hear this gun go off, run like hell. Don't look behind you and don't stop until you get back to civilization."

They hurried to the kitchen, opened the back door. Just as Lily started across the backyard, Mary grabbed her arm.

"I'll give you a five step lead," she said as she pulled out her gun. "If I see him I'll shoot. You just keep going, whatever happens."

Lily nodded, her eyes wide, then she took a deep breath, and with trembling legs, ran into the snow, her snowshoes clacking against her loaded pack. Why had she not thought to carry them quietly, under her arm? Anybody within five miles could hear them!

Still, she lowered her head and ran on, ignoring the pain in her ankle as she bounded through the deep snow, seeking the cover of the wood-shed. With every stride she expected the tracker to jump out and grab her, but she finally reached the darkness of the shed and the sharp aroma of cut pine. A few seconds later, Mary Crow came up behind her.

"Which way now?" Mary gasped, clutching her gun.

"There," she pointed to the left.

"Go!" said Mary. "Hurry!"

Holding her snowshoes to keep them quiet, Lily plunged back into the night. The thick trees that would hide them stood fifty feet away. Again she ran, picturing the tracker drawing inexorably closer. Her chest burned and she slipped on something covered by the snow, but she kept on. Finally, as a low pine branch dumped snow on her head, she reached the woods.

"Keep going," Mary called, right behind her. "Don't stop."

She went on, following the same route she'd taken two nights before. Through the pines, across a creek, then along the rocky creek bank to hide her tracks. Mary Crow trailed her only by a few feet, breath-ing heavily, but never stopping to rest.

Mid-point in the circle, under a huge oak tree, Lily stopped. "Here's where I looped back, the other night," she said as Mary leaned over, gasp-ing for breath. "Do you think he's following us?"

"Maybe. If he's got night vision equipment."

"Seriously?" Lily pictured storm troopers from Star Wars, tracking them with lasers.

Mary said, "It wouldn't surprise me, since he and his buddy pin-pointed your cabin in the middle of a snowstorm."

Lily felt sick inside. Was there no escape from these people?

Mary touched her shoulder. "Come on, honey. Let's go."

Weaving through the trees, they made their way closer to the hideaway. Lily forged ahead while Mary kept a close eye on the woods around them. Half an hour later they came to a massive oak tree that had wooden steps nailed to one side of the trunk.

"There." Lily pointed to the deer blind hidden thirty feet off the ground, in the crotch of the tree.

"These steps okay?" asked Mary.

"They were two days ago."

"Let's get up there, then."

"I'll go up first," said Lily. "And send a rope down for your pack." Tightening her backpack, she climbed up the rungs. When she got to the blind, she pushed opened the trapdoor and crawled inside. Unlike her bedroom closet, nothing here had been disturbed.

She lowered a long rope with a grappling hook to the ground. A few moments later she pulled up Mary's pack, then helped Mary climb up herself.

"Wow," said Mary, looking around the little box. "A two man deer blind, with gun slots on four sides."

"I've got heat, too," said Lily, reaching for a fat emergency candle. "And blankets and water."

"Pretty cozy." Mary gave her the sharp frown that Lily remembered as always preceding a question. "Why didn't you just hole up here when the men came? Why trek all the way to Unaka?"

Lily felt her cheeks flush. She didn't want to admit that she'd trekked through a blizzard to meet a boy who had never even shown up. "I promised Edoda I would call you," she finally said. "I knew I could get a signal at Unaka. You couldn't have gotten to Shagbark Ridge."

"I see." Mary shot her a skeptical look, but questioned her no further. Instead, she said, "Which way is the cabin from here?"

"There." Lily moved to the wall behind her and lifted the canvas that covered one of the gun slots. "In daylight you can see the roofline, at about two o'clock. The boathouse is closer, at about seven."

Mary studied the area where Lily pointed. "I can't see anything or any-body now," she finally said.

"You think the tracker might have given up?" asked Lily.

"No," said Mary. "I think he might have just begun."

CHAPTER 24

Chet was snoring to Megadeath's *Rust In Peace*, when Leroy burst through the camper door. Chet bolted upright to see blood covering the lower half of his Leroy's ski mask, red splotches dotting his winter camouflage like holly berries on a snowy bush. When Leroy yanked the mask off, his nose was the size of a turnip.

"Holy shit," cried Chet. "What the fuck happened to you?"

"Turn the music up," Leroy said urgently. "I don't want Crazy Horse to hear this."

Chet reached to turn his ancient boom box up to full volume. As Megadeath started rattling the windows of the camper, Leroy sat down close beside him.

"Kimmeegirl's back at the cabin," he whispered.

Chet snorted, thinking Leroy must have bloodied his brain along with his nose. "Along with Santa and the reindeers?"

"She's there with another woman," Leroy went on. "Sitting in front of the fireplace."

"Doing what?"

"Just sitting there. Kimmeegirl was rubbing her ankle. The woman just looked pissed."

"Probably Kimmeegirl's mother," said Chet.

Leroy frowned. "I don't know. Kimmeegirl never mentioned her mother being up here."

"It doesn't matter who she is," said Chet. What did you do?"

"I sneaked around the back of the cabin, to see if anybody else was there."

"And?"

"Nobody but Kimmeegirl and her pal," said Leroy. "They'd cleaned all the snow off that truck. I figured they were planning on driving out tomorrow, so I slit their tires."

Chet eyed Leroy's bloody nose. "And did one of those tires bite back?"

"I fell down and banged my nose against your damn gun." Leroy wiped blood away from one nostril.

Chet blinked. "Let me get this straight. You say Kimmeegirl and a woman who could be her mom are right now in that cabin, with no way out?"

"Not unless they walk. Or fly."

Chet felt a sudden throb of desire. He'd always dreamed of doing two women at the same time, arms, legs and lips all intertwined together. Now, according to Leroy, his dream lay twenty cold minutes away in a cabin, just waiting to become reality.

"Are you thinking what I'm thinking?" asked Leroy.

"Leave the Indian here. Go to the cabin, do whatever the fuck we please with mother and daughter, then take Crazy Horse to Oklahoma and collect our ten grand."

Leroy giggled. "Right."

"What does the other woman look like?"

"Older," said Leroy. "But still pretty."

They double-checked the lock on Crazy Horse's cave and left Megadeath yowling at full blast. Then they followed Leroy's blood-speckled path to the cabin. The walking was easier in the tamped-down snow, and the clouds parted briefly, revealing an anemic moon. For a moment the landscape looked like a fantasy world, tree limbs glittering in rime ice. But new clouds quickly rolled across the moon and Chet again felt as if they were walking through pocket lint.

They crested the rise that allowed them a view of the cabin. Chet had envisioned a Christmas card scene, the women having candles flickering and smoke rising from the chimney, but the cabin stood cold and closed up, with not even the dimmest glow coming from the front windows.

He frowned. "Leroy, if this is some of your bullshit, I will fucking kill you."

"I swear to God they're in the front room," said Leroy. "They pulled a mattress in there, close to the fire."

Chet was tempted to run up and blast open the door again, but that might be a repeat of their first disaster. The women might be sleeping in shifts; one might be standing at a window keeping watch. The mother might well have a gun. He turned to his brother.

"You sneak around the cabin and guard the back door. I'll go in the front. When you hear the bullpup, come in."

"Okay," said Leroy.

As Leroy lumbered awkwardly towards the rear of the cabin, Chet headed east, to the far end of the little parking lot. He strode through the snow carefully, but moving with purpose. After pausing behind a bank of snow-laden rhododendrons, Chet took the safety off the bullpup and made a run for the porch.

He reached the corner and pressed himself against the logs. The angle made him invisible to anyone looking out of the cabin, so all he had to do was stay below the windows and slither to the entrance.

Dropping to his knees, Chet crawled along the porch until he reached the front door. Then he stood up and checked his watch, giving Leroy another three minutes to get into position. When he figured that even his flabby brother could have made it to the back door, he unstrapped the bullpup and took a deep breath. Operation Cutie was about to begin.

He kicked open the front door, rifle at the ready, expecting screams, terrified women running for their lives. Instead, he found only an empty mattress pulled in front of a dying fire. Rushing down the hall toward the bedrooms, he heard Leroy coming in the kitchen door. "Nobody by the fire," Chet yelled. "Check the bedrooms."

Chet headed into the nearest one. By the crap strewn all over the floor, he guessed it was the girl's. Clothes had been dumped from the closet, pictures piled on the floor. When he found no one hiding under the bed, he raced down the hall, almost running into Leroy.

"They're gone, Chet," his brother announced sadly. "I saw fresh tracks outside."

"Are you kidding me?"

Leroy shook his head. Chet muscled past him, into the kitchen and out the back door, where a line of footprints dotted the snow from the back porch to the smokehouse.

Just as before, Chet followed them, around the smokehouse, across a small field and into the woods beyond. For fifty yards he read the tracks easily, but then thick trees shielded the undergrowth from snow, and the footprints vanished in tangles of weeds and bushes. He tried to pick up the trail deeper in the woods, but he knew it was pointless. The girl owned this terrain; he could not beat her in these woods.

WHITE TREES CRIMSON SNOW

He turned and went back to the cabin, seething. This was all Leroy's fault. He was clumsy and loud. He'd probably cried like a baby when he broke his damn nose and they'd heard him. Furious, Chet stalked back into the kitchen. Leroy was in the bathroom, leaning over the toilet, as if he might vomit.

"Find them?" Leroy looked up, bleary eyed.

"No." Chet unzipped his parka. "I lost them in the damn woods."

"You didn't follow them?"

"I can't make a miracle, Leroy. They know their shit here. You probably sounded like a wounded elephant when you fell on that gun. They heard you and took off. You blew it, you dumb fuck."

"I did not sound like an elephant," Leroy insisted.

Chet glared at his brother, his finger twitching on the trigger of the bullpup. At this moment he could blow a hole in Leroy and not think twice about it.

As Chet stood there in a murderous rage, Leroy turned around and pulled up his shirt. The gut wound that had just oozed blood before had now flooded his menstrual pad, dripping a stream of fresh blood onto his pants.

"Good Lord, Leroy," said Chet, his own stomach clenching at the sight of his brother's gut. "You're bleeding like a stuck pig."

"Look in the closet," whispered Leroy. "Grab me another one of those pads."

Chet rummaged through the linen closet, pulling out a box of pads and a handful of Band-Aids. "Damn. They've got enough shit in there for a fucking sorority house."

"Could you help me here?" said Leroy, ripping away the bloody pad. "Get a new pad on?"

"Ugh." Holding his breath against the stink of the rotting wound, Chet grabbed a clean menstrual pad and pressed it Leroy's belly. As he taped the thing on with Band-Aids, he again thought about the women. They could be miles away by now. Or they could be just minutes away, watching this cabin, maybe sighting down the barrel of their own rifle. His mood turned even fouler as he realized that Leroy had once again suckered him into another disaster. Last time it was Spitfire, tonight Kimmee-girl.

"There," he said, as he slapped the last Band-Aid in place. "That should hold you for a while. Let's get the fuck out of here."

"You don't want to wait for them?" Leroy sounded surprised. "Try to find them?"

"Leroy, I want to take the Indian and leave. I'm done with the snow and the cold and the ice and your stink and the two cuties you claimed were here."

"But..."

"You can wait here if you want. But tomorrow, I'm driving out. Be at the camper if you want to come, too."

Leroy looked at him a long moment, as if plumbing the depths of Chet's fury. He soon realized that arguing was pointless, so he stood up and began filling his pockets with more pads and Band-Aids. "Okay," he said, disappointed. "I guess you're right."

Angrily, Chet headed out the back door, Leroy bobbing like a cork in his brother's furious wake. They'd just turned the corner of the driveway when Chet spotted a small gas-powered generator under the eave of the roof. He walked over, kicked the snow off the thing, and gave Leroy a sly grin.

"Wanna leave 'em something to remember us by?"

"Okay," said Leroy, knowing that the best way to de-fuse Chet was to let him blow off his steam.

"Go inside and turn on their propane stove, full tilt. I'll bleed the gas off this generator and slosh it all over the inside. Once we get back in the woods, I'll fire a round from the bullpup into the kitchen. This whole cabin will go off like a rocket."

"And then what?"

"And then nothing. If Kimmeegirl and her mom are out there laughing at us now, they won't be laughing much longer."

CHAPTER 25

Mary was dreaming a disjointed scenario where her divorce client JimAnn Ponder was testifying that *Walkingstick got kilt with his shoes on!* She was about to tell JimAnn that she was wrong when a blast like a bomb rocked the deer blind. Jolting awake, she grabbed her pistol and looked around for Lily. The girl was wide awake too, sitting up in her sleeping bag.

"What was that?" she cried, her voice high and thready. "It sounded like a bomb!"

Wondering if another big tree had fallen victim to the snow, Mary crawled over to peer out one of the rifle slots. "Oh my God!" she whispered. "The cabin is on fire!"

Lily crawled over beside her. They peered out the rifle slot as flames soared up into the night sky, orange fingers of fire piercing a shroud of gray snow-mist. The tops of the trees started gyrating in a spasm of cracking ice and roaring flames. As they watched tears began to roll down Lily's cheeks. "All my pictures were in there," she cried. "Mom and Alenna. My whole life."

Mary put an arm around her shoulder. "Thank God we weren't there."

"Do you think the Snow Men did it?" she asked.

"I don't think the little maple log we left burning did."

"But why?" Lily's voice cracked. "Why would they burn down a stupid cabin?"

It was a question similar to others Mary had heard many times before. *Why did they kill my husband? Why did they steal my child?* After years of listening to the heartbreak of anguished victims, she still hadn't come up with a satisfactory response. "I don't know, Lily. Your father would say some people are just mad-dog mean."

Wrenching away from Mary, Lily stood up and grabbed her bow. "I'm going to kill them."

"You can't, Lily," Mary said, immediately regretting that she'd quoted Jonathan. This girl launched into attack mode as fast as he did.

"Why not?"

"Because you only have a bow and arrow. They have guns."

"Then give me your gun."

"No."

"But you're supposed to protect me. That's why Edoda made me promise to call you."

"And that's exactly what I'm doing."

"How? By sitting here and watching our house burn down?"

"By keeping you away from men who apparently want to capture you. I imagine your grandfather's probably put out a reward for you, just like your dad. To those guys, you're a nice, fat paycheck, hiding in the snow."

Her words brought the girl up short. Lily moved to a different rifle slot and continued to watch the cabin burn. As she did, Mary again pondered these skip chasers. If Fred Moon had put money out for Lily, she could understand these men hanging around, hoping to grab her. But why burn down a cabin? Why not build a warm fire, light the lights and keep watch until Lily sought shelter from the storm? Unless, of course, Jonathan was dead and Lily was the one remaining person they could get money for.

"So what's our plan now?" Lily asked sarcastically. "We still walking back to Murphy?"

Feeling sick inside, Mary nodded. She didn't know what else to do. For she and Lily to go up against men who just blew up a cabin was insanity. "With luck, we should get there late tomorrow. You'll be safe and we can turn the sheriff on to these people."

"But they're still here! We can still save Edoda!"

"Lily, these men mean business, and I'm not willing to risk either of our lives. I'll help your father when they deliver him to Oklahoma."

"Fine," snapped Lily. "Then let's go right now. No point in wasting time."

Knowing that more sleep was impossible, Mary agreed. She secured her sleeping bag to her frame as Lily strapped her bow and quiver across her chest. Carefully, they made their way down the ice-slicked rungs Jonathan had nailed to the tree. The wind was cold and blustery, carrying savage little bits of snow, mixed with flecks of ash. Unbelievable, thought Mary. First blizzards, now fires. Maybe tomorrow we'll have floods and a plague of locusts.

"Do you remember the way to Unaka?" asked Lily when Mary reached the bottom of the ladder.

Mary pointed to her left. "Around the lake, up that steep ridge. After that, follow your blazes to the road."

"Good. Then you'll be okay."

"What do you mean, I'll be okay?"

"I mean you can make it back to town on your own. I'm going to find my father." She gave Mary a cold, dismissive smile that was all Ruth Moon. "Thanks for your help. I really appreciate it."

With a jaunty little wave, Lily ran towards the cabin, bow slung over her shoulder. Mary stood there, dumbfounded.

"She's as crazy as Ruth Moon," Mary finally whispered. "And way beyond my help." *Just get to Murphy*, she told herself. *Call Sheriff Ray and let him take over. You've fulfilled your promise to Jonathan—hell, you never promised Jonathan anything in the first place.*

Fully intending to do just that, she strode down the path toward the lake. But twenty paces on, she stopped. As angry and used as she felt, she could not abandon the girl she once loved. Lily Walkingstick was a lethal combination of fear, rage and adolescent bravado. Somebody needed to save Lily from herself.

"Okay," Mary whispered bitterly as she turned to follow the head-strong girl. "This is for you, Jonathan Walkingstick. And for you, Ruth Moon. For here on out, I owe you nothing."

By the time Mary caught up her with her, Lily was standing behind a large tree, surveying the remnants of the cabin. It looked like someone had fired a missile at the place—nothing remained but a shell of charred logs crumpled in a circle of muddy slush.

"Not much left, is there?" Mary said, her eyes watering from the acrid stink lingering in the air.

"Everything I own is in this backpack," the girl murmured, stunned.

"Then please, let's get back to Murphy." Mary tried once more, still hoping Lily might see reason. "The sooner I can get an APB put on these guys, the sooner we can find your dad."

"No way." She shook her head. "I can find him now. I know exactly where he is."

"Where?"

Lily pointed to two sets of faint footprints that disappeared into the snow of the driveway. "Those tracks weren't here before. The Snow Men must have broken open the gates to the park roads and driven up here. They probably parked near the front gate and sneaked up to the cabin."

"And you think they're still hanging around?"

Lily shrugged. "Like you said before, Mary. Why would they leave if they're waiting for me?"

Mary's heart sank. She'd hoped the cabin's utter destruction might have changed Lily's mind about things. Instead it had only strengthened her resolve. "Lily, it's still you against two men with at least two guns." Mary looked at the circle of scorched earth that surrounded what was left of the cabin. "With apparently no small knowledge of explosives."

"I don't care," she replied. "They aren't more than a mile away. And unless Edoda is dead, he's still with them. I can't come this close and not try to save him. You'd do the same thing, if it was your dad."

Mary had to admit that was true, but she also knew this was crazy. But what could she do? Lily was too stubborn to change her mind and too big to pick up and drag to Murphy. The only thing she could think of was to go along, and try to keep the girl from getting herself killed.

"Okay," Mary said. "Lead the way."

Lily drew back, surprised. "You're coming too?"

"I can't let you go alone. I love your father too much to do that."

"I thought you loved that Victor guy."

"I love them both."

Lily gave her a strange look. "Then follow me. I know a path we can take and stay hidden."

Mary followed Lily into the dark trees that grew above the driveway, feeling as if she were clinging to a runaway horse. Please let Jonathan be alive and the Snowmen be gone, she prayed as she unzipped her parka to keep one hand on her Glock. Let this torched cabin be their parting shot as they take Jonathan to Oklahoma.

By the time they reached the end of the drive, it started to snow again, the flakes coming down furiously, big as quarters. Lily stopped and pointed at a wide yellow gate that stood unlocked, a chain dangling from one end.

"I locked that Friday, when Edoda and I came back from town," she whispered. "They must have cut it and sneaked in."

Keeping to the tree line, they walked west, looking for a van or a truck pulled to the side of the road. After twenty minutes, when they'd seen nothing but an empty, snowy road, they turned around and retraced their steps. They passed the open gate again, passed a faded PAINT CREEK CAMP sign, then, as the sky lightened slightly ahead of them, Lily grabbed Mary's arm. Twenty yards away, a blanket of snow covered what looked like a small camper, pulled off at a wide spot in the road.

They ducked into the trees that bordered the road. "Let's get closer," whispered Lily. "And try to see what they're doing."

Mary allowed the girl to lead—she was almost as good as her father in the woods. Even limping she walked noiselessly, aware of every sound and scent around her. They crept through the trees until they were about forty feet away. No lights or noise came from inside the camper. Mary was trying to figure out if the Snowmen were awake or sleeping when Lily peeled off her pack and grabbed her bow and quiver.

Mary grabbed her arm. "What the hell are you doing?"

"I'm going to flatten one of their tires. Just like they did to our truck."

"With an arrow?" Mary was horrified. The light was just a shade above dawn, and snow covered all but the tops of the tires. If Lily missed and hit the aluminum side of the thing, the men would wake up and fly out like hornets from a nest.

Lily pulled out one arrow. With a black shaft and a lethal triangular point, it didn't look like anything Jonathan had ever made. "Edoda calls these man killers, in honor of some chief."

"Wilma Mankiller," said Mary. "A great chief in Oklahoma."

"Yeah, well, that's what they're for. Man killing."

"Lily, please don't do this. You don't know if your father's even in there!"

"If he's not in there, then he's dead." She looked at Mary, her eyes flat with hatred. "Don't worry. I've got this."

Before Mary could protest further, Lily was crawling through the laurel, bow in hand. Mary pulled the Glock from her holster and aimed at the door of the camper. If the girl missed and someone came barreling out with a gun, she could at least get the first shot off.

She waited, her gaze trained on the camper. As the Glock grew heavy in her hand, she saw a flash of movement, heard a soft *thunk*. Squinting at the camper, she saw the fletched end of a black arrow protruding from the front tire.

"Damn," she whispered, amazed. "She's good."

She kept her gun trained on the camper, waiting for somebody to wake up. But the occupants had either not heard the arrow or had attributed it to snow, falling off the heavily laden trees. A few moments later, Lily returned.

"See?" She grinned as if she'd made an A on some test. "I told you."

"Good job," Mary admitted. "But why didn't you flatten both their tires?"

Her smile turned bitter. "I'm saving my man killers for bigger game."

Mary gave an inward shiver, picturing one of those arrows in the middle of someone's chest. "Look," she said, offering her plan for the third time."We know where they are and that they aren't going anywhere on that tire. We've got the whole day to hike back to town and get some real help."

"No way am I leaving my dad now," said Lily. "One way or the other, I'm going to find out what happened to him."

CHAPTER 26

_____

Tuesday

Victor sat up, shivering. His night under Coza's tent had been neither warm nor comfortable, but sheer exhaustion had plunged him into a deep and dreamless sleep. Now, the luminous numbers on his watch read 6:07 and as he peeked outside, he saw that the snow continued to fall, turning their once robust fire into a soggy mound of ash. Reaching in his parka, he retrieved his SBI phone—a state-of-the-art instrument which, according to the asshole Spencer, would connect them with headquarters from anywhere shy of Mars. He punched the thing on, keyed in a code and held it to his ear. As a din of static roared in his ear, he realized he may as well as have been on Mars.

"Worthless piece of shit," he whispered, wondering why he bothered with the thing in the first place. He was history, as far as the NC SBI was concerned. He put the phone back in his pocket and leaned across the tent to shake Coza. "Wake up," he said. "We've got to get moving."

She slowly came to life, immediately complaining about being cold and hungry. She left the tent to pee and returned to smoke two cigarettes and open another can of Vienna sausages. "Wish I had a hot cup of coffee," she said, her voice husky with sleep.

Victor rubbed his forehead, unconcerned about the lack of coffee. Where was Mary? And who was she with? Walkingstick's daughter? Or Teo? Was Coza covering for the bastard with this crazy Mexican story? Suddenly a new nightmare popped into his head—one of Mary, captured by neither Walkingstick nor Teo, but some older, unknown enemy, bearing a long ago courtroom grudge. For prosecutors, it was an occupational hazard.

"Hurry up," he told Coza sharply as he rose from his sleeping bag. "The longer we wait, the further we'll get behind."

They packed up their camp and returned to the pine trees where Coza had found the tracks. Overnight the snow had obscured a lot of them, but enough of the bluish depressions were still visible. Coza led the way, while Victor followed, struggling to keep a vicious west wind from blowing him into her. He saw no sign of Mary, and his mind spun back to the original question—why had Walkingstick's daughter called Mary in the first place? Somebody hurt or ill would call paramedics—not a prosecutor.

Maybe it was personal after all. Maybe Walkingstick had decided that Mary really was his own true love and sent his daughter as an envoy, to help mend the shattered fences between them.

"Oh, come on," he whispered under his breath. What kind of man would send his teenaged daughter out in three feet of snow to reconnect with an old girlfriend?

With his brain spinning with more questions than answers, he finally decided just to keep his gun close and follow the funny little orange-haired woman who was leading him deeper into the frigid wilderness.

They'd followed what tracks they could see for an hour when Coza suddenly ran over to stand beside a tree. "Look!" she cried. "Over here!"

Victor followed her. Grinning, Coza pointed to what looked like a backwards 7 carved about five feet up from the base of a smooth-barked tree. "Somebody's made a blaze!"

He frowned, his knowledge of blazes minimal. What hiking he'd done had been with a compass and topo map. "Marking a trail?"

Coza rolled her unswollen eye. "Boy, you're not SBI for nothing, are you? Of course that's what they're doing!" She touched the bark where a knifepoint had scored it. "It's a fresh cut, too. The wood's still yellow."

Victor brightened. If someone was blazing a trail, it meant they must not know this part of the forest. Teo Owle would not have needed help like that, and he certainly wouldn't have left a trail for anybody to follow. He looked at Coza, his trust level rising a few degrees. Maybe she really was telling him the truth.

They went on, now looking for blazes on the trees as well as tracks in the snow. Along the way Coza volunteered her life story. He'd heard similar ones—some guy hooks a needy girl on drugs, and starts pimping her out to feed her habit. Coza's story differed in that she'd had a daughter, whom Florida protective services took away when the child was three months old. "I named her Tesoro," Coza said, her voice trembling slightly. "That's Italian for treasure. I heard it on a perfume commercial. It's the most beautiful word I've ever heard."

"You see her much?" asked Victor.

"Not since they took her away. They told me some nice people adopted her, but they won't tell me who."

Victor made no comment. His sister Maura had given up a child when she was seventeen. She was forty now, and still mourned the loss. He changed the subject. "So how did you wind up with Teo Owle?"

Coza gave a bitter laugh. "My pimp came up three grand short on a drug deal. He offered me to make up the difference and Teo said okay."

"Does Teo pimp you out?"

"He would if he lived closer to town. Mostly I just clean his house and cook his food. Have sex when he wants it. Just like any old wife."

"But how did you learn all this stuff about the woods?"

"I go with him on his drug runs. No point in staying cooped up in that shitty trailer."

"Why do you stay with him?"

"Because until you showed up, I had nowhere to go, and no way to get there."

They kept on following the blazes, when suddenly Coza came to a stop.

"What's the matter?" said Victor, almost bumping into her. "Do you see something?"

"That blaze goes straight," she said, pointing in the direction they were walking. "But those tracks turn left." She nodded at a line of bluish depressions that led to a steep ridge that loomed high above them.

Victor frowned. "Why would they change directions? This path is a lot flatter."

"I don't know." Coza pointed to one of the still visible cross-hatched tracks. "But here it looks like Snowshoe switched over to boots, probably to dig into that ridge."

"Is there anything up there?" asked Victor.

"I told you before–cabins of Florida's rich and famous," replied Coza. "Maybe they were planning on breaking into one of them."

Victor looked up at the towering ridge. Somebody must have wanted to get somewhere badly to risk that steep a climb in snow.

"It's your call, SBI. We can follow those new tracks, or we can stick with the blazes. I don't know which way will get us to your girlfriend."

Victor looked at the blazed trail, then the steep ridge. Both seemed like thick miasmas of snow and fog. "Door number two," he finally said. "Let's do the ridge."

"It looks awfully slick," Coza warned. "So be careful. I'm no nurse."

"Lead on," said Victor. "Don't worry about me."

"What you want to do is turn sideways," explained Coza. "And then go up like you're climbing stairs." She walked to the base of the ridge, turned sideways and started stepping up the ridge. "See?" she called. "Like this."

Imitating her actions, he followed her, but the deep snow made the going hard and treacherous. When she was twenty feet up the ridge, she called down to him.

"You okay?" she asked.

He shot her a thumbs-up. "Doing okay," he said with a confidence he did not feel.

He made slow progress, testing his footing with every step, trying to keep up with Coza. But the higher he went, the icier the snow became. Sweating under his clothes, he labored on when suddenly, he heard Coza yell. He looked up. Twenty yards ahead of him, she'd lost her balance. She teetered backward for a moment, then started tumbling down the ridge, somersaulting like a kid. She could not gain any purchase on the ice-glazed snow, and he realized sickly that she was heading straight for the massive tree he'd just passed. If she careened into that tree, it would kill her.

He ditched his pack and rushed to get between her and the tree. If he could tackle her, or even slow her down, this might be okay. Though the snow was like glass, he told himself it would be just like the miserable year he'd played tackle on his junior high football team. Throw yourself on top her, he told himself. Your weight will slow her down.

He crouched down as she tumbled towards him, a look of utter terror on her face. Skidding downhill fast, she came closer and closer. When she was six feet in front of him, he leapt forward, trying to wrap his arms around her. They tangled like awkward lovers, his arms around her butt, his face smacking into something hard.They rolled together in a manic slide until the world turned to nothing but crystalline ice that raked into them like a thousand frigid knives.

CHAPTER 27

Mary and Lily hid behind the thick, snow-draped laurel, keeping watch on the trailer. Though Mary kept trying to persuade Lily to leave, or at least move to a safer location, the girl refused to budge. They staked out the camper for hours, but no sound came from inside, nor did anyone emerge into the cold, white morning. Blowing up cabins must take a toll, Mary thought acidly. The bombers must need some extra sack time.

As Lily huddled motionless in her Canadian coat, the cold damp seeped into Mary's bones. Shivering, her eyelids grew heavy and her thoughts turned to Victor and the way he'd whispered *eres mi corazón*. But in the surreal fluidity of dreams, Victor morphed into Jonathan, only not Jonathan as a man, but as a boy of seventeen—his arms embracing her beneath the fronds of a willow tree. Suddenly she returned to that long ago afternoon, when soft moss cradled them as they'd first come together and felt something as new and fresh as the wildflowers that bloomed around them. How young they'd been. How wild and heady!

"Mary! Wake up!"

Lily's urgent whisper jerked her from that distant spring into the frigid reality of now. She opened her eyes to see a man coming down the steps of the camper.

He was six feet at least, husky with a scruff of a beard. He wore snow camo and an orange hunting cap. Stretching his arms out, he twisted from the waist and did a few back stretches, as if he'd overslept in a lumpy bed. He started to go back inside the camper when suddenly he stopped and tilted his head. He walked a few steps towards the front of the camper, then he saw it. Lily's black arrow protruding from the flattened tire.

"Chet!" he screamed, rushing towards the tire, the cap flying off his head. "Chet, get out here!"

A moment later, a second man flew out of the camper, carrying a rifle. He seemed almost a clone of the first—tall and barrel-chested, but with his bare head shaved to cue-ball smoothness.

"What?" he cried, pointing his rifle at the woods that surrounded them.

"Look at this!" said his friend.

The second man backed toward the side of the camper in a military crouch, scanning the forest as if enemy troops were about to pour from the trees. He kept his guard up until he reached his companion and looked down at the tire with the arrow protruding from it. "Aww, shit!" he cried.

While Mary studied the two men, Lily silently nocked another arrow and rose up on one knee. Before Mary even realized what she was doing, she aimed through the laurel and drew back her bowstring. With a soft phffft, her arrow zipped through the laurel and caught the man with the rifle in the side of his head.

Blood spurted all over his face in a red arc. Screaming, the man turned and started firing his rifle blindly in their direction. Mary pulled Lily to the ground as bullets zinged through the branches above them, peppering them with frozen branches and snow. Mary felt a sharp branch scrape her cheek, but she continued to hold the girl tightly. "Rattle these leaves and they'll kill us for sure," she whispered.

The Rifleman must have emptied his clip, because loud cursing quickly replaced the gunfire. As the sharp smell of cordite tinged the air, Mary lifted her head to peek through the laurel. Blood streamed down the side of the Rifleman's head. Lily's arrow had missed the man's right eye by millimeters, leaving a long bloody gash from his upper cheek to his temple. The first man grabbed the rifle while the bleeding man hurried back into the camper, stumbling up the steps. Mary figured the other man would rush to tend his wounded friend, but instead, he leaned the rifle against the camper and turned to face the woods.

"Kimmeegirl?" he called, awkwardly stooping to pick up his cap. "I don't know if you're out there, but I'm Bryan's Uncle Jake. Honey, I think we've gotten our wires crossed pretty bad."

Lily began to squirm. Stunned, Mary gave her arm a hard squeeze, willing her to be still. Who was Kimmeegirl? What was this guy talking about?

"I'm sorry we couldn't meet you like we'd planned. We got hammered by the snowstorm and didn't get to Unaka until yesterday. Then this crazy van full of yahoos came screaming down the mountain and about ran us off the road. When you didn't show up, we kinda followed our noses here. Bryan tore up his knee trying to push us out of a ditch, and now somebody's almost put out my brother's eye."

Lily started to stand up. Mary clamped down harder on her arm.

The man held his hands out, innocent and imploring. "Anyway, girl, if you're the one shooting the arrows, there's no need to. We don't mean you any harm."

He bobbed on his feet, as if trying to think of something else to say. "Well, I'm gonna go inside and see about Bryan and my brother. If they aren't too bad off, we'll change this tire and get on our way. If you can hear me, I hope you know you've got no reason to be afraid. Bryan's sleeping off a pain pill; otherwise he'd be out here talking to you himself. He was mighty excited about meeting you."

With a final apologetic shrug of his shoulders, he picked up the rifle, and headed back into the camper, closing the door firmly behind him.

They waited to see if anyone else was going to come out. When the camper remained still, Mary turned to Lily furious, blood from her cheek dripping on to the snow. "Lily, we are going back to that deer blind. And you are going to tell me what the hell is going on."

Lily gulped. "But..."

"Now!" said Mary.

"Follow me," Lily finally said. "I know a closer place."

They waited a few more moments, then Lily started crawling through the laurel, away from the camper, finally stopping at the edge of a small creek. After scurrying along the rocky bank, she ducked inside a little hollow beneath an outcropping of rocks.

"They won't find us here." She flopped down, breathless.

Mary stared at the girl in a stone cold rage. She thought she'd heard her call "Bryan" when she first drove up to Unaka. Now one of the men in that camper claimed that "Bryan" had been excited to meet somebody named Kimmeegirl, until he tore up his knee. If Lily didn't come clean with her about this, she was going to walk out of these woods without a backward glance. Then Lily or Kimmeegirl or whoever the hell it was would have to work this mess out on her own.

"Okay. Truth time. Who are these people. Why did you shoot that guy?"

"I thought he was the tracker," she cried. "His voice sounded the same. Raspy."

"Then why did the other guy call himself Uncle Jake? And start talking about Bryan? And who is Kimmeegirl?"

For a moment, Lily's eyes blazed with their usual dark defiance, then she broke down, weeping heavy, wrenching sobs. "I don't know," she sobbed. "I don't know what to believe anymore."

"Then start with what you do know," said Mary coldly, pressing some snow against her bleeding cheek. "And don't leave one damn thing out."

Hiccoughing, Lily began to explain. "Last fall I met a boy online. Bryan, from Kentucky..."

Mary listened closely as Lily went on. She was familiar with the stories of lonely teenagers who sought their soul mates via the Internet. Most wound up just shamed or humiliated; but a number of them either vanished or turned up dead—raped and murdered by sexual predators. As Lily talked, a chill far colder than the blizzard ran down Mary's spine. She realized that the men she'd assumed to be bounty hunters could well be something far worse. If that was the case, what had happened to Jonathan? Had they shot him? Tried to staunch his wound with a menstrual pad? Had he bled out anyway and they'd dumped him in that lake?

Sniffling, Lily went on. "We'd planned to meet at Unaka, just like Uncle Jake said. But then the trackers broke into the cabin. That's when I called you. I was really scared."

Mary said, "And you thought I was Bryan when I drove up."

Lily gave a miserable nod. "I hoped so. But it was you."

"What were you and this boy going to do? Elope?"

"I just wanted to get away from Edoda," she cried. "Get away from this stupid life!"

Mary was seething inside. Never had she been played for such a fool. "And do you stilll want to go with this Bryan?"

Lily looked up, her eyes full of a desperate confusion. "Now I just want to find Edoda. But I'd like to see Bryan, too. You know? Just meet someone who loves me. Is that so bad?"

She started crying again. Mary wanted to slap her, but then her own thoughts flashed back to the afternoon she was seventeen and had lied to her mother, so she could linger with Jonathan under that willow tree. Had she really behaved more rationally than Lily, back then? Probably not, she decided. But at least Jonathan had been a real, flesh-and-blood boy, not some Internet fake.

Mary frowned at the weeping girl, not knowing what to say. She didn't know what these men were, except monstrously dangerous. Now she had to convince Lily of that.

"Lily," she finally said. "I think Uncle Jake is lying. I see lots of holes in his story."

"I figured you'd say that.

"Listen to me. He said they came up here from Unaka yesterday. The Unaka road has been blocked ever since that tree fell on my car."

"Maybe those other people moved it," said Lily. "The ones with my dad."

Mary wanted to scream, wanted to tell her that these men were likely predators and there was no Bryan and that her father was probably dead, but the words wouldn't leave her mouth. Though Lily talked bravely about Jonathan being dead, it was an abstract notion. The reality of it would shatter her like glass. Mary could barely wrap her own head around the idea. "I still think you've been conned."

Lily looked up, her face blotchy with tears. "No way. Bryan would never do that..."

"There is no Bryan!" Mary snapped. She knew her words would hurt, but she didn't care. This girl's stupid crush had probably gotten Jonathan killed.

"He was just asleep, Mary. They'd given him medicine."

"Have you ever spoken to him on the phone?"

"No, but I have pictures of him. And lots of texts."

"Lily, if that rifle fire didn't wake him up, he must be dead."

"Shut up!" Lily cried. "He is not dead!"

"Listen to me! I truly think those men came up here for you. And not for any reward from your grandfather."

"Oh, yeah?" Lily stood up, her anger flaring. "You're as bad as Edoda, thinking you know everything. Well, I think Bryan is real and alive and I'm going to prove it!"

Before Mary could answer, Lily turned and ran back toward the camper. Mary watched, aghast. How could this girl not see the danger she was heading towards? Why could she not see that these men were conning her? Because she's fifteen, Mary realized. In the full rut of first love. Not a rational time of life, as she recalled.

Mary watched Lily cross the creek; then she left the little overhang and followed her, praying to the mountains a muddled prayer that Jonathan was still alive somewhere, that there really was a hurt boy inside that camper and that Uncle Jake and his gun-toting pal were nothing more than bumbling enablers of young love.

CHAPTER 28

———

Victor felt something hard hit the back of his head. Worse than any bone-jarring check he'd received playing soccer, the blow sent him into an inner snowfall, where a hazy, formless world spun around him. He lay inert, inwardly trying to assess the damage to his body. He felt more in shock than in pain, and as he tried to wiggle his fingers and toes, he answered the concussion questions the trainers always asked on the soccer field. My name is Victor Galloway. I live in Hartsville, North Carolina. It's Tuesday, January 23 (or is it still Monday, the 22nd?) I'm engaged to Mary Crow.

He lifted his head. The motion made him dizzy, and he spat out a mouthful of bloody snow. But other than one wobbly tooth, he seemed okay. Extricating his arms to push himself up, he realized that he and Coza had both tumbled into the tree he'd tried to avoid. She lay in a heap next to him, a purple bruise blooming on her forehead. Still, neither of her legs were bent in grotesque angles and he saw no blood in the snow around her. Gently, he touched her shoulder.

"Coza? Can you wake up?"

She did not move. He wondered if she'd died—if she'd broken her neck in the fall he'd tried so desperately to prevent. Gently, he turned her over on her back, and cupped his hand beneath her nostrils. Her respiration was slow, but her breath still warmed his fingers.

"Coza?" He tapped her shoulder. "Can you open your eyes?" When again she didn't move, he scooped up some snow and rubbed it on her cheeks. She flinched; a moment later, her good eye opened.

"Don't Teo," she whimpered. "That really hurt."

"It's not Teo, it's Victor," he told her. "SBI."

She looked at him dreamily. "Where are we?"

"I have no idea. You slipped and started sliding down the ridge. I tried to catch you and we both slammed into this tree."

"How fast were we going?"

"Fast enough," he said, remembering how the topsy-turvy landscape flew by. He felt a sudden, sharp pain in his side. Digging down into his parka, he pulled out Spencer's cell phone. The worthless thing had probably broken one of his ribs. He decided to ignore that and concentrate on Coza. "Can you move? Wiggle your fingers and toes?"

Looking like an overturned beetle, she slowly waved both arms in the air, then made a feeble attempt to straighten her legs. "Help me up. I need a cigarette."

With his own arms tingling, he helped her to sit up against the tree. "Get me a smoke, will you? They're in my pack."

Her pack had tumbled down the ridge, a good fifty feet beyond the tree. Victor stood up, but his dizziness returned to the point of nausea. Finally he dropped to his knees and crawled down to the pack and dragged it up the hill to her.

She dug a cigarette out and lit up. He collapsed beside her, gazing up at the snowy ridge, grateful they were both alive and in one piece. He should thank the mountains, he supposed. But he couldn't remember the name Mary always called them.

They sat in silence. He made another pointless attempt on Spencer's cell phone, while Coza finished one cigarette and lit another. Halfway through the second smoke, she hurled the cigarette into the snow and started to cry.

"I was so scared," she sobbed. "I tried to stop but I couldn't. I couldn't grab the ice."

He put his arm around her, tried to comfort her, but she twisted away.

"You know what I was thinking about? The whole time I was sliding down that fucker?"

He shook his head.

"My little girl. Tesoro. I knew I would die up here on this shitty mountain and never know what happened to her."

She covered her face with her hands and began to cry for real, her shoulders heaving, her body wracked with huge, gulping sobs. Again, he tried to put his arm around her. He'd offered Maura the same comfort, twenty years ago.

"It's okay," he whispered. "You're alive. You can look for her after she's grown up.

"No, I can't. They make you sign a paper and promise never to try and find her."

"Coza, there are ways to get around that."

She lifted a face streaked with tears. "How do you know? Did you learn that at SBI school?"

He shrugged and revealed something he'd only ever told Mary. "Because my sister went through the same thing."

Coza blinked, shocked. "Your sister got knocked up?"

"One summer in high school," he told her. "The next spring she had a little girl."

"What did she do?"

"She gave her up. A couple in Savannah were over the moon about getting a child."

"Has she seen the baby since then?"

He shrugged. "I don't know. When the baby turned 18 my sister had her DNA done and signed up on all these adoption websites. If that baby ever decides to look for Maura, it'll take her about five minutes to find her."

"So I could do that, too?"

"I don't know why not."

She looked at him for a long moment, then she leaned forward and kissed him, full on the mouth. It took him by surprise, and though her lips and tongue were all lush and warmth in the middle of a frozen landscape, her lips were not the ones he wanted. He took her face in his hands and ended the kiss as gently as he could.

"What's the matter?" she asked, hurt and puzzled. "I thought you liked me."

"I do like you," he said. "But I love someone else."

They sat in an awkward silence, Coza smoking another cigarette while Victor gazed at the top of the ridge, entertaining a crazy notion that Mary was up there, waiting for him. In a few minutes, he turned to Coza and asked,

"Do you feel like you can go on?"

"And help you find your fiancé?" she asked, sarcastic.

He shrugged. "If you'd rather go back to Teo's, I understand. I'll still give you a ride to an airport."

She whirled around to face him, her good eye hard. "SBI, there's something you should know. Before I left Teo's house, I raided his little secret cache and stole every dime the bastard had. For Teo, I may as well have sawed off his dick with a dull knife. So going back to Teo's house is not on the table. I 've seen what he does to people who cheat him."

"Oh," said Victor, realizing that this truly was a one-way trip for Coza.

"So the only question for me, is how do we want to go on? Up the ridge like before, or back downhill, to those blazes on the trees."

"How do you feel?"

"Sore as hell," she cried. "But nothing's broken now that wasn't broken before."

He looked up the ridge. Since they were both shaken up, neither option seemed all that great. But climbing back up held more promise than retreating back down to the trees. They would at least get to where they were going faster, if they didn't kill themselves first.

"Let's go up, if you're game."

Another cigarette later, she was ready to go. They resumed their climb up the ridge, using their backpacks to stabilize their steps, feeling for any more of the icy spots that had sent her tumbling. For Victor, every step was both a fight and a prayer that he would find solid footing. As he climbed that notion remained in his head—that once they reached the top of this ridge, *something* would be there. Either a fancy cabin or a road or even a tent with Mary in it. But when they finally reached the top of the ridge, they found nothing beyond a million more trees, all pushing up through a carpet of snow.

As they stopped to let their racing hearts slow, Victor looked at Coza closely. Though she'd made no complaint, she now stood with her whole body tilted to the right.

"How do you feel?" Victor asked, hoping she felt well enough to guide him further.

"I'll live," she replied gruffly, rubbing one shoulder.

"You think Mary made it up here?"

"Somebody did," Coza replied. She pointed to the right side of the ridge, where a distant tree sported the same blaze they'd followed before. "Good thing they thought to do that," she added. "The way the snow blows up here, we would never have found their tracks."

"Okay," said Victor. "Let's go."

They turned east, Coza limping. The snow continued to fall from a thick cotton sky, the wind sometimes gusting it sideways, into their faces and eyes. Victor had no sense of time; only when he checked his phone did he realize it was just past noon. They'd been out in this weather for twenty-four hours; it felt like twenty-four days.

After a while Coza went behind a tree to pee. When she came back, her eyes were brighter, as if some wonderful idea had struck her while she had her pants pulled down. "I might know where these people are trying to go."

"Where?"

"I remember Teo complaining about some fish camp up here, built around a lake. It's crowded in the summertime, but we never could get any business there. The fishermen were old farts, into Scotch and Bourbon more than weed or coke."

Victor frowned, leery of any enterprise Teo might have come up with. "But why Mary would go to a fish camp?"

"Because there's nowhere else to go in this direction," said Coza. "All the summer cabins are west, near the Unaka road. These tracks are going east. The only things this way are more game lands and that camp."

Victor still doubted that Mary would hike through the snow to a fish camp, but here, in the middle of a thousand snow-bloated acres, it sounded as likely a destination as anywhere else.

CHAPTER 29

Leroy paced inside the camper like a big dog in a too-small cage, clutching the album of cuties as he peeked out every window in the vehicle. Though he considered his *aw, shucks, please don't hurt poor Uncle Jake* act a sudden stroke of genius, it was not having the effect he'd hoped for. If Kimmeegirl had been the one shooting at them, she was not coming forward either to apologize or to rush to her injured Bryan. The surrounding trees stood motionless and silent, fine flakes of new snow sifting down like powdered sugar on a cake.

"Well, at least no one's shooting our tires anymore," he muttered. If they lost another tire, they would be in deep shit. Right now, he figured Chet could get them back to civilization on the spare.

Abruptly, he heard Chet begin a new round of retching in the bathroom. He put the album on the dinette table and went to check on his brother.

"You okay?" He tapped softly on the door, hoping Chet would tell him to go away. Visceral noises emanating from bathrooms always made him nervous.

"No, I'm not okay," bellowed Chet, sliding the door open. He stood naked from the waist up, his own line of Band-Aids closing the wound near his eye. Leroy swallowed a bubble of hysterical laughter. Chet looked like some bizarre version of Frankenstein, pieced together with plastic tape.

"Do you know how close I came to losing an eye?" Chet's voice came out in a growl.

Leroy's amusement withered. Chet scared him, when he got this angry.

"This is all your fault." His brother pointed an accusing finger at him. "I ought to kill you right now, along with that goddamn Indian."

Leroy realized he needed to do some fast talking—Chet was veering into a murderous rage.

"I'm sorry, bro," he said, trying to mollify him. "I'll change the tire and shovel us out. We'll get the Indian to Oklahoma and you can have the whole ten grand. You deserve it."

"Damn straight about that, Leroy," said Chet. "But I'm not going anywhere until I get that girl."

"Get the girl? Last night you just wanted to leave."

"Last night I had two good eyes. Now I want to teach that little bitch a lesson."

"But you don't even know if she's the one who shot you. It could have been her mother."

"Then I'll teach both of them a lesson," snarled Chet.

Leroy nodded, knowing it was best to go along with him. He sat down at the dinette and held the album to his chest, watching while Chet put his shirt back on.

"Does it hurt bad?" Leroy tried to sound like their mother, in one of her rare moments of sympathy.

"Bad enough," Chet replied, wrestling a wool sweater over his head. "I mean, fuck, man. What if you'd had to pull an arrow out of my eye?"

The thought of that sent a wave of nausea through Leroy. "Don't talk about it. It didn't happen."

"Yeah, well. When I find those bitches, something *is* gonna happen. Something real bad."

"But how are we going to find them?" Leroy asked, still in mollify-mode. "You said at the cabin you'd lost the girl's tracks in the woods."

Chet went to the windows on the other side of the camper. "She was shooting from those bushes. The bow I saw in that cabin was an old-fashioned thing, with not much range at all. She probably wasn't twenty yards away when she shot me."

"But have you seen those bushes? Up close? They're all twisted up, like a maze."

Chet scowled. "Yeah. Just like the ones I got lost in yesterday."

"Yesterday you had two good eyes. Today you're already down one eye. You might get poked in your other eye crawling around a bunch of bushes. And the shooter might still be out there, waiting with another arrow."

Chet fingered his cheek, considering his brother's words.

"It's a lose-lose, bro," Leroy continued, trying to close the deal. "I like your first idea better. Cut our losses and get the Indian to Oklahoma. You could have a lot of fun with ten grand."

For a long moment, Chet stared out the window. When he turned back to Leroy, a wicked grin spread across his face. "I just thought of what we can do."

Leroy's heart sank. Thinking had never been Chet's strong suit. "What?" he asked glumly.

"Make Crazy Horse track her. He leads, we follow. Nobody can shoot us that way."

"He'd never do it," said Leroy.

"Sure he would. You can make him. You charm the pants off people every day. I know you can make a poor worried father track his frightened child." Chet grabbed the lethal looking arrow that winged him and ran the tip down Leroy's left cheek. "You need to make this happen, bro," he said, his eyes dark with fury. "Remember, all this is your fault."

Jonathan had spent the morning listening. Last night had been a maelstrom of noise—the trailer had shaken with loud music, then a noise like an explosion, deep in the woods. Just a few minutes ago, he'd heard shrieks, the rapid fire of an assault rifle, slamming doors and yelps of pain. Wondering if they were in the middle of some kind of police firefight, he crawled close and pressed his ear to the panel, but now all he could hear was the two men, arguing. He only hoped that they wouldn't kill each other. If they did, he would die locked up in this berth. Nobody would find him until spring. He would never see Lily again.

During his dark imprisonment, he'd put together what was going on. His initial assumption had been far too innocent—these men weren't bird dogs; these men were pedophiles. The little girl whose bra he'd found had written more, on the underside of the carpet. *So scared. So sorry.* Then he'd found another inscription on the carpet, a simple *J.A.T. 11-4-15.* It was fainter than the first one, written not in pink marker, but something brown, that looked like dried blood. He'd passed his locked-up hours by giving this girl a name and a history—Judy Ann Turner. Chubby, with pimples. Neither brain nor athlete, she was just a nobody who got teased at school and harassed on the Internet. These bastards had woven some kind of fake boyfriend fantasy around her and grabbed her from the mall, when her mother thought she was at the movies. After they'd had their fun with her, they'd killed her. Now she lay in a shallow grave that might or might not ever be found. And Mr. and Mrs. Turner, her parents, would wait and wonder for the rest of their lives.

He wondered how many more sad little inscriptions might be written underneath this carpet? After finding two, he didn't have the heart to look for more.

What he couldn't figure out was how they'd found Lily. He'd been so careful, kept her so close, lived so quietly. And yet they had burst into an isolated cabin in the middle of a blizzard, to grab her. It made no sense.

But as he'd gone over that last night for the thousandth time, he remembered something. Lily had suggested Kentucky as their next destination. One of these bastards drank from a plastic mug with a UK logo on it. Was that some kind of connection? Or just some crazy coincidence?

In a way, it didn't matter. The only thing that mattered now was that Lily had done what he'd taught her—what he'd drilled her since day one. She was probably with Mary now, back in Murphy or Harstville. She would not meet the same fate as poor Judy Ann Turner.

He decided to knock on the panel and ask for the bathroom, when the panel burst open. Handgun stood there nervous, sweat beading on his upper lip.

"Breakfast time," he announced.

Careful not to bump his shoulder, Jonathan climbed out of the berth. For the first time in twelve hours, he stood straight rather than curled in a fetal position. "What the hell's going on?" he asked. "Who's doing all the shooting?"

"We had a regrettable incident this morning," Handgun began, his voice wobbly. "I believe it might have involved your daughter."

His heart stopped. That wasn't possible. Lily was far away, maybe with Mary Crow.

Handgun held up two arrows. Jonathan recognized them immediately—-razor sharp broadhead points on black carbon shafts. Lily's man killers. He gulped down a sick, rising panic. Lily wasn't with Mary Crow at all. Lily was here.

Handgun went on. "This morning I found one of these in the front tire of the camper. When my partner came out to have a look," he held up the second arrow, "someone shot this one at him. It barely missed his right eye."

"And?" asked Jonathan, too scared to breath.

"He didn't know what was happening, so he fired off a clip from his rifle. We heard someone scream. We think it might have been your daughter."

Jonathan knew Lily's aim was true, but her range was limited. She didn't have the upper body strength to shoot very far. That rifle could have cut her in half. "Did you look for her?" he said, his heart running like a hamster in a wheel.

"We couldn't find any trace of her." Handgun cleared his throat, sheepish. "We were wondering if you might help us find her. She might be hurt."

He grabbed Handgun by his camouflage jacket and pulled him so close their noses almost touched. "I'll find her," he said. "But if my daughter has as much as a broken nail, you and your buddy are going to have a whole lot more to worry about than arrows in your eyes."

CHAPTER 30

Handgun cut the zip ties from Jonathan's wrists, allowing him to shove his arms into his coat sleeves as he tied a noose around his neck. The pain in his left shoulder flared up like a hot poker, but Jonathan ignored it. He was upright, he was walking, he was about to look for Lily. With ten feet of rope between them, Handgun opened the door and shoved him down the stairs. Rifleman was waiting, sporting a camo cap that shielded a patched-up gash that went from the corner of his eye up to his scalp. Jonathan felt a swell of pride. Lily had aimed well.

"Your little bitch almost put out my eye," Rifleman muttered.

"You got off lucky," Jonathan replied, squinting against the bright, glaring snow light. "She was probably aiming for your heart. Where were you when she hit you?"

Rifleman pointed at the bushes. "She shot from over there."

Turning, Jonathan hurried to the laurel that bordered the opposite side of the road, terrified that he would find Lily bleeding, Lily struggling to breathe or worse, Lily dead.

"Uweji!" he called. "It's Edoda. Atli, if you can!"

No sound came from the bushes. With Handgun holding on to the end of the rope around his neck, he plunged into the thick green maze at the point where Lily would have taken her shot. A swath of snow was packed down at one place, as if someone had kept watch on the camper. Then he saw tracks and a dribble of bright red blood. Part of him wanted to weep with relief; another part wanted to howl with rage. She was not dead, but she'd been bleeding. What had happened to her? Where had she gone?

His shoulder throbbing, he backed out of the laurel.

"Any sign of her?" asked Handgun.

"Only boot tracks," he replied. "And blood." He gazed at the snow-covered bushes, sick with fear. Though the blood loss seemed minimal, it didn't mean that Lily wasn't badly hurt. She was probably wearing that wooly Canadian coat. That by itself could absorb a lot of blood. But regardless of her wounds, she was still injured, alone in deep snow.

Handgun poked him. "Get going and find her. We promised her grandpa we'd bring her home."

He almost called them out; almost told them that he knew exactly what they'd come for–the sad little bra and the bloody scribblings beneath the carpet had revealed their secrets. But at the last second, he stopped himself. If they knew he was on to them, they might kill him right here. He needed to find Lily first, or at least draw these bastards away from her

"She went through this laurel hell," Jonathan pointed back at the bushes. "I'd have to track her through there."

"That's okay," Handgun assured him. "We've tracked before."

Jonathan glared at them. "Brother, your buddy's got a bad eye and you've got a gut wound I can smell from here. Neither one of you looks exactly trail-ready."

Rifleman sneered. "Don't worry about us, Crazy Horse. Worry about your kid."

Jonathan stood a little taller. The Rifleman had unknowingly paid him a huge compliment–the great Lakota Crazy Horse had always been his hero. "*Tasunkowitko*," he whispered to the ghost of the dead warrior. *Be my strength now.*

They tightened the noose around his neck and he crawled into the bushes, the men creeping after him. The bloodstains neither lessened nor grew worse—they remained consistent, all small splatters on the right side of the path. Strangely, he began to find a second set of tracks mixed with Lily's. Slightly larger, with a different tread, but still a woman's shallower, narrow footprint. He paused to feel the crisper edge of the new print and caught his breath. Had Lily called Mary Crow and gotten her to come up here? That had never been his intention—Mary was to be Lily's escape route. Yet what other woman would be up here? In that instant he wanted to laugh because Mary had come back to him and to cry at the reason she had. He reached out and put his hand over that bootprint until the warmth from his body began to melt the edges.

"Pick it up, Crazy Horse." Rifleman poked him in the hip. "It ain't getting any warmer out here."

He got to his feet, silently cursing himself, these men, and the uselessness of his left arm. Then he plunged ahead, realizing that now he needed to protect two people from these monsters.

He led them on through the laurel. It went just as he'd figured, with Handgun sucking in air while Rifleman walked with his head canted to the right. Still, Jonathan knew that if Lily or Mary were close by, they would smell Handgun's stink and hear the whistle of Rifleman's cheap camo pants in plenty of time to hide.

He faked them out easily, obscuring Lily's tracks as he led them along. Eventually, the laurel petered out at a small creek and they were able to stand upright. While Handgun rubbed his stomach, Jonathan searched for Lily's actual trail. Instinct told him that she would have crossed this creek and gone up to higher ground. But with Mary's greater experience in the woods, they could just as easily have followed the creek west, to Unaka and Murphy.

Jonathan turned to regard his captors. They stood close together, caps pulled off, small curls of steam rising from their sweaty scalps. As they stood close together, he realized they were brothers. Handgun had gone to seed while Rifleman still had a few muscles, but they were both big men with pale blue eyes and strange little curlicues of cartilage for ears. Wonder what fucked up family hatched them, he thought.

As Handgun rubbed his festering gut, Jonathan suddenly knew what to do. He would pretend to track Lily up to the highest ground he could find. These men were almost spent now; another steep, fast mile up a snowy mountain might kill Handgun and it wouldn't do Rifleman any good. If he picked up Lily's trail again, he would simply lead them in the opposite direction. He almost laughed at the irony of it all—for the first time in his life he was guiding people on a hunt and doing his best not to find a damned thing.

After they'd rested he led them on, following a fake path of bent twigs, claiming that Lily had made all of them. As they climbed the wind grew stronger, blowing sharp little bits of snow into their faces. Halfway up a steep ridge he stopped at a fallen log. Rifleman was squinting badly and Handgun was lagging a good twenty yards behind him. Jonathan smiled. His plan was working.

"I need to stop," Handgun called as he flung himself down on the log.

No shit, thought Jonathan, holding his coat close around his aching shoulder. He scanned the trees, wondering if Lily and Mary were watching. He'd seen no sign of them, but they were both good in the woods.

Just let them be far away from here, he thought. Past Unaka and heading back to town.

"Is the girl's mother with her?" Handgun called as he tried to catch his breath.

Jonathan pretended to be surprised. "What do you mean?"

"The woman with her. Older. Dark-haired. We saw them at the cabin."

Jonathan made no reply, wondering when they'd seen Mary at the cabin. He'd thought they hadn't known about Mary at all, but like every other assumption he'd made, he'd been wrong.

"Well?" Irritated, Handgun repeated his question. "Who is she?"

"I don't know what you're talking about," Jonathan lied. "I found only one set of tracks coming out of that laurel, and that's what I've been following."

After Handgun rested another five minutes, they went on, up another steep climb until they reached the top of the ridge. In clear weather, the view would have stretched west into Tennessee, south into Georgia. Today, those states were occluded by snow that faded into a thick soup of swirling grey clouds.

"She's in Tennessee now," Jonathan lied, his breath white as woodsmoke.

"Tennessee?" said Handgun, incredulous. "How do you know that?"

"There's her trail." Jonathan pointed down the ridge, to a small branch dangling from a pine sapling. A bear had probably scratched against it, but he needed to convince these two that it was Lily's trail. "She has friends down in Sycamore Creek. She's probably halfway there by now."

"Bullshit," said Rifleman. "No girl's that fast."

"This one is." Jonathan gave a bitter laugh. "You just blinked your one remaining eye and missed her."

"Watch your mouth," said Handgun. "Piss him off and he'll shoot your ass to kingdom come."

Jonathan stepped towards Handgun. As much as he hated both of them, he hated Handgun more. "Buddy, if anybody's headed to kingdom come, it's you. And by the looks of it, you'll be going there pretty soon."

"Oh, yeah?"

"You smell like rotting meat. My knife probably pierced your bowel, which means your shit has gone into your bloodstream, circulating all through your body. By the way you're sucking air, I'd say it's already infected the linings of your heart. Maybe your lungs, too."

"Bullshit."

"I was a medic in the Army," said Jonathan. "I learned what untreated puncture wounds do. In a day or two, your fever will go up while your blood pressure will tank. You won't be able to piss and it'll feel like fire ants are crawling under your skin." He paused, relishing the terror in Handgun's eyes. "You'll want water, but you won't be able to swallow. You'll try to breathe, but your lungs won't fill up. Then, bang," he snapped his fingers. "You're history."

Handgun started rubbing his belly. "What should I do?" he asked, his voice high and quivery.

"If I were you, I'd get to a hospital. If you're real lucky, they might be able to save you." Jonathan pointed towards the hazy mist that was Tennessee. "You can follow the Tellico River to a clinic about twenty miles that way. Or you can put the spare on that camper and drive like hell to Murphy."

A look passed between the two men. Fear, love, panic. Jonathan couldn't read it exactly, but he guessed it was a kind of *knowing* between creatures who'd been raised together.

"Arneeshar?" Handgun actually looked as if he might cry.

"Doss," Rifleman snapped. "Doss de looj."

They argued in their strange fraternal language for a moment longer, then Handgun wrapped the end of Jonathan's rope around one hand and gave it a sharp tug. "Come on. We're going back to the camper."

"Osda," Jonathan replied, adding to the polyglot conversation with Cherokee for *good*. Good that they were going downhill. Good that he'd scared them both shitless. Good especially, that he had managed to lead them far away from Lily and Mary Crow.

CHAPTER 31

Victor and Coza slogged along the ridge, following the blazes that had become welcome little signposts in the snow. Victor had a ripping headache that throbbed down his neck to his shoulder, while Coza stumbled along like someone drunk. As she struggled, he carried her pack, which rattled with every step, no doubt filled with cigarettes and cans of Vienna sausages. An awkwardness had grown between them since she'd kissed him. He figured his rejection had hurt her, but he couldn't help it. Sex was Coza's coin of the realm. It was a currency that had no value to him.

Just when Victor thought the ridge would go on forever, it descended to the edge of a half-frozen lake. Near the shore, thick white ice looked strong enough to walk on, while the middle remained a slushy dull gray.

"Is this the fishing camp's lake?"asked Victor.

"I think so." Coza pointed to some vaguely mashed up snow. "But the tracks go this way."

They walked on, the lake on their right, a million snowy trees on their left. Every so often Coza would announce that she could still see tracks, raising his hopes rose that he might soon find Mary. This had to be the right trail— there was simply no other place to go.

They passed a snow-covered bench that overlooked the lake, then the path made a hard left turn. Suddenly, a couple of small sheds came into view close to a red truck, covered with only a few inches of snow. Victor stopped, unbelieving. Walkingstick's pickup! The truck of Mary's dreams and his nightmares.

They quickened their pace, Victor sick inside, readying himself to see a love nest burrowed in the snow, full of light and cozy warmth. Instead, he only saw a single stone chimney rising from a rubble of charred logs.

"Holy shit!" cried Coza. "Looks like somebody nuked the joint."

Victor couldn't speak. He dropped both packs and raced ahead, unmindful of snow or ice or the blustery wind. He couldn't imagine what had happened here.

He slipped, fell, and scrambled to his feet, rushing toward the pickup, hoping Mary might be inside. The snow on the hood had been blown into little drifts, and the paint beneath was puckered, as if blistered by some inferno. He wiped snow from the passenger window and looked inside, but the cab was empty.

"What the hell?" he whispered. Grabbing his pistol, he hurried to what was left of the cabin. He found the soot-covered remains of a generator and some blackened kitchen appliances, but beyond that, the whole structure had burned to charred logs and shingles curled from the heat. He searched frantically through the remains, kicking through chunks of logs, terrified of finding scorched bodies twisted in agony. But when he reached the far corner of the structure, the black dust and gray ash covered no human remains. Mary may have died, he thought, but she did not die here. At least she had not burned to death. Suddenly, Coza's voice broke the stillness.

"Hey! SBI!"

He turned. She stood in front of the truck, pointing a rifle straight at him. Instinctively, he raised his pistol and aimed at her chest. This is the con, he thought. *She's led me here on purpose. This is why she wanted to come so badly.*

"Stop!" Coza shrieked, throwing the rifle to the ground. "I'm not going to shoot. I just found this in the truck!"

It took him a second to process what she was saying; he'd been trained to draw his weapon the instant someone drew on him. But he quickly realized she was simply showing him something she'd found. Shaking with adrenaline, he lowered his pistol and walked over to scoop the rifle out of the snow. It was an old Remington .22, just a varmint gun. Then he looked at Coza. Tears were streaming down her cheeks, and she was waving her hands as if to cool off her face.

"Are you fucking crazy?" she cried. "Did you really think I was going to shoot you?"

"You were pointing a rifle at me. What was I supposed to think?" he replied with matching anger. "Don't you know better than to point a gun at someone? Didn't life with Teo at least teach you that?"

"Fuck you!" She drew back one small, ineffective fist and punched his chest. "You're a bigger asshole than Teo."

Weeping, she turned and ran around the truck. He stood there, his knees weak, his heart still pounding. He'd come within an eyelash of shooting her, just because she hadn't known shit about guns. For a moment he thought he might vomit. He tossed the rifle back in the truck and walked over to where she was standing, huddled and small against the snow.

"Look," he began, awkwardly reaching for her shoulder. "I'm sorry. I'd just finished looking for Mary's body. Then I turned around and saw that rifle. It caught me by surprise."

She whirled around, still angry. "You should have seen your face!" she cried. "You looked like you wanted to kill me!"

Did he want to kill her? Of course not. He wanted to kill the snow and the cold and the pain in his shoulder and the sad, sick fear that he would never see Mary again. Those were his targets. Not Coza.

He put his arms around her and held her close. "I'm so sorry," he whispered. "I didn't mean to scare you."

She stood there crying in his arms, and lifted her face to look at him. Tears had streaked the remains of her mascara and snow peppered the dark roots of her hair. He knew she wanted him to kiss her, to share a moment of warmth in the middle of this cold hell. But just as before, she was not the woman who held his heart. He kissed the top of her head and said, "Just for the record, don't *ever* point a gun at someone unless you intend to shoot them."

Hurriedly, he let her go and walked back over to examine the cab of the truck. Beyond the melted paint job, he found nothing but typical vehicle trash—gas station receipts, a utility knife, two empty Coke cans. Reaching to check the glove box, he pulled out a battered map of the Eastern United States and a pink envelope addressed to someone named Alenna Prosper, in Jackman, Maine. The return address read Lily Walkingstick, Middle of Nowhere.

He gaped at the envelope, realizing that this truly was Walkingstick's truck and that Lily Walkingstick had recently been inside it. He sat down in the driver's seat and ripped open the envelope. It was an unsent birthday card that showed a shirtless young body builder holding out a piece of cake. Inside, in round, girlish handwriting, someone had written *Hope you get a piece just like this for your birthday!!!!!* It was signed *Love, Lily* with the addendum, *see you this summer, if the Warden lets me out.*

Victor turned the card over, trying to piece together a scenario. Father must have cleaned the snow off this truck, not too long ago. Daughter had made some kind of emergency call to Mary and had met her at Unaka. They may have come back here, but where were they now? And how did they figure in whatever the hell had happened to this cabin?

He put the card in his pocket and got out of the truck.

"What are you going to do now?" asked Coza, checking her mascara in the side mirror of the truck.

"Treat this place as a crime scene," Victor replied. "And start collecting evidence."

He walked over towards the cabin and studied the area. The pine trees closest to the structure were green—totally devoid of snow. Those further away were still iced in white. It reminded him of old films he'd seen of A-bomb tests, where the trees were blown backward from the heat of the blast. Snow had once been melted from the gravel drive in front of the place, but new snow had covered what tire tracks or footprints that might have remained..

With Coza limping along behind him, he walked to the cabin, into what had once been the kitchen. A propane tank sat curled open like a can of sardines and he thought he caught a wispy, lingering odor of gas. Frowning, he turned to her. "You smell anything?"

She lowered the hood of her parka and sniffed. "Gas," she said. "Not the rotten egg kind, but gasoline, for a car."

"Me, too," said Victor. He walked over and knelt down to pull the plug on the generator. Gas came out in drops, where it should have gushed out in a heavy stream. When he got up to examine the valve of the propane tank, he found it wide open.

He looked at Coza. "You know, I'm wondering if somebody doused everything with gasoline, opened this propane valve and set the whole thing off."

"Like tossed in a match?"

He shook his head. "If they'd done that, body parts would be hanging in the trees."

"I know somebody messed with the truck," volunteered Coza. "They slit two of the tires. I've watched Teo do that a lot."

He remembered the rifle inside the truck. "So maybe they disabled the truck and drained off the gas from the generator. After splashing that all over the cabin, they turned on the propane and somehow set everything off."

"Wow," she said. "They must have meant business."

"But no bodies are inside the cabin. It doesn't make any sense."

"Unless they killed them first, ditched the bodies, and then blew the place up," said Coza. "You know, to get rid of the evidence. Teo's done a lot of that, too."

That possibility had been at the back of his mind since he first searched the rubble of the cabin. He just hadn't wanted to face the fact that Mary might be dead, her body gone. He still couldn't think of this rescue mission turning into a search to recover bodies.

As he looked around, he realized that he'd ignored the two small outbuildings that remained unscathed by the fire.

"I'm going to have a look over there," he told Coza. Though he knew that anybody alive in there would have called out to them, he hurried towards the shacks anyway. Finding Mary, in any shape, was better than never knowing anything at all.

The first one was made of long-silvered wood, with a door secured by two latches. Quickly, he unhooked them and looked inside. He saw that it was a smokehouse–the interior was dark and smelled delicious. Two hocks of some kind of game hung from the low rafters, directly above an old-fashioned woodstove. Beyond that, it stood empty.

Relieved, he hurried over to search the woodshed. A three-sided structure, stacks of different kinds of wood had been placed in order of their diameters—slender kindling becoming piles of thick logs. The arrangement was tight and efficient, and gave no room to hide bodies, living or otherwise.

He stepped back from the structure, frustrated. Coza came up behind him.

"Find anything?" she asked.

"Nothing."

"What are you going to do now?"

"Keep looking," he said. "Around the lake. Deeper in the woods."

"I'm really hurting," she told him. "All over. I'm going to lie down in that smokehouse."

As Coza hobbled over to lie down, he turned and headed toward the lake. There must be some trace of Mary here, somewhere. "Just don't let it her be dead," he whispered. "Let her be hurt or wounded or even have run off with Walkingstick. Nobody deserves to die this cold and alone."

CHAPTER 32

Mary had to hurry to catch up with Lily. The girl had taken a different route back to their hiding place near the camper, crossing the rushing creek several yards upstream. She'd forded the stream by hopping on rocks—Mary could see her footprints on the snow-covered stones. It was a move only a love-crazed teenager might risk. One slip would dunk you into frigid water on an already frigid day. This far away from heat and warmth, hypothermia would be a given.

"Damn," whispered Mary. "Why did she have to go this way?" Probably to get rid of me, she decided. She had to keep following her, though. Every second she wasted staring at an icy creek meant that Lily was only getting closer to that camper. And she doubted Uncle Jake's story about changing the tire and leaving. That might have happened if Lily hadn't shot that arrow. But now the men in the camper knew she was here. They weren't going to give up on Kimmeegirl.

"Just watch the rocks and go fast," she told herself, eyeing the rocky creek. "You've crossed wider streams than this before."

Holding tight to the Glock, she stepped on the first of five stones. It was slippery, but rough enough to gain traction on. Two rocks later she'd reached mid-stream, eyeing the fourth rock, a small stone hump that barely broke the surface of the water. It was farther away than the first three. But a good leap would get her there. Then she could push off and propel herself to the opposite bank.

"Okay," she whispered, eyeing the greenish-gray rock. "Here goes nothing."

She leapt forward. Her right foot landed squarely on the rock, but before she could transfer her weight for the last leap, she slipped off the icy, wet surface. Down she went, face first. She threw her arms out and arched her back like a cat, trying to stay dry. As the knee-deep water roiled around her, she floundered to the other bank. When she got there, her arms were wet to the elbow, but she managed to hold on to the Glock.

Clambering away from the stream, Mary ran on. A quarter mile away, she caught up to Lily. The girl was walking fast, no doubt determined to prove that Bryan really existed. Mary lagged a few steps behind her, keeping an eye on the surrounding woods. The snow continued to fall, but it now wafted down slowly, as if the storm had exhausted its fury, but couldn't bear to leave without a few parting shots. She thought of how Victor had wanted to take her skiing. Maybe next winter, she thought. If she survived this one.

Lily stopped among some snow-laden cedar trees and turned to look at Mary. "I guess you're coming with me?"

Mary nodded. "Sorry to disappoint you."

Lily gave a disgusted shrug and went on, again taking a different path from the one they'd made coming up here. Clever, Mary had to admit. No point in giving Uncle Jake an easy trail to follow.

When they reached the broad coil of laurel, Lily paused. Mary saw that the edgy look had returned to the girl's face.

"What's the matter?" asked Mary.

"Nothing," Lily replied. "I just thought we should probably stay closer together."

They crawled back into the thick, leafy maze. They'd only gone a few yards when Lily stopped.

"Look," she said, pointing to the right.

Mary turned. Where the ground had before been uniformly smooth and white, now a path of tracked-up snow went through the bushes, along the route they'd taken earlier.

Crawling forward, Lily studied the ground more closely. "People are following our first trail," she whispered. "I see at least two sets of big boot prints."

"Uncle Jake and his brother," said Mary. "Coming after you."

"Which means Bryan might still be in the camper," Lily insisted, her eyes brightening. "I'm going to find him!"

Before Mary could stop her, Lily wiggled on through the bushes, following the path that the men had made. Just as Mary figured, it led straight to the tiny clearing where Lily had shot that arrow.

"Hold on!" Mary cried, grabbing Lily just before she hurried across the road.

"What?" Lily said, wresting her arm out of Mary's grasp.

"First let's see if anybody's in there. Those men might have doubled back a different way and be waiting for you."

"So what?" cried Lily. "I just want to see Bryan!"

Mary wanted to scream: how could this girl be so stupid? "Lily, you don't know what these men are. Maybe they're your boyfriend's uncles, maybe they're bounty hunters running a very long game. Plus we still don't know where your father is. Could you at least let me check out that camper before you go rushing in?"

Sighing, Lily flounced down in the snow. "You've got the gun, Mary. You make the rules."

Gritting her teeth, Mary reached for her Glock. Keeping one eye on the camper, she crept down to the shoulder of the road, feeling beneath the snow for any rocks that might have loosened from the pavement. With her left hand numb from the cold, she unearthed two half-eaten walnuts, forgotten by some squirrel. Quickly, she crawled back into the laurel and sat down beside Lily.

"Okay," she said in a whisper. "Don't take your eyes off that camper. I'm going to poke the hornet's nest."

She rolled the walnuts in the snow, compressing them into the tight, bruise-producing snowballs she'd thrown as a kid. After molding them in her bare hands to give them an even harder glaze, she crept back down to the street.

She heaved one walnut at the side of the camper. It landed dead on, thudding like a drum. She crouched down, ready for someone to come flying out the door, but nothing happened. After a moment she raised up and threw the other walnut. This one pinged sharply against the window of the truck, causing a shower of snow to fall from the side mirror. She waited another moment, just in case Jonathan or some injured kid might actually be trying to hobble to a window, but not a noise nor a person came from inside the vehicle.

Slowly, she crawled back up to Lily.

"Well?" the girl said. "Happy now?"

"Not at all," Mary replied. "But a deal's a deal."

Lily rose to a crouch beneath the low bushes. "So are you coming with me or what?"

"I'm not letting you go alone," said Mary.

With another disgusted sigh, Lily crawled out of the laurel and strode across the snowy road, desperate to find the young man who loved her.

As Lily hurried to the camper, she tried to get as far away from Mary Crow as she could. Meeting Bryan with an old woman behind her was the most pathetic thing she could imagine, but it was better than no meeting at all. Anyway, if she didn't make her move now, Uncle Jake and his brother would soon be on their way back to Kentucky.

She ran towards the door, her footsteps squeaking in the snow. She wanted to rush in and surprise him, but as she neared the camper, her courage faltered. She'd never gone into a boy's room before—hadn't even spoken with a boy since Marc Freneau in Maine. What if Bryan was lying there naked? Or stoned? Or jerking off? Suddenly she felt as if she were about to barge into an alternate universe, uninvited.

"Get a grip," she whispered. "This is Bryan." The boy who'd come all the way from Kentucky, who had seen her bare breasts and still found her beautiful.

Nonetheless, she was nervous as she walked up the steps and tapped softly on the door. She didn't want to startle him if he was sleeping. She listened, heard nothing. Moving closer to the door, she risked a whisper. "Bryan? Are you there? It's me, Lily."

All she heard was a gust of wind whistling around the camper.

"Try the door," whispered Mary, coming up behind her.

Lily opened the door opened, revealing a dark camper that stank of spoiling food and unwashed bodies. "Bryan?" she called a little louder. Still no response.

She glanced over her shoulder at Mary. Even though her face betrayed no emotion, Lily knew what she was thinking. *Told you so, Lily. Your boyfriend was a big fake. Nobody would want a loser like you!*

Screw you, Mary Crow, she thought. Angry, she jerked the door open wide and climbed into the camper.

"Bryan? Edoda?" she called. "Are you here?" She looked around. To her left was the cab of the truck—driver and passenger seats littered with cast-off paper cups and empty candy wrappers. Above that an upper berth was closed off by a strange wooden panel decorated with decals from a dozen different states. The rest of the camper consisted of a small dinette table, a galley piled high with dirty dishes, and at the very rear, a bedroom that looked as if someone lay sprawled under a dirty brown blanket.

Somebody's in there, she decided. As she heard Mary Crow climbing the steps behind her, she hurried to the rear of the camper, determined to find either her father or a boy with a bad knee. For once she was going to prove Mary Crow wrong.

She approached the bedroom door, whispering "Bryan? Edoda?" When no one stirred, she stepped inside. The bed was a mass of rumpled sheets and a lumpy blanket. Slowly, she tiptoed forward. and reached for the blanket. But instead of a dreaming sleeper, her fingers felt only dingy sheets, twisted as if someone had fled the devil in a nightmare

Tears came to her eyes. Where was her father? Where was Bryan? Had Mary Crow been right all along?

No, she told herself, peeling all the sheets and blankets back until they lay in a heap on the floor. Somebody must be here. They must be in that berth above the driver's seat.

She hurried out of the bedroom and squeezed past Mary, who stood flipping through some kind of album on the little dining table. Grabbing the stepladder that gave access to the upper berth, she climbed up and swung open the panel that closed it off. With her heart skittery in antic-ipation, she knew in seconds she would see Bryan, even surprise him, all snugged up in his den. But when the panel swung open, she found only a small room totally covered in smelly old carpeting. The windows had been painted black; the only light came through a small slit someone had scratched near the bottom of one window.

She reached forward, dug her fingers into the carpeting. Had Bryan ever been here? Was there really no boy, no sweetness, no escaping to Kentucky? Had she truly been that big a fool?

"Lily," Mary's voice cracked like a whip.

Here it comes, she thought. The old I-told-you-so. I'm a lawyer and I've been to court and I know how bad people think and blah-blah-blah.

"Lily!" Mary called even more sharply.

"What?" she snapped, miserable.

"We need to get out of here. Now."

She heard the urgency in Mary's voice and looked over her shoul-der. Mary was standing at the back bedroom door, staring out the win-dow. "What's the matter?"

"Uncle Jake and his brother are coming back," Mary said, hustling for-ward.

Lily craned her neck, trying to peer around Mary. "Is Bryan with him?"

"I don't know. And we aren't waiting to find out."

Before Lily could speak, Mary whipped her around and shoved her out the door. Down the steps and into the snow she stumbled, Mary pushing her away from the camper and Bryan and all her dreams that were now never going to come true.

CHAPTER 33

Mary tried to drag Lily deep in the woods, but the girl balked, as obstinate as her father.

"Let go of me!" she whispered, jerking away as she turned back towards the camper. "I want to see Bryan."

Mary was pretty sure Bryan was not among the figures she'd seen nearing the camper, but she'd learned that convincing Lily of anything was almost impossible. Had the girl been younger or smaller, she would have picked her up and carried her to safety. But Lily stood as tall as she did, plus she was now gripped by the ferocity of first love.

"Then at least hide," Mary said. "And watch from the cover of the trees."

Mary pulled her farther from the camper, where they took cover behind a massive old basswood with scrub brush growing thick at the roots. Lily stood and peeked around the wide trunk while Mary knelt in the bushes. In the gray light she could see three figures coming up the snowy road. The first two looked big and tall and trudged with exhaustion. The third person walked tall, with a proud tilt of the head. As the figure grew clearer, she gasped. It was Jonathan! Though he had a rope around his neck and one arm in a makeshift sling, he was alive!

Lily gave a whimper as she, too, recognized her father. She started to reach for her bow, but Mary grabbed her. "Not now!" she whispered. "Too risky!"

For once Lily did what she told her. Motionless, they watched as the men came nearer. The man Lily had winged with an arrow held his rifle at the ready while Uncle Jake clutched the rope that tethered Jonathan. They plodded slowly, heading for the camper. Jonathan followed behind them, scanning the woods, as if searching for a trail or a clue. Wonder if he knows we're up here, thought Mary.

They reached the trailer door. Uncle Jake pulled it open, pushed Jonathan up the steps. The man with the rifle paused to survey the surrounding woods, then followed them inside, slamming the door shut.

Quickly, Mary reached to drag Lily down into the bushes. The girl looked wide-eyed, stunned. No boy, no lover, no Bryan; just two men leading her father like some captured beast. "I guess they were bounty hunters," she whispered. "I guess I was wrong."

"Don't worry about that now," Mary whispered. "I need to tell you something that's going to be hard to hear."

"What?"

"That you've been tricked by experts."

"What do you mean?"

Mary pulled two sheets of paper from inside her coat. "I found these in that album, on their dining table."

She gave them to Lily. One showed an apple-cheeked blond boy grinning from a lawn tractor; the other a dark-eyed Goth teen smoking a cigarette as he sneered at the camera. To the side of both photos was a list of girls' names. Heather, Doris, Becca, Renee and Lily were scrawled on the blond boy's photo, while another set of names were listed on the Goth kid's snapshot. On both pages, a thin black line had been drawn through every name but Lily's.

Lily frowned at the pages as if Mary had presented her some document in Chinese. "I don't understand. That's Bryan—but what's this list beside his picture? And who's this other boy?"

Mary spoke softly. "Lily, there is no Bryan. There never was. These men have been scamming you."

"Why?"

"To trap young girls like you."

"But I was careful. I never went on those creepy sites."

"Remember all those decals on that door in their camper?"

Lily shrugged. "Yeah, I guess."

"I counted twelve decals from twelve different states. There are twelve crossed-out names on these sheets. I think yours would have made the thirteenth."

She blinked, unbelieving. "Are you saying they've kidnapped twelve girls?"

Mary answered obliquely, not wanting to reveal the horror she'd seen in some of their pictures. "I think that if things had gone as they'd planned, they would have crossed through your name and added a North Carolina decal to their collection."

"But everything Bryan wrote..." she began, her voice shaking. "He talked about algebra class and football practice and bands he liked."

"Predators know all the tricks, Lily. And these men seem like pros."

For a long moment Lily just stared at the image of the boy she knew as Bryan. He looked as healthy and straightforward as a tall stalk of corn. But he was just a photograph. Nothing more than pixels on paper.

"So I could be dead now?" Lily asked again, her voice sounding closer to five than fifteen. "These men could have killed me?"

Mary said, "I'm betting we could match each of those names to a dead girl and a decal."

"How can you say this?" she cried, wiping away tears. "How can you even stand to think these things?"

"Because I flipped through that binder. Every girl has a nickname, a picture, and a report card."

"A report card? About what?"

"One girl's tits got 100. Another's ass got a 70." Mary gulped. "Their words, not mine. I won't elaborate further, but it gets much, much worse."

Lily rubbed her eyes hard, as if doing that might change two lying pedophiles into Bryan, her ardent young lover.

"But why did they take Edoda? Are they bounty hunters too?"

"I can't figure out that piece of the puzzle," said Mary. "I'm thinking maybe he told them there was a reward out for him, to lead them away from you."

"What should we do now?" she finally asked. "How can we save Edoda?"

Mary didn't know what to tell her. She hated the thought of leaving Jonathan, but her first responsibility was to get this girl to safety. "Let's wait a bit and see what they do. If they try to leave, we can get their license plate. If they stay here, then we'll walk to Murphy and the sheriff."

For once, Lily offered no resistance. While Mary kept watch on the camper, the girl put Bryan's picture in her pocket and wept, her sorrow as cold and deep as the snow that surrounded her.

After Chet wrangled Jonathan back in the cave, Leroy collapsed at the dinette table. He took off his jacket and lifted his shirt to check on his wound. Oozing pus, it resembled a swirling hurricane of infection, with pink bands spiraling out from a burning red eye.

"Crazy Horse might be right," he said hoarsely, his face ashen. "I think I do need a doctor."

Chet stood next to the table, wishing Leroy would lower his shirt and shut up about doctors. The sight of his brother's belly made him want to vomit, and the idea of hauling him to a hospital with Crazy Horse in tow was more than he could deal with. "I'll get you something to drink," he said, opening the refrigerator.

"Hand me some aspirin. And the rest of that Mountain Dew," Leroy gasped.

"Here." Chet tossed his brother the bottle of pills and handed him a half-empty can of Mountain Dew. Leroy managed to catch the pills, but the soda slipped from his grasp. It bounced on the table, spewing yellow liquid as it fell to the floor.

"Aw, shit, Chet!" cried Leroy. "You're messing up the album!"

Scooping the open binder from the table, he gathered it up and shook the mess off their pictures, one by one. When he'd shaken off the last page, he frowned up at Chet.

"Where are the pictures of the boys?"

Chet slumped wearily against the refrigerator. "The who?"

"The boys. Bryan and Lance. Look on the floor."

Disgusted, Chet stooped down and peered beneath the dinette. "No pictures down there."

Leroy looked at him, unbelieving. "What?"

"They aren't on the floor, Leroy. Last time I saw them they were in that binder, on this table. Right where you left them before I got shot in the eye."

Leroy went through the binder again. He looked under the table himself. Coming up empty, he scooted out of the dinette and searched through the kitchen drawers. When he still didn't find the photos, he hurried to the back bedroom, his footsteps shaking the camper. A few seconds later he called out, irritated.

"Why the hell did you dump all the blankets on the floor, Chet?"

"I didn't do anything to the damn blankets," his brother replied. "You're the one who slept in there last."

There was a long silence, then Leroy started shrieking. "Oh, shit. Oh, holy fucking shit!"

"What?" Chet cried. "What's the matter with you?"

Leroy didn't answer. He hurried out of the bedroom to feel between the cushions of the sofa. After he rifled through the cabinets in the galley and bathroom, he re-checked the dinette and the litter-strewn cab of the truck.

Finally he turned to Chet, empty-handed, sweat beading on his forehead. "Somebody's been here."

Chet looked at him with his good eye. "Huh?"

"Somebody's been in here, you moron." Leroy spoke a notch below a shout, as if Chet had suddenly gone deaf. "They took the pictures of the boys. *The pictures with all the names on them!*"

Chet blinked. "Maybe Crazy Horse took them."

"Crazy Horse has been with us," said Leroy, pacing up and down the camper. "With a rope around his neck. It's Kimmeegirl. And her friend."

"But Kimmeegirl's in Tennessee," said Chet. "According to Crazy Horse."

"She must have doubled back"," insisted Leroy. "To save her dad. It's the only thing that makes sense. Kimmeegirl would have recognized Bryan and taken the picture. She's probably on her way to the cops, right now!"

"Goddamn you, Leroy." Chet's voice cracked with rage. "You've fucked us up again!"

"No, I haven't," said Leroy. He bounced on his feet, clutching his hair, as if he might pull some new idea out his brain. "Here's what we do," he said, his face flushing scarlet. "Burn that album and get the fuck out of here."

"What about Crazy Horse?"

His eyes narrowing, Leroy made a gun with his thumb and index finger and pointed it at the cave. "Just do what you've wanted to do since day one,"

Chet raised a brow, surprised. "And forget about Oklahoma?"

Leroy nodded. "We'd never sleep a wink as long as that Indian was alive and talking. Give me your lighter fluid. I'll take care of the album while you change the tire."

"I've got a better idea," said Chet, a slow grin creasing his face. "Let's let Crazy Horse change the tire. May as well put him to good use while he's still breathing."

While Coza holed up in the smokehouse, Victor took the rifle from Walkingstick's truck and started off to search around the lake. He felt safer walking with the old Remington in his arms. Though it was a smaller caliber weapon, the rifle's range was longer than his pistol and God only knew what he might run into up here.

He walked across the back of the ruined cabin to the lake. A pier extended out into the water, ice moaning against the pylons. Though he'd never fished much, he imagined the place would be beautiful in the summertime—a little blue sapphire of a lake surrounded by green mountains. Today, though, it was stark. Not a single speck of color interrupted the gray and white expanse of snow and ice.

He crossed the pier, slipping on the frozen boards, and walked over to what he guessed was a boathouse. Thinking it might be a good place to hide a body, he approached it cautiously. Though the door was chained and padlocked, he scraped thick frost off one window and peered inside. A half-dozen small boats were stored keel-up on racks. Orange life jackets hung along one wall, while the opposite wall displayed a bulletin board with pictures of fisherman, grinning with their catches. Nothing looked like it had been touched in months.

A wave of anger flashed through him, and he had to fight the urge to put a fist through the windowpane. He desperately wanted to figure out what had gone on here, but everywhere he looked he came up empty.

He checked the exterior of the boathouse. He found no tracks leading into the woods, but there was a narrow path that led around the edge of the lake. Hoping that might hold some clue as to what happened, he started following it, but realized that a hike around the lake might take anywhere from an hour to a day, and it was already mid-afternoon.

"Go twenty minutes," he said, setting the timer on his watch. "Then head back. You'll be frozen by then anyway."

He pulled the hood of his parka close and started off. The snow was a pristine carpet of white—untracked and sculpted only by the wind. As he walked he wondered if someone could have hidden a body or bodies in that frozen lake. It would have required a lot of dragging over the thick ice and onto the slushy stuff that skimmed the middle of the lake. Too crazy, he decided as the ice gave a low groan.

"But you're dealing with somebody crazy," he reminded himself. "Who the hell else would light off a mixture of propane and gasoline?"

Holding Walkingstick's rifle closer, he soldiered on, seeing the same white nothingness he'd seen before. Finally, the alarm on his watch beeped, and he started back to Coza, his latest search and research mission coming up as empty as all the others.

He expected to find Coza sleeping in the cold, spicy-smelling darkness of the smokehouse. But when he opened the door, he found her sitting by a glowing fire that winked from the woodstove, a pile of money spread out across her sleeping bag.

"Come on in and warm up," she called, patting the ground beside her, a tentative invitation for sex again riding on the edge of her voice.

"Thanks," he said, sitting down well away from her. "When did you build this fire?"

"When I saw this stove and that woodpile. I put two and two together and used my lighter." She looked at him and laughed. "Rocket science, huh?"

"Where did all this money come from?"

"Teo. 3700 U.S. dollars, in twenties and fifties," she said proudly. She looked up at him as she began to re-roll all the bills. "Think that'll get me to California?"

"Several times," said Victor. He unzipped his parka. Though the wood stove was too small to generate much heat, he was thankful for it. It was still the warmest place he'd been since they'd left Teo's kitchen.

"How about you?" Coza asked. "Find any trace of your girl?"

"All I found was a boathouse full of boats," he replied. "No bodies floating in the lake, no tracks leading into the woods."

"I'm sorry," she said.

"Teo must be a part of this," Victor whispered. He leaned back against a rough-hewn post and stared at the red truck through a crack in the chinked walls. "Otherwise, it doesn't makes sense. If Walkingstick persuaded Mary to go with him, why not take the truck? Even if Walkingstick torched his own cabin and wanted to make it look like some other kind of crime, why not take the truck?"

Coza busily stuffed her money back into the bottom of her backpack. "Teo usually brags about what he's going to do. He didn't say anything about this–he was too excited about getting money from those Mexicans."

"Maybe Teo killed them all." Victor ignored her and continued with his theory. "And torched the cabin to cover his tracks."

"Except Teo's going northeast, to Del Rio," said Coza. "We're headed north. Read your map, SBI."

"But maybe he ran into them. Saw Mary and saw his chance to get rid of her."

Coza shook her head. "Teo knows the way Del Rio. He wouldn't be wandering around up here."

Victor stared at the truck a moment longer; then he pulled the Walkingstick girl's birthday card from his pocket. *Hope you get a piece like this for your birthday!!!!!* Lily had written, with the addendum, *See you this summer, if the Warden lets me out.*

"Maybe the kid did it," he muttered, as the warm little stove made his eyelids grow heavy. "Maybe the kid just couldn't stand life with the Warden anymore. Maybe she wanted to go back to Maine, and have some young stud feed her birthday cake."

Coza scowled at him. "That's stupid, SBI. Why would she call her dad's old girlfriend and blow up his cabin if all she wanted to do was run away?"

"I don't know," he said, his head feeling muzzy.

"Lie down and take a nap," she said. "You're not making any sense. I'll keep watch and wake you up if the bad guys come calling."

CHAPTER 34

Not far away, Lily Walkingstick had fallen asleep. Whether from shock or depression or pure exhaustion, she nestled inside her huge coat, her only movement the rise and fall of her respiration. Mary knew they should start back to Murphy, but she decided to allow the girl five more minutes of sleep. In the past two days, her whole world had exploded as violently as that cabin. A small respite from reality might do her good.

Mary kept watch on the camper, weak with relief over Jonathan. He was still alive, his gaze defiant. How many times had she seen that look? In eleventh grade history, when he'd poked out Andrew Jackson's eyes on a twenty dollar bill. A year later, when he'd gone into the woods to hunt her mother's killer. Years beyond that in Oklahoma, when he'd walked out of a courtroom and fled a custody decision. Always proud. Often too proud for his own good.

"Jonathan, you are God's own Tsalagi," she whispered. A full blood, just like her mother. Both were natural children of the forest, mindful of the wind and the weather and the secrets the trees whispered, deep in the night.

What would it have been like, she wondered, if he'd just accepted the court's decision? Probably they would have married, moved to Oklahoma and shared custody of Lily with her maternal grandparents. The girl had a right to know her mother's people—what would it have harmed? But Jonathan had allowed his hatred of Fred Moon to poison his reason. Ultimately that loathing had resulted in this—him a wounded captive, his daughter a desperately lonely teenager, and her—a woman whose patched-up heart resembled a crazy quilt.

Despite all that, he still had a place deep inside her. Though he'd cost her nights without sleep and years without happiness, seeing him today was like seeing him for the first time, on the rickety tribal bus that carted them to school. She'd loved him then; she guessed she would love him until the day she died.

Don't go there, she warned herself, suddenly aware of Victor's ring on her left hand. You and Jonathan don't work. Never have. Never will.

Lily moaned softly, deep in a dream. Mary turned to look at her. As big a brat as she'd been, Mary couldn't blame her, either. In a single day she'd lost her home, her first love and every memento she hadn't stuffed in her backpack. Maybe when they got out of here, *if* they got out of here, those wounds might heal. With real boys and a real life that included friends and school and all the things Jonathan was so afraid of.

She sighed, deciding to take two minutes of sleep for herself. With one ear to the camper, she closed her eyes and began to nod off into little micro-dreams, when she jumped awake. Someone had slammed the camper door.

She reached for Lily. "Wake up!" she whispered. "And be quiet. They've come outside."

Lily sat up. They watched as Jonathan stood by the flat tire, the rope still around his neck. While the Rifleman covered him with his gun, Uncle Jake handed him a shovel.

"Okay, Crazy Horse," said the Rifleman. "Get busy."

Jonathan knelt down and started to dig out the snow from around the tire. When his shovel finally started scraping the asphalt surface of the road, Uncle Jake tossed him a lug wrench and jack.

"Don't jack it up yet," he told Jonathan. "I need something from inside."

The man disappeared into the camper, returning a few moments later with the album that held all the photographs of those girls. He cleared off a circle of snow from behind the camper, and started making a pile of the album's pages on the ground.

"Damn it," Mary whispered, watching as he pulled a can of lighter fluid from his parka.

"What's he doing?" asked Lily.

"Burning evidence. They must have missed those pages I took. They know someone's been in there."

The words had barely left her mouth when Uncle Jake doused the papers with lighter fluid and dropped in a lit match. A bright flame leapt up, making a fierce circle of orange fire in a while field of frozen snow.

Lily watched as oily-smelling smoke rose in the cold air. "What will they do now?"

"Beat it out of here, if they're smart," Mary said, silently cursing her own stupidity. Why had she not left that binder in tact? The greenest rookie would have known better than that. Because, she reminded herself, if you hadn't shown Lily that picture, she'd still be insisting that Bryan was real.

"But what will they do with Edoda?" asked Lily.

They'll kill him, Mary realized, the obvious solution to the trackers' dilemma hitting her like a kick to the gut. Jonathan was not stupid. He'd probably figured out exactly what these men were up to. A ten thousand dollar reward in Oklahoma was tempting, but staying off of death row was priceless.

"Mary?" Lily repeated, shaking her arm. "What will they do with Edoda?"

"I don't know," she lied, feeling sick inside. Would they march him into the woods and kill him there? Or just put a bullet in his brain right here by the side of the road?

"They're going to kill him, aren't they?" Lily's voice skated on the edge of panic.

Mary didn't answer. Frantically, she considered their options, desperate to come up with a plan.

"Get your gun!" Lily whispered. "Shoot them!"

Mary shook her head. "If I killed one, the other would kill your father. Then he'd come after us." She'd seen death up close, many times. It was nothing like what they showed in the movies. Forget the fake blood and the plastic guts. The real horror was the invisible shimmer of a soul no longer there, the universe altered in an instant. Too many fifteen-year-olds suffered the trauma of gun violence—she wasn't prepared to let Lily go through that. Suddenly, an idea came to her.

"Give me your bow," she snapped at the girl. "And your quiver."

Lily looked at her as if she'd gone nuts. "Why? You can't shoot a bow."

"No, but I can buy us some time with one." Mary glared at the girl—eyes hard as flint. "This is the plan, Lily. And for once, you are going to do exactly what I tell you. We don't have much time."

"What?"

"Your *Atli* promise." Mary put the safety on the Glock and gave Lily her gun. "Get to where you can get a signal on your phone. Call 911. Tell them there's a hostage situation at whatever this camp is called. Tell them they need to come immediately, that the park roads have been breeched."

Lily shook her head. "I'm not leaving Edoda—"

"Yes, you are," Mary said sharply, full of tough love. "If you love him at all, you'll leave him."

"But I can't. He would never leave me like this!" Tears welled in the girl's eyes. Suddenly, she reached for Mary. "I don't want to go! I'm scared!"

Mary took her in her arms and held her as she had years ago, when Lily wept over skinned knees and broken-winged owls.

"Lily, it's our only shot," she whispered, as the girl's body shook with silent tears. "I know it's scary, but you can do it. You're strong and you know these woods. Two days ago you wanted to be a grown up—here's your chance to act like one."

That stopped the girl's tears. Mary pulled away from her, giving a quick whispered lesson in pistol shooting. "You've got nine shots, but this gun won't fire until you take the safety off. If these men find you, push this button, aim at their stomachs and squeeze the trigger."

"But..."

"This is it, Lily. Be brave, just like your dad."

Lily stared at Mary wide-eyed, but she handed her the bow. "Okay, *uji*," she said, tears streaking her face. "I'll do it."

"Good girl," said Mary, weak with relief. "Remember what I told you?"

"Call 911, tell them there's a hostage situation. The park roads are open."

"Okay." Mary gave her a quick hug. "Now go and don't look back!"

Lily gave Jonathan a long last look, turned up the hood of her coat and vanished into the trees. Mary watched her with an ironic smile. *Uji*, she repeated to herself. *Mother*. Never had Lily called her that before. "Watch over her, *dodahluh*," she invoked the mountains in a whisper. "Guard her with your fiercest wolves."

CHAPTER 35

Rifleman sagged against the camper, his wounded eye swollen shut. "Pick it up, Crazy Horse," he muttered wearily. "We need to get going."

Jonathan knelt in the snow, trying to fit one end of the lug wrench on to one of the nuts. With his left arm in a sling, he had to work right-handed, against his natural preference. At first he chalked up the uncooperative nuts to unscrewing them the wrong way. Finally he realized that he'd compensated correctly: all five had simply frozen to the wheel.

But that was okay. It gave him time to piece together what had happened. Mary and Lily had fled into the woods after nicking Rifleman with that arrow. Then they'd doubled back to the camper, probably hoping to rescue him. But Mary had discovered something in that album that had put the fear of God in these men. That it was connected to the little girls who'd scribbled farewell notes in his prison, he was certain. That Lily was to be their next victim, he was equally sure. What he just couldn't figure out was how these two had come across his little girl, who three months ago had only wanted to go back to Maine and make out with Marc Freneau. If he hadn't been so scared, he would have laughed—last spring he would have killed Freneau if he'd touched Lily. Now, he would give the gawky, pimply-faced boy his blessings and the keys to his truck if he could magically show up and drive his child away from this madness.

At least she's gone now, he told himself as he pushed hard against one nut. Mary was probably halfway to Murphy by now, Lily in tow. For that, he was so grateful he wanted to cry. At least neither of them would have to watch him die.

That these men would kill him, he had no doubt. Rifleman, especially, took great pleasure in pressing that bullpup into the back of his skull. He would die quickly, a good death he'd dispatched to a number of hurt and wounded animals. But he would not see his child again. Would not attend the story of her life. He realized that this was his tragedy, the missing out. Not the rest of *his* life, but Lily's. However he could, he decided, he wasn't going down without a fight. Even with a bad arm and one stupid little Swiss Army knife.

"Hurry up, Crazy Horse!" Rifleman poked him with the gun. "You work like an old woman!"

"The lug nuts are frozen," Jonathan said. "I can't loosen them with just one arm."

The man snorted."Oh, come on. You're goldbricking."

"See for yourself." Jonathan stood up and backed away from the wheel, watching to see what Rifleman would do. If the bastard put the rifle down to struggle with the lug wrench, he might be able to grab it. He would have to move fast, and immediately start firing an unfamiliar weapon, but it was his only chance. He held his breath and waited.

Rifleman glanced at Handgun, who was staring at his burning papers, then with a long-suffering sigh, he walked over to the lug wrench. He slung the rifle over his shoulder, held the wrench in place with one hand and pressed down on the thing with his foot. The nut still wouldn't budge. He switched the wrench to different lug and gave another kick, with the same result.

"Shit," he whispered. Frowning, he unshouldered the bullpup and leaned it against the side of the camper. As soon as he grasped the wrench with both hands, Jonathan made his move.

He leapt toward the gun. His eyes were focused on the barrel of the weapon when something flitted across his field of vision. Instinctively he flinched, as a new arrow pinged against the side of the camper, ricocheting off to plummet harmlessly into the snow. Lily! Jonathan realized, terrified. She was still here, shooting her man killers!

He lunged for the bull pup, but Rifleman had heard the ping of the arrow as well. He turned, and with a vicious kick to Jonathan's torn shoulder, pushed the rifle just out of his reach.

"You bastard," he cried. "I'm gonna kill you, but only after you watch me kill your kid."

Jonathan rolled over to face the snowy woods beyond. "Atli!" he screamed. "Atli now, Lily! And don't come back!"

He heard a sharp click, followed by a thunderous volley of bullets. Hot shell casings rained down on him like sparks from a fire.

"Leroy!" Rifleman yelled. "The girl's back!"

As Chet fired off another volley, Leroy ran over to Jonathan, grabbing the rope around his neck. He pulled him to his feet and shoved him forward, turning Jonathan into a shield from any incoming arrow.

"She must have been watching from those bushes," said Chet as he put another clip in the rifle. "Her aim's gone to shit, but she still means to fucking kill us."

"Hang on, Chet," replied Leroy. "I've got an idea."

With Chet holding the bull pup at the ready, Leroy put his pistol to Jonathan's temple. Clearing his throat, Leroy began to speak. "I'm sorry this has turned out so badly, Kimmeegirl. We didn't mean for it to happen this way."

Jonathan scanned the woods, desperate to see a shadow or the movement of a bush. But he only saw still, green pine trees that shouldered a thick blanket of white snow. If she's hiding, she's hiding well, he thought.

Leroy went on. "We know you've been in our camper. We know you've taken things that don't belong to you. So we're going to put an end to this now. You come out, return those pages you took, and everything will be just fine. If you don't come out," he said as he drew his pistol, "we're going to make your father pay for it. That will be most upsetting for you to watch. I'm sorry it has to be this way, but you've treated us very unfairly. We'll give you one minute to make up your mind."

"Atli, Lily," Jonathan called one final time, sending his words out on the frigid air, praying that she was too far away to hear them. "Atli now. And never forget I love you."

A throbbing in her left leg awakened Coza Lambert. At first she thought it was simply part of the nightmare she was having about Teo, but when she opened her eyes she knew it was real—some new injury she'd sustained when she'd pinwheeled down that ridge. Yawning, she rubbed her eyes and scooted closer to the woodstove, in hopes that heat might soothe her aching back and legs. But the warmth provided no relief.

Propping up on one elbow, she saw that SBI was still asleep on the other side of the stove. She reached for her backpack, undecided about whether to smoke a cigarette or one of the joints she kept in her sock. The joint might ease her pain, but it would make her fuzzy and hungry. A cig-

WHITE TREES CRIMSON SNOW

arette would at least make her more alert. Plus SBI wouldn't go off on her with his drug mule rap.

She dug a smoke out of her backpack and lit up. As she enjoyed her cigarette, she gazed at SBI, wondering what he looked like naked, how he might make love to someone. Probably pretty nice, she decided. A guy like SBI would take his time, mindful of her pleasure. Not like Teo and the rest of them, three poke wonders who couldn't wait to put their pants back on. The notion of sex with SBI begged the question of Mary Crow, the woman he loved. What had happened to her? Had she gotten cold feet about marriage? Decided to dump SBI for her old flame who was living in this shack?

"Not unless she's fucking nuts," Coza whispered. What then? She tried to think of everything Teo had said about this Mary Crow. Usually she ignored his rants, but she remembered the unending venom with which he'd raged about this woman. "She's smart and she's Cherokee," he kept saying. "That's like fighting a snapping turtle. She'll bite and hang on and pull me down until I drown." She'd laughed at the image of Teo being drowned by a turtle until she realized how scared he was.

Suddenly, a new worry sizzled through her. What if SBI had gotten it right in the first place? What if Teo was behind all this? What if those Mexicans had been his stooges? Maybe he'd just told her they were illegals wanting to go to DC when they were really going to help him kill Mary Crow. If Teo got caught, he would pull her down with him, telling the cops some ridiculous lie, like she'd put him up to all the drug selling. Then she would wind up in prison while his fancy lawyer would get him off.

"No," she told herself, trying to put the brakes on her own panic. She'd seen those illegals—a raggedy-looking Latino couple with three kids, scared of being caught by ICE or shot by the grubs. Still, she knew how clever Teo was at setting things up. She was wondering if she ought to crawl over and tell SBI her suspicions when she heard a series of distant *pop-pop-pop-pop-pops*. Most people would think someone was shooting firecrackers. But she knew better. She'd heard automatic rifle fire before.

Immediately, she reached for SBI. "Hey," she said, giving his leg a rough shake. "Wake up."

"What's going on?" He sat up, immediately reaching for his pistol.

"Rifle fire," she said. "Not close, but definitely in the hood."

Before he could answer, another series of pops floated through the air.

"Shit." He got to his feet and peered out a crack in the smokehouse door. "Can you tell where it's coming from?"

"That way, I think." She pointed past the remains of the cabin. "I've heard it twice, in the past two minutes."

"Okay." SBI took the safety off his pistol. He scooped up the rifle, then stopped. "You stay here. I'll be back."

"No way!" Coza struggled painfully to her feet. "You're not leaving me here for Teo to shoot."

"Teo?" He looked at her, his gaze turning so cold it scared her. "If Teo's here you need to tell me, now."

"I had a kind of dream," she explained, floundering with her words. "That he hadn't told me the truth about those Mexicans. That maybe he really is behind all this. I never told you, but Mary Crow was all Teo talked about, last weekend. He hates her big time. She scares him."

"I wish you'd mentioned that before, Coza."

"It wouldn't have made any difference," she said. "I haven't lied to you. And I've led you on the only trail I saw. If Teo comes here and finds me with all his money, he'll kill me. And it won't be a quick bullet in the head, either."

She tried to hold back her tears, but they came anyway. She was scared. She did not want Teo to kill her in the middle of this frozen hell. She wanted to go to California and walk on the beach. She wanted to see Tesora once again before she died.

"You can barely walk," said SBI. "Just find someplace to hide and you'll be fine."

She shook her head. "He'll find me. Please," she begged. "Let me go with you."

He frowned as he strapped Walkingstick's old Remington over his shoulder. "Have you ever shot a rifle before?"

"A couple of times."

"Then you know what to do. You've got a range of about a hundred yards with this one. The length of a football field."

His words buzzed inside her head like bees. "How am I going to shoot the rifle if you're carrying it?"

"If Teo's the one doing the shooting, I'll give it to you. Otherwise, just stay behind me and try to keep up."

CHAPTER 36

Mary stood frozen, her heart beating like crazy. The big basswood tree had given her cover, and she'd aimed an arrow at the guy with the rifle. But instead of flying true to its mark, the thing had skittered down the side of the camper, barely missing Jonathan. Nonetheless, her shot had caused a stir. Rifleman had peppered the woods will bullets while Uncle Jake had grabbed Jonathan to use as a shield. Now Uncle Jake held a pistol to Jonathan's head while Rifleman stood slightly behind them, ready to start blasting again. Jonathan, however, looked strangely calm. He's probably thinking it's a good day to die, she decided, remembering how he used to quote the great Crazy Horse. Or maybe he thinks Lily's still here and he doesn't want his daughter to see him afraid.

Uncle Jake's voice rang out. "Make up your mind, Kimmeegirl. Trigger fingers are getting itchy here!"

Mary didn't know what to do. Then suddenly, JimAnn Ponder, her needy divorce case, popped into her head. JimAnn was exactly the attitude she needed—a tough, Scotch-Irish mountain woman. Channeling JimAnn would be perfect. From behind the tree she threw the bow onto the snow-covered road. "Well, don't start scratching them fingers yet!" she called. "You got me treed."

She walked out of the woods slowly, her hands above her head. To a man they looked astonished, the trackers scowling while Jonathan gaped in surprise. As she drew closer, he didn't look at her at all, but lowered his head to study the knee-deep snow at his feet.

The one who claimed to be Uncle Jake turned his pistol from Jonathan's head and aimed it at her while Rifleman nudged his weapon up against Jonathan's neck.

"Where's the girl?" asked Uncle Jake.

"Halfway to Tennessee, by now," Mary replied. "She took off an hour ago."

"Then why are you still here?"

"Cause that's my idiot brother," she called loudly, pointing at Jonathan, hoping he would catch on. If they could keep this family act going, they could buy Lily some time.

"So you're not Kimmeegirl's mother?"

She shook her head. "Her Aunt Mary."

Keeping his pistol trained on her, he walked closer, studying her face. "I've seen you before," he said. "In a picture by your brother's bed. You didn't look like any sister there."

Mary shrugged, as best she could with her arms raised. "I can't help what the fool keeps by his bed. All I'm telling you is that he is my brother, Jonny Walkingstick. I'm Mary Walkingstick."

He drew closer and with one hand unzipped her coat. "Take it off," he said, his eyes glittering bright and feral.

She lowered her arms and let the parka drop to the ground.

"Now spread your legs."

Again, she did as he asked. With Lily's bow too far away to grab, she stood helpless before him.

"Okay, Sis. Let's see what you've got on you."

He frisked her, starting in the back, going from bottom to top. He must have been the subject of several prior pat-downs, because he knew exactly where to feel for hidden contraband–knives stuffed inside socks, guns carried in the small of the back. With Jonathan and the other man watching, she stood there stone-faced as he squeezed her bottom. When he did the same to both her breasts, Jonathan jumped, and took a step forward, but the other tracker held him fast by the rope around his neck.

"Sweet," Uncle Jake cooed, relishing her embarrassment.

Mary longed to kick his balls into the next county, but she knew how that would go, so she tamped down her rage for the moment. Everything hinged on how she dealt with this man.

"Where are the pictures you stole?" he asked. "Or did your niece take them to Tennessee?"

She squinted up at him. "I don't know. She took something out of your camper, but she didn't show it to me. I told her she was trespassing, but she's stubborn as a mule. So's he." She pointed at Jonathan, for the first time telling Uncle Jake the absolute truth.

Keeping his gun pointed at her, he grabbed the coat and fumbled through her pockets. A moment later, he came up empty-handed. "Aw, fuck!" he whispered.

"I warned her y'all would come back and be pissed. But nothing stops that one. I kept watch outside while she messed around inside. When I saw y'all coming back, I hollered, and we ran away."

Uncle Jake cocked his head. "So how do you figure in all this?"

"Come again?"

"You. How come you're up here with her?"

"Two nights ago I was watchin' TV when she called me, out of the blue. Said men had busted in to their cabin in the middle of the night and to come help her. What was I gonna do? Say sorry, honey, I'm busy, I'm about to buy a big ol' fake diamond on HSN?" She frowned at Jonathan. "Anyway, I ain't heard from either one of these two in years. He owes me five hundred dollars that I'd like to get back."

"Where do you live?"

"Yonder." She pointed her thumb over her shoulder, to the mountains behind her. "Tennessee. I sent Lily back over there, to fetch my boys."

"How far away is your place?"

"Half a day on foot. Couple of hours by car."

"And what's at your place? A husband? A boyfriend?"

"I got two big old boys and a stack of bills a foot high. You don't believe me, come and see." As she spoke Mary simply repeated JimAnn's endless litany of complaints.

Uncle Jake stared at her, still not quite buying her story. "So what do you think's going on up here?"

She blinked against the harsh light. "Besides all this snow?"

"No. Why do you think we're holding your brother with a noose around his neck?"

"That ain't hard. Jonny's been runnin' from the law for years. I reckoned right off you two were bounty hunters, who'd tracked him down. What I couldn't understand was Lily's boyfriend bullshit." She cocked her head and looked at him with a coy little smile. "But I figured that out, too."

"Oh?"

"Yeah. You set a trap for both of 'em. There's as much cash on the girl's head as his. I ought to turn her in myself and make some money for traipsing around in all this damn snow. I'll probably come down with pneumonia."

Uncle Jake's eyes grew narrow. Mary realized she might have gone too far. Interjecting her own interest in Lily's reward money might have reserved her own personal bullet from that gun.

"Get on over there," Uncle Jake said, pointing his pistol at the camper.

"Can put my coat back on? I'm right cold without it."

"I guess."

She remembered JimAnn's addiction to Marlboro Lights. "You got a cigarette on you?"

"No."

She grabbed her coat, dusted off the snow. Uncle Jake grabbed her elbow and pulled her to within mere feet of where Jonathan stood with Rifleman.

"Argonish," Uncle Jake said to his brother. "Keebot."

Rifleman stepped around Jonathan. "Sit down," he said, leaving the rope around his neck. As Jonathan sank to the ground, Uncle Jake turned to her.

"Go sit across from him. We need to talk." He watched her as she went over and sat in front of Jonathan. "And don't do anything stupid. I'm keeping this gun pointed straight at you."

CHAPTER 37

For once, Lily did as she'd promised. With Mary's pistol heavy in the pocket of her coat, she circled through the woods, running when she could, sliding down embankments where the snow had iced over. As she hurried along she listened, praying that she wouldn't hear the sound of more gunfire. Already she'd heard two bursts from that big rifle, but she figured that was just Uncle Jake's brother, trying to scare Mary. She knew if she ever heard two single shots close together, that would be the end. Edoda and Mary would lie dead, the white snow turning crimson with their blood. The thought made her sick inside. She ran faster, the gun banging against her thigh, trying to outrun everything—the sound of the shots, the memory of her father standing with that noose around his neck, the monstrous guilt she felt for causing this whole mess.

Two hundred yards west of the camper she ran out of the woods and onto the frozen road. For a moment she stayed on the straight path to Unaka, but she soon realized that doubling back to their burned-out cabin and scaling the ridge where she'd first texted Bryan would be better. If she could get up there, she might be able to get a cell signal to Murphy faster.

"Just go," she whispered. Turning, she slipped into the trees that grew above the road to their cabin. For a moment she walked silently, out of habit, as Edoda had taught her. Then she remembered she had no need of silence; speed was what mattered now. She had to get to that ridge, before those final two gunshots would ring in her head forever. She slid down another bank and reached the road that fishermen would start driving down in just a few months. Rods and reels would jiggle in the backs of their cars, whisky and poker chips clattering in their trunks. How disappointed they would be, to find the cabin burned to ashes and the guide Walkingstick dead. Though they would, of course, continue to catch the bass and crappie the lake was famous for, this year they would have to live in tents and find the fish all by themselves.

"Shut up!" she shrieked, willing the image away. "Just shut up!"

"Hold it right there!"

A man stepped from behind the trees, directly in front of her. His voice was gruff and male and serious. She fumbled in her coat for the pistol, but the Canadian pockets were too deep; she couldn't get it out. Finally she turned and started to run, back in the direction she'd come.

"I said hold it," came the male voice again, louder now.

She started to run faster, but another voice came from behind her. A woman's voice, scratchy, but speaking in a slightly kinder tone.

"Hey, girlie. You need to stop, right now. You've got a bad ass SBI agent pointing a pistol right at you."

She stopped; something about the woman's voice carried the ring of truth. Again she was tempted to reach for Mary's gun, but she realized that by the time she got the thing out of her pocket, whoever stood behind her would probably have shot her dead.

"Raise your hands and turn around slowly," said the man.

She turned around terrified, trying hard not to wet her pants. Two people stood side-by-side. A tall, serious looking man, flanked by a short woman with spiky orange hair. The man pointed a pistol at her, but had Edoda's old rifle slung over his shoulder. More trackers, she decided. Ones she hadn't seen before.

Her last hope was to get away. She leaped from the road and tried to barrel back into the trees, but the man came running after her. He was quick, strong. He caught her easily, grabbing her by the collar of her coat. He pulled down her hood and scanned her face closely, as if checking her against some wanted poster.

"Who are you?" he asked, the orange-haired woman limping over to stand next to him.

She wasn't going to answer.

The man reached beneath his parka and withdrew a black wallet that held a silver badge next to a photo ID. "I'll ask you one more time. Who are you?"

She glanced at the ID, incredulous. "Are you Victor? Mary Crow's Victor?" Her heart leapt. Could these people possibly be here to help?

"I am," Galloway held on to her, his eyes blazing. "Who are you? And what do you know about Mary Crow?"

"I'm Lily Walkingstick," Lily squeaked, pointing in the direction of the trailer. "Mary's at my dad's fish camp. Men have captured my father. Maybe Mary, too," she managed to reply.

"What kind of men?" the orange-haired woman blurted, looking ready to cut and run the other way. "Is one a short little guy with spider tats on his hands?"

Lily shook her head. "They're both big. They're driving a camper from Kentucky." She gulped down air; her throat burned. "Mary thinks they've done bad things to a bunch of girls. Here." She reached in her coat pocket and handed the picture of Bryan to Victor. "Mary says all those names are girls they've killed."

Victor glanced at the paper. "What about Mary now?"

"I left her about twenty minutes ago. She was going to try and talk them out of killing my father." Lily tried to keep her voice steady, but she couldn't do it. She started to sob, her tears coming hot and fast. "Please, go help them! If you don't, those men are going to kill them both."

CHAPTER 38

———

Mary had not seen him in five years; now she sat across from him guarded by a man with a gun. He looked older, with deeper laugh lines. Though his hair was still Cherokee black and his eyes sharp, his mouth seemed drawn, as if the burden of raising a daughter alone had been much harder than making bows and tracking bears. She'd last gazed at him after a long night of love in an Oklahoma motel. She'd said "see you after court" and he'd said "okay." He'd left to put on his one suit; she'd seen him at court, but he'd walked out in the middle of her testimony. When she went back to the motel to explain everything, she'd found an empty room with a note, asking forgiveness and understanding. It took her two seconds to understand, but she still wasn't sure she'd forgiven him.

Now he sat, with a wrecked shoulder, staring at his boots. She glanced at the men, arguing in their own strange tongue, one pointing towards Tennessee, the keeping an eye on her. She doubted they could understand Cherokee, so she drummed up what words she could remember.

"Gawoniha!" she told him softly. *Say something!*

He lifted his gaze to her face. As always, she could read his eyes. At that moment they were full of pain, anger and something she once knew as love.

"Hatlu Lily?" he replied. "Tennessee?"

"Murphy," she whispered, if the girl had, indeed, done as she'd told her.

He brightened at her answer, knowing that Murphy would mean safety for Lily, a future unmarred by memories of murder and assault. But neither Murphy nor Tennessee could help the two of them. Too many miles and too much snow lay between them and any hope of rescue.

"Wado," he said. "I owe you. For her."

She didn't know whether to laugh or cry. Yes, he did owe her. But not for Lily. He owed her for all the days and months and years that had brought them here, tied up and staring at each other while two crazy men argued over how to kill them. For a moment her outrage boiled; then, just as quickly, it cooled. She had chosen to respond to Lily's plea. She had elected to leave her warm bed and venture up here in a blizzard. The choice had been hers-—Jonathan was just trying to save his child.

She looked at him and suddenly saw him in a different way. Though she knew his voice and his smell and his body as well as her own, there was a new strangeness about him. He'd traveled far away, made new friends, laughed at different jokes. No longer was he the familiar extension of herself.

"How bad is your shoulder?" She switched to English, her Cherokee reaching its limits.

"Shot to hell. But I'm better off than Leroy."

"Who's Leroy?"

"The asswipe who frisked you."

Mary glanced at the chubby man Lily called Uncle Jake. "What's the matter with him?"

"Septicemia," said Jonathan. "That first night, I threw Ribtickler at him and nicked his bowel."

"So all that blood in the bathroom was his?"

Jonathan nodded. "If he doesn't get to a doctor soon, Chet's going to have to drop him off at the morgue."

"Chet?" Mary looked at Rifleman, who cradled his weapon like a precious child.

"Leroy and Chet. Kentucky's answer to Romulus and Remus."

"So septicemia's bad?"

He nodded. "Basically, you turn into a pile of pus. Then you die."

"Ugh." Mary shuddered.

She watched the two men arguing. Leroy kept pointing down the road and lifting his shirt to reveal the flaming wound in his abdomen. Chet kept shaking his head, pointing at her. When their eyes met briefly a chill went down her spine. She'd seen similar expressions before, in court. It was the angry, feral look of men accused of doing monstrous things to women. Usually they stood cocky, their attorneys insouciantly claiming that their victims were to blame, with their fancy makeup and provocative outfits. *You can't fault a boy for just being a boy* and *he was only being playful, and he never heard her say no.* Mary always took special pleasure in putting men like that away.

But that one brief look told her volumes. She knew what would come next. Rape, for sure. *They'll put us in that camper, assault me, make Jonathan watch and then kill us both. Or maybe they would make me watch while they killed Jonathan and save the raping for later. Maybe I'll get to be their little party doll all the way back to Kentucky.*

The certainty of it made bile bubble up in her throat. She glanced at Jonathan, who was watching the men, a look of pure hatred on his face. Should she tell him her fears? Warn him? Would it do the least bit of good?

No, she decided. What could he do, anyway, with a rope around his neck and one arm in a sling? She would fight in the way of all women—kicks to the groin, thumbs in the eyes.

"I think they've killed a lot of little girls," Jonathan said abruptly.

She thought of the decals she'd seen in the camper and the pictures she'd given Lily. "What makes you say that?"

"I found a little bra where they kept me locked up. Some kid had written inside it. Somebody else had written on the backside of the carpeting. I think that one was written in blood."

Mary closed her eyes, appalled at the men and furious at her own stupidity. Why had it taken her so long to figure this out? Only a freak snowstorm had kept Lily from becoming another victim.

"Got any bright ideas about getting out of here?" she asked.

He shook his head. "Julunahuhski."

Fight hard. She gave a deep sigh, thinking of sweet Victor and the life they would not be sharing.

"Nigohilvuh," he said. *Always.* Suddenly, all the anguish left his face and he smiled at her—the same bright grin he'd flashed that morning on the school bus, so many years ago. "Guhgeyu, Mehli Koga. I always will."

Before she could respond, they came, marching in tandem, their footsteps squeaking in the snow. Uncle Jake jerked her to her feet and pulled her coat off. Rifleman watched, snickering while he kept the bullpup pointed at Jonathan.

"Get your filthy paws off me!" Mary sputtered, once again channeling JimAnn Ponder.

"Since you sent Kimmeegirl to Tennessee, you're gonna have to take her place." Leroy grinned at her, his small, pig eyes sly. "I'm going first, then it'll be my brother's turn."

Mary laughed. "You sure you're up to it? You stink like bear meat gone bad."

"Shut up!" cried Leroy. "Lay that coat in the snow and get down on your knees. You're older than I like, but you've got a pretty mouth, when it isn't yakking."

Jonathan lunged forward, but Chet grabbed the rope and jerked him back against the camper. Mary gasped, terrified that the man was going to shoot him right there.

"Don't you worry about your brother," said Leroy. "We aren't gonna kill him yet. We want him to enjoy this, too."

Before Mary could answer, Uncle Jake or Leroy or whatever the hell his name was, squeezed the top of her shoulder so hard it brought tears to her eyes. "Down on your knees, sis. We're gonna see just what that little hillbilly mouth can do."

He pushed her down in front of him. Slowly, he unbuckled his belt with his left hand as he put the pistol up against her temple. "I think you know what to do. But just in case you get any bright ideas about using your teeth, there's a pistol on you and a rifle on your brother."

A wave of revulsion went through her as he unzipped his fly and pulled her into the ripe aroma of rotting flesh.

She swallowed quickly, trying hard not to retch. She wondered what vomiting on him might do. It might repulse him–men usually recoiled from puke. But it could also enrage him to the point of murder. No, she decided. Gagging was too risky. She would have to try something else.

"Come on, mama," he said. "Give that boy a juicy little kiss."

Humiliated that Jonathan was watching all this, she concentrated on the stains on Uncle Jake's underwear as she reached for his penis. She groped for it clumsily—it was a soft, limp thing that felt more like a turd than an appendage—but when she finally managed to grasp it, she knew what she was going to do.

She pulled his dick out with her left hand, quickly turning her head away from the gun, spitting out the saliva that was flooding her mouth. With her head still turned away, she reached up further into his underwear and grabbed his testicles. She heard him gasp as she clenched her hand like a claw and squeezed his scrotum as if extracting the last drops of juice from a withered lemon.

He screamed; the gun went off somewhere above her head, ringing her left ear like a bell. She lunged into his stomach, flattening him on the ground. He rolled in the snow, still screaming as she held on tight.

"You little bitch!" He gave a high, thin howl, like an animal caught in a trap.

They thrashed in the snow. He tried to cover his crotch, and roll away from her, but she clung to him, squeezing him even harder. Suddenly, he started to scream.

"Argonish! Jurnosk!"

"Luradoo!" Chet yelled back.

A loud volley came from the rifle. Mary looked up, expecting to see Jonathan, lying dead on the ground. But Jonathan was on his feet, frantically trying to saw through his rope with the point of Mary's arrow. The gunshot had come from Chet, aiming at her. He rushed toward her, clutching the bullpup, intent on murder.

"You fucking bitch!" he roared. "I'm going to kill you!"

"Mary!" she heard Jonathan bellow. "Let him go! Now!"

She loosened her grip on Leroy's testicles and tried to extricate herself from him. But somehow he'd sensed his brother coming to his rescue. Wrapping his legs around hers, he pinned her to the ground. As they struggled like co-joined insects, she realized her only chance was to drag herself away, back into the snow. But it was pointless. She'd only crawled a few feet when a heavy weight crashed down on the back of her neck. She looked up, over her shoulder. Chet's foot was on her neck as he pointed the rifle at her temple.

A few feet away, Leroy groaned in agony, curled up in a ball. "Just shoot her, Chet," he whimpered. "Shoot her now."

Chet pressed his right cheek against the gun and sighted down the barrel. Leroy kept moaning about something, but Mary couldn't make it out. All she could do was stare at that gun. Soon a bullet would come out, destroying her face and her brain. Suddenly, her life started to play out inside her head. She saw her mother, Jonathan, Irene Hannah, Victor. How sweet it had been, even the awful parts. How sad she would be to leave it. She watched as if in slow motion as Chet put his index finger around the trigger. He drew his lips back in a smile of pure evil, then he squeezed the trigger. She heard a huge blast, but felt no heat, no pain, nothing. Instead a warm spray of liquid splattered over her face as the world went dark and silent.

CHAPTER 39

———

Mary floated, warm and weightless, with muted golds and lavenders coalescing around her, dissipating only when she felt a tapping on her shoulder.

"Mary?" asked a soft voice. "Can you wake up?"

She tried to respond but the effort was herculean–her tongue seemed too thick, her eyelids glued together.

"Here," said another voice. "Let me give her another blow."

The pungent aroma of tobacco smoke assaulted her. As she recoiled from the odor, her eyes fluttered open. Lily Walkingstick and a woman with a crown of bright orange hair knelt beside her. I am dead, Mary thought. And so is Lily. This woman must be some kind of spirit guide.

But the spirit guide seemed firmly anchored in the here-and-now, taking another drag on a cigarette and poking Lily in the ribs. "See?" she said, sounding a lot like JimAnn Ponder. "That trick always works, unless they're dead. I'll run get SBI."

Orange Hair left, leaving Lily. "Are you okay?" the girl asked.

"I don't know," Mary replied. "What happened?"

Breathlessly, Lily recounted running into Victor and Coza. "When I told him what was happening, Victor left me with Coza and ran ahead. By the time we got here, the Rifleman was dead. Victor shot him."

Mary remembered the barrel of the man's assault rifle, pointed an inch away from her face. "What happened to Uncle Jake?"

"He's over there." Lily pointed to the far end of the camper. "Tied up. Victor arrested him."

"Good for Victor," Mary whispered.

"I know. I really like him." Lily smiled, then lowered her gaze and stared at Mary. "I need to tell you something before everybody comes over here," she said, her tone urgent. "I've been really shitty to you, and I just wanted to say, you know, I'm sorry."

Mary looked at her, the planes of her young face suddenly looking less like a child's and more like the woman she would become. "It's okay. You were just being a kid."

Lily grabbed her hand. "Then come back to me and Edoda," she whispered, her voice cracking with tears. "Put us back together again. It'll be like before."

Before Mary could answer, another face appeared above her. Victor.

Lily scurried away as he knelt down beside her. "Hey, sweetheart. How do you feel?"

"I'm not dead, am I?"

"No." He smiled. "I dropped the rifle guy, who fell on you. That bullpup gave you a lick on the head. Can you answer some questions for me?"

"Okay."

He made her go through the concussion drill, asking her who she was, what year it was, who was president. When she scored a hundred on his test, he asked one thing more. "What's the last thing you remember?"

"Wrestling with someone who was screaming. Jonathan…"

"It's okay," said Victor. "More will come back to you."

"Did I a woman with orange hair just blow smoke in my face?"

"She did. She's Teo Owle's former girlfriend. She said it would wake you up."

Mary frowned. "How did Teo' Owle's girlfriend get up here?"

Victor explained how he'd enlisted Coza and how they'd tracked Mary and Lily to the fish camp. "She heard those first volleys and we came running. Halfway here we ran into Lily."

It didn't make much sense to her, but she did remember the pages she'd given to Lily. "Did Lily give you those pictures? With the girls' names?"

"She did. I've already locked up their camper to preserve evidence."

Mary smiled. "That should impress Spencer. Collaring two pedophiles in the middle of a blizzard."

Softly, he kissed her forehead. "You and Lily did the heavy lifting here. You want to try and stand up? You can go warm up next to Walkingstick."

Trembling, she grabbed his hand, the world spinning as she got to her feet. Victor wrapped his arms around her, steadying her. "I love you," he whispered, holding her close.

"I love you, too."As she burrowed into his embrace, everything started to feel real again. The snow crunching beneath her feet, the shock of cold air, the solid warmth of his body against hers.

He put his arm around her, helping her over to the small fire that was warming Jonathan and Lily.

"Can you make room for the acting DA?" he asked.

Lily scooted over. Mary sat down between them.

"I kept your gun safe," Lily said, returning the heavy pistol. "And I didn't shoot anybody."

"Good for you," said Mary. "The best guns are the ones you don't have to use."

After Victor walked over to check on Uncle Jake's handcuffs, he returned to Jonathan and Mary.

"Could you two keep an eye on him while we're gone? I've given him his Mirandas."

"Where are you going?" asked Mary.

"Lily says she can take me to a ridge where I might get a call out to Spencer. If so, I'll try to get a CSI unit up here right away." Victor looked at Jonathan and Mary, sitting together, then turned to Coza, who was putting a few more branches on the fire. "Why don't you come with us, Coza. These folks may have some catching up to do."

"Is that part of my airport deal?"

"Yeah," he said, again glancing at Mary and Jonathan. "It is."

The three walked off together, Coza limping beside Victor while Lily led the way.

Mary turned to Jonathan. She was trembling so hard her teeth chattered. "Lily didn't see Victor shoot that guy, did she?"

"No. Your friend came around the camper and plugged Rifleman with my .22. By the time Lily and Coza showed up, we'd covered him up with a blanket from the camper."

"Thank God," said Mary. "At least she won't have nightmares about that."

They sat silent for a moment, then Jonathan cleared his throat. "So, Lily tells me this Victor is your fiancé."

"You could say that." For some reason, she didn't want to show him the ring she now wore.

"He seems like an okay guy."

She fought back a twinge of resentment. Victor was so much more than okay. Victor was kind; Victor was funny; Victor would never walk out of her life with one crummy note of explanation.

"He sure loves you," said Jonathan. "But then, a lot of people love you."

"I don't know about that." Mary gave a bitter laugh. "Though Lily seems to like me a little better."

"My daughter's learned a lot. I have, too."

"Like what?"

He swallowed hard. "Like I should never have skipped out with her. It wasn't fair to her or to you. It was just me, being a selfish asshole."

Mary looked at him, astonished. Never before had such a frank admission come out of Jonathan Walkingstick's mouth. "Hindsight's twenty-twenty, Jonathan. You can't rewrite history."

"But I can change the future," he said. "I can take Lily back to Oklahoma. Turn her over to Fred Moon."

"That would be a good start," said Mary. "She deserves to know her mother's people. But more than that, she needs friends her own age. You know, proms and pow-wows and football games on Friday night."

"We both had that, didn't we," he said, gazing into the snowy wilderness. "Back in the day."

In that moment Mary remembered everything—the first time she'd seen him, the first time he'd kissed her, the first time they'd made love. How incredibly they'd fit together that afternoon. They'd struggled to recapture that first perfection ever since.

He held his hands out towards the woefully insufficient fire. "If I took Lily back to Oklahoma, would they put me in jail?"

"I don't know. You've broken the law and defied a court order. But you'd be turning yourself in, plus you'll be a huge material witness against that bastard, over there." She nodded at Leroy. "I think those pictures I gave Lily will help solve a lot of cold cases. That album he burned was sickening—full of young girls."

"I can't believe how close Lily came to being one of them," Jonathan said, barely above a whisper. "If it hadn't been for you..."

She took his good hand, stopping him. "Hey—I owed you. You saved me from Mitchell Whitman, all those years ago."

For a long moment they watched the fire as flames sputtered around some dry cedar branches Lily had scrounged up. Finally, Jonathan broke the silence that had sprung between them.

"I know I'm many days late and a million dollars short, but I don't suppose you'd consider saving me a seat again?"

It was their old line from high school—save me a seat on the bus, at the pep rally, in your life. Even today, when their eyes first met, a part of her still longed to feel his kiss again. But she knew it would not be the same. Better to leave that sweetness in memory only, a small, delicious pleasure she could revisit when she was old, and the world's coldness would be for keeps.

She reached to wipe some dirt from his cheek. "I'll always love you, Jonathan. But I can't save your seat anymore. I'm a different person on a different bus, and so are you."

He looked at her, his eyes glistening. He'd started to say something else when Uncle Jake began howling.

"None of this was my fault," he cried. "Chet made me do everything. He threatened to kill me if I didn't cooperate. He was sick, a real pervert."

"Shut up," said Jonathan.

"But it wasn't me!" Leroy insisted. "It was Chet. All along!"

Suddenly, Jonathan grabbed Mary's Glock, pointed it at Leroy. "You have terrorized my daughter, messed up my shoulder, and God only knows what you've done to little girls inside that camper. If I were you,

I'd be real quiet and not piss me off. Up in the mountains, It's funny how often firearms go off by accident."

Leroy started to say something else, but thought better of it. His shoulders slumped and he crumpled, rocking back and forth, mumbling to himself in the strange language he now spoke alone.

"Asshole," said Jonathan, returning the gun to Mary.

They said no more after that, just watched the small orange flames dance against the blue snow. Maybe there's nothing more to say, thought Mary. Maybe Walkingstick and I have finally said it all.

As the fire flickered down to embers, Victor and Lily returned, tromping through the snow.

"I've got good news and bad news," Victor announced. "The bad news is that the crime scene guys can't get here until tomorrow. The good news is that Coza's got a warm fire going in the smokehouse stove. We can huddle up there and at least stay a little warm until they get here in the morning."

"What about him?" Jonathan cocked his head at the weeping Leroy. "Shall we just leave him here to freeze?"

Laughing, Victor took the rifle from his shoulder and returned it to Jonathan. "We'll have to take him with us. Would you and Lily like the pleasure of escorting him to the smokehouse?"

Jonathan looked at Mary one final time. She could read everything in his gaze—love, desire, apology. But she made no response beyond a warm smile that wished an old love well. He held his good arm out to his daughter.

"Help me up, Lily."

Lily pulled her father to his feet. Together they prodded Uncle Jake away from his brother's body and headed toward the ruins of the cabin.

"I'm telling you," Uncle Jake insisted as he waddled along. "None of this was my idea."

"Shut up, you stinking pile of shit." Jonathan poked the barrel of the rifle into the man's butt. "And don't forget where this gun's pointed."

Mary stood up. The wide spot in the snowy road looked like a crime scene. The burned photo album was now just ashes and soot, Lily's arrow was stuck point down in the snow, and the puddle of crimson blood visible under Chet's blanket had darkened to black. The snow, though, had finally stopped. She turned and looked up into the western sky, where a band of the palest pink light shone over the tops of the mountains in Tennessee.

"Wado, Dodaluh," she whispered.

"What did you say?" Victor walked over, put his arm around her.

"I thanked the mountains. Everybody I love is going to walk out of here alive."

"Thank them for me, too." He pulled her closer. "But I've got another question to ask you."

"What?"

He looked at her, his eyes serious. "It's about life beyond these mountains. Is yours going to be with Walkingstick? Or with me?"

For an instant she hesitated, as if choosing between those two roads that diverged in a snowy wood. Then she removed her glove and held up her left hand. The diamond ring glittered brightly in the pale winter light. "Not once did I ever take this off."

He wrapped her in his arms. "Are you absolutely sure?"

She nodded. "Jonathan talked. I listened. When he finished, he hadn't convinced me of anything I didn't already know."

"Such as?"

"Such as he is my used to be. You are my now."

"Even if we leave here?"

"Yes," she whispered. "Even if we leave here."

He kissed her hand, but before they started to the fish camp, she stopped and turned again toward the far blue peaks, now rimmed in a bright pink sunset. The Dodaluh. The beautiful and perilous Old Men. Along with Jonathan and Lily and a dozen other people, she would carry them in her heart for the rest of her life. But the silver thread in her mother's tapestry was leading her in a new direction. It was time for her to seek a newer world and leave these mountains to somebody else.

"Wijadoligi," she whispered to the land that had sheltered her people since the world began. "Be well and live long. I will miss you."